KT-567-991

AUTHORS' CHOICE 2

A companion volume

AUTHOR'S CHOICE

Stories chosen by

GILLIAN AVERY	HESTER BURTON
PAULINE CLARKE	EILÍS DILLON
LEON GARFIELD	ALAN GARNER
JANET MCNEILL	WILLIAM MAYNE
JAMES REEVES	IAN SERRAILLIER
NOEL STREATFEILD	ROSEMARY SUTCLIFF
MARY TREADGOLD	GEOFFREY TREASE
ELFRIDA VIPONT	BARBARA WILLARD
URSULA MORAY WILLIAMS	

AUTHORS' CHOICE 2

STORIES CHOSEN BY

JOAN AIKEN HONOR ARUNDEL

JOHN CHRISTOPHER VERA & BILL CLEAVER

ELIZABETH COATSWORTH HELEN CRESSWELL

PETER DICKINSON JANE GARDAM

MOLLIE HUNTER JOAN LINGARD

ANDRE NORTON SCOTT O'DELL

JOAN PHIPSON ANDREW SALKEY

IVAN SOUTHALL JOHN ROWE TOWNSEND

JILL PATON WALSH PATRICIA WRIGHTSON

ILLUSTRATED BY KRYSTYNA TURSKA

HAMISH HAMILTON
LONDON

This anthology first published in Great Britain 1973
by Hamish Hamilton Children's Books Ltd
90 Great Russell Street London WC1B 3PT
© in this collection Hamish Hamilton Children's Books Ltd 1973
Illustrations © Krystyna Turska 1973
All rights reserved
Printed in Great Britain by
Western Printing Services Ltd, Bristol
SBN 241 02335 1

Publisher's Note.
Where stories originated in the United
States of America, and are by American
writers, American spelling and usage
have been retained

Acknowledgements

The Publishers are indebted to the following for the use of copyright material: The Executors of the Laurence Housman Estate for permission to include *The Gentle Cockatrice* from MOONSHINE AND CLOVER by Laurence Housman; T. Werner Laurie Ltd., London, for permission to include abridged material from THE BOOK OF MAGGIE OWEN; E. J. Carnell Literary Agency, London, for permission to include *The Graveyard Reader* by Theodore Sturgeon, © 1958 by Theodore Sturgeon; Paul R. Reynolds, Inc., N.Y., for permission to include *The Purple Moccasin* by MacKinlay Kantor, copyright 1937 by The Curtis Publishing Company; The Literary Trustees of Walter de la Mare and the Society of Authors, London, for permission to include *Visitors* from COLLECTED STORIES FOR CHILDREN by Walter de la Mare; the Author and the Scott Meredith Literary Agency, Inc., N.Y., for permission to include *The Ruum* by Arthur Porges; Methuen & Co. Ltd., London, for permission to include *The Gay Goshawk* from THOU SHALT NOT SUFFER A WITCH by Dorothy K. Haynes; Jonathan Cape Ltd., London, and the Devin-Adair Company, U.S.A., for permission to include *The Wild Goat's Kid* by Liam O'Flaherty from THE SHORT STORIES OF LIAM O'FLAHERTY; Faber & Faber Ltd., London, and Hawthorn Books, Inc., N.Y., for permission to include *The Star Beast* from MAINLY IN MOONLIGHT by Nicholas Stuart Gray; *Bim* Magazine, Barbados, edited by Frank Collymore, for permission to include *The Water Woman and Her Lover* by Ralph Prince; Constable Publishers Ltd., London for permission to include *A Piece of Pie* from TAKE IT EASY by Damon Runyon, U.S. rights controlled by The Estate of Damon Runyon Jr.; Hogarth Press Ltd., London, and Harcourt Brace Jovanovitch, Inc., N.Y., for permission to include *The Story of Jorkel Hayforks* from A CALENDAR OF LOVE by George MacKay Brown, copyright © 1967 by George MacKay Brown; A. D. Peters & Co., London, and Harold Matson & Co., Inc., N.Y., for permission to include *The Invisible Boy* from THE GOLDEN APPLES OF THE SUN by Ray Bradbury, copyright 1945 by Street & Smith Publications Inc.

The Publishers acknowledge with thanks the help of the authors who have co-operated in the preparation of this volume by supplying

ACKNOWLEDGEMENTS

introductory notes and biographical details; the latter can be found at
the end of the book from page 237 onwards.

Every effort has been made to trace holders of copyright material.
If, however, any query should arise it should be addressed to the
Publishers.

Contents

CONTENTS

For Honor Arundel
In Memoriam

The
Gentle Cockatrice
by Laurence Housman
chosen by Joan Aiken

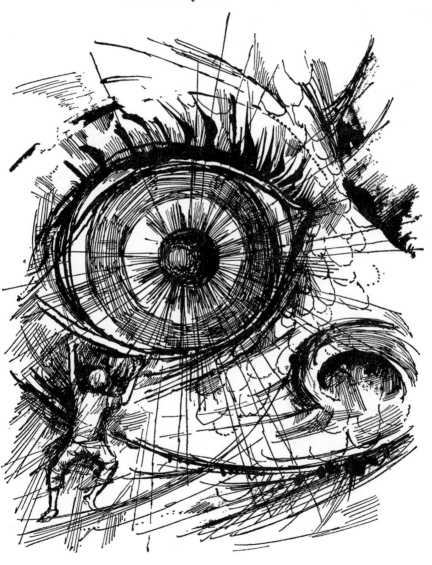

WHEN asked to choose a story for this anthology, I thought I would like to find one that was a favourite of my own but was rare and might not be very well known. In fact I picked even better than I'd planned, for it seemed there wasn't another copy to be found of the book I have, called MOONSHINE AND CLOVER—stories by Laurence Housman—from which I chose *The Gentle Cockatrice*. And what a hard choice *that* was. All the stories are lovely: there's a most haunting one about a castle with its roots going down into a deep cliff and an old ancestral duke snoring away in a vault down below, all ringed with red-and-blue flame; there is a sad beautiful one about rocking-horse land; a cheerful, satisfying one about a Chinese Old Master who pops back out of one of his pictures to help a poor little studio apprentice; as well as more traditional ones about princesses and witches and magicians. But I think the cockatrice one is my favourite because the cockatrice himself is such an endearing character, although this story, too, is rather sad.

A brother of the poet A. E. Housman, Laurence also wrote many books, plays, and poems, and illustrated them as well. He began writing in the eighteen-nineties, and his first stories were published not long after Oscar Wilde's *The Happy Prince*, and have something of the same quality. But I think Housman's stories are better than Wilde's: they make less use of stock ingredients, they are funnier, and less heartless; above all they are beautifully written and most deeply mysterious and imaginative. I can't think why no one has yet got round to republishing any of them—he wrote four or five collections of stories which are tantalisingly listed at the beginning of the two books I'm lucky enough to own, but they are all out of print. They have enticing names—THE BLUE MOON, A FARM IN FAIRYLAND, THE HOUSE OF JOY, THE FIELD OF CLOVER—*somebody*, somewhere, must have copies of them!

Although born in 1865, while Palmerston was still Prime Minister, and long before motor cars were dreamed of, Laurence Housman didn't die till quite recently, for he lived to be over ninety. Probably his best-known works are the plays about Queen Victoria, VICTORIA REGINA, and the LITTLE PLAYS OF ST. FRANCIS. But I think that his stories are absolutely special. I'm very glad to have one of them reprinted.

JOAN AIKEN

FAR above the terraces of vine, where the goat pastures ended and the rocks began, the eye could take a clear view over the whole plain. From that point the world below spread itself out like a green map, and the only walls one could see were the white flanks and tower of the cathedral rising up from the grey roofs of the city; as for the streets, they seemed to be but narrow foot-tracks on which people appeared like ants walking.

This was the view of the town which Beppo, the son of the common hangman, loved best. It was little pleasure to him to be down there, where all the other lads drove him from their play: for the hangman had had too much to do with the fathers and brothers of some of them, and his son was not popular. When there was a hanging they would rush off to the public square to see it; afterwards they made it their sport to play at hanging Beppo, if by chance they could catch him; and that play had a way at times of coming uncomfortably near to reality.

Beppo did not himself go to the square when his father's trade was on; the near view did not please him. Perched on the rocky hillside, he would look down upon a gathering of black specks, where two others stood detached upon a space in their midst, and would know that there his father was hanging a man.

Sometimes it was more than one, and that made Beppo afraid. For he knew that for every man that he hanged his father took a dram to give him courage for the work; and if there were several poor fellows to be cast off from life, the hangman was not pleasant company afterwards for those very near and dear to him.

It happened one day that the hangman was to give the rope to five fellows, the most popular and devil-may-care rakes and roysterers in the whole town. Beppo was up very early that morning, and at the first streak of light had dropped himself over the wall into the town ditch, and was away for the open country

3

and the free air of the hills; for he knew that neither at home nor in the streets would life be worth living for a week after, because of all the vengeances that would fall on him.

Therefore he had taken from the home larder a loaf of bread and a clump of dried figs; and with these hoped to stand the siege of a week's solitude rather than fall in with the hard dealings of his own kind. He knew a cave, above where the goats found pasture, out of which a little red, rusty water trickled; there he thought to make himself a castle and dream dreams, and was sure he would be happy enough, if only he did not grow afraid.

Beppo had discovered the cave one day from seeing a goat push out through a thicket of creepers on the side of the hill; and, hidden under their leaves, he had found it a wonderful, cool refuge from the heat of summer noons. Now, as he entered, the place struck very cold; for it was early spring, and the earth was not yet warmed through with the sun. So he set himself to gather dead grass, and briers, and tufts of goat's hair and from farther down the hillside the wood of a ruined goat-paddock, till he had a great store of fuel at hand. He worked all day like a squirrel for its winter hoard; and as his pile mounted he grew less and less afraid of the cave where he meant to live.

Seeing so large a heap of stuff ready for the feeding of his fire, he began to rise to great heights in his own imagination. First he had been a poor outlaw, a mere sheep-stealer hiding from men's clutches; then he became a robber-chief; and at last he was no less than the king of the mountains.

"This mountain is all caves," he said to himself, "and all the caves are full of gold; and I am the king to whom it all belongs."

In the evening Beppo lighted his fire, in the far back of his cave, where its light would not be seen, and sat down by its warmth to eat dried figs and bread and drink brackish water. To-morrow he meant to catch a kid and roast it and eat it. Why should he ever go home again? Kid was good—he did not get that to eat when he was at home; and now in the streets the boys must be looking for him to play at their cruel game of hanging. Why should he go back at all?

The fire licked its way up the long walls of the cavern; slowly

4

the warmth crept round on all sides. The rock where Beppo laid his hand was no longer damp and cold; he made himself a bed of the dried litter in a niche close to the fire, laid his head on a smooth knob of stone, and slept. But even in his sleep he remembered his fire, dreading to awake and find himself in darkness. Every time the warmth of it diminished he raised himself and put on more fuel.

In the morning—for faint blue edges of light marking the ridged throat of the cavern told that outside the day had begun —he woke fully, and the fire still burned. As he lay, his pillow of rock felt warm and almost soft; and, strangely enough, through it there went a beating sound as of blood. This must be his own brain that he heard; but he lifted his head, and where he laid his hand could feel a slow movement of life going on under it. Then he stared hard at the overhanging rock, and surely it heaved softly up and down, like some great thing breathing slowly in its sleep.

Yet he could make out no shape at all till, having run to the other side of the cave, he turned to see the whole face of the rock which seemed to be taking on life. Then he realised very gradually what looked to be the throat and jaws of a great monster lying along the ground, while all the rest passed away into shadow or lay buried under masses of rock, which closed round it like a mould. Below the nether-jaw bone the flames licked and caressed the throat; and the tough, mud-coloured hide ruffled and smoothed again as if grateful for the heat that tickled its way in.

Very slowly indeed the great Cockatrice, which had lain buried for thousands of years, out of reach of the light or heat of the sun, was coming round again to life. That was Beppo's own doing, and for some very curious reason he was not afraid.

His heart was uplifted. "This is my cave," thought he, "so this must be my Cockatrice! Now I will ride out on him and conquer the world. I shall be really a king then!"

He guessed that it must have been the warmth which had waked the Cockatrice, so he made fires all down the side of the cave; wherever the great flank of the Cockatrice seemed to show, there he lighted a fire to put heat into the slumbering body of the beast.

"Warm up, old fellow," he cried; "thaw out, I tell you! I want you to talk to me."

Presently the mouth of the Cockatrice unsealed itself, and began to babble of green fields. "Hay—I want hay!" said the Cockatrice; "or grass. Does the world contain any grass?"

Beppo went out, and presently returned with an armful. Very slowly the Cockatrice began munching the fresh fodder, and Beppo, intent on feeding him back to life, ran to and fro between the hillside and the cavern till he was exhausted and could go no more. He sat down and watched the Cockatrice finish his meal.

Presently, when the monster found that his fodder was at an end, he puckered a great lid, and far up aloft in the wall of the cave flashed out a green eye.

If all the emeralds in the world were gathered together, they might shine like that; if all the glow-worms came up out of the fields and put their tails together, they might make as great an orb of fire. All the cave looked as green as grass when the eye of the Cockatrice lighted on it; and Beppo, seeing so mighty an optic turning its rays on him, felt all at once shrivelled and small, and very weak at the knees.

"Oh, Cockatrice," he said, in a monstrous sad voice, "I hope I haven't hurt you!"

"On the contrary," said the Cockatrice, "you have done me much good. What are you going to do with me now?"

"*I* do with *you*?" cried Beppo, astonished at so wild a possibility offering to come true. "I would like to get you out, of course—but can I?"

"I would like that dearly also!" said the Cockatrice.

"But how can I?" inquired Beppo.

"Keep me warm and feed me," returned the monster. "Presently I shall be able to find out where my tail is. When I can move that I shall be able to get out."

Beppo undertook whatever the Cockatrice told him—it was so grand to have a Cockatrice of his own. But it was a hard life, stoking up fires day and night, and bringing the Cockatrice the fodder necessary to replenish his drowsy being. When Beppo was quite tired out he would come and lay his head against the monster's snout: and the Cockatrice would open a benevolent eye and look at him affectionately.

"Dear Cockatrice," said the boy one day, "tell me about yourself, and how you lived and what the world was like when you were free!"

"Do you see any green in my eye?" said the Cockatrice.

"I do, indeed!" said Beppo. "I never saw anything so green in all the world."

"That's all right, then!" said the Cockatrice. "Climb up and look in, and you will see what the world was like when I was young."

So Beppo climbed and scrambled, and slipped and clung, till he found himself on the margin of a wonderful green lake, which was but the opening into the whole eye of the Cockatrice.

And as soon as Beppo looked, he had lost his heart for ever to the world he saw there. It was there, quite real before him: a whole world full of living and moving things—the world before the trouble of man came to it.

"I see green hills, and fields, and rocks, and trees," cried Beppo, "and among them a lot of little Cockatrices are playing!"

"They were my brothers and sisters; I remember them," said the Cockatrice. "I have them all in my mind's eye. Call them—perhaps they will come and talk to you; you will find them very nice and friendly."

"They are too far off," said Beppo, "they cannot hear me."

"Ah, yes," murmured the Cockatrice, "memory is a wonderful thing!"

When Beppo came down again he was quite giddy, and lost in wonder and joy over the beautiful green world the Cockatrice had shown him. "I like that better than this!" said he.

"So do I," said the Cockatrice. "But perhaps, when my tail gets free, I shall feel better."

One morning he said to Beppo: "I do really begin to feel my tail. It is somewhere away down the hill yonder. Go and look out for me, and tell me if you can see it moving."

So Beppo went to the mouth of the cave, and looked out

towards the city, over all the rocks and ridges and goat-pastures and slopes of vine that lay between.

Suddenly, as he looked, the steeple of the cathedral tottered, and down fell its weathercock and two of its pinnacles, and half the chimneys of the town snapped off their tops. All that distance away Beppo could hear the terrified screams of the inhabitants as they ran out of their houses in terror.

"I've done it!" cried the Cockatrice, from within the cave.

"But you mustn't do that!" exclaimed Beppo in horror.

"Mustn't do what?" inquired the Cockatrice.

"You mustn't wag your tail! You don't know what you are doing!"

"Oh, master!" wailed the Cockatrice; "mayn't I? For the first time this thousand years I have felt young again."

Beppo was pale and trembling with agitation over the fearful effects of that first tail-wagging. "You mustn't feel young!" said he.

"Why not?" asked the Cockatrice, with a piteous wail.

"There isn't room in the world for a Cockatrice to feel young nowadays," answered Beppo gravely.

"But, dear little master and benefactor," cried the Cockatrice, "what did you wake me up for?"

"I don't know," replied Beppo, terribly perplexed. "I wouldn't have done it had I known where your tail was."

"Where is it?" inquired the Cockatrice, with great interest.

"It's right underneath the city where I mean to be king," said Beppo; "and if you move it the city will come down; and then I shall have nothing to be king of."

"Very well," said the Cockatrice sadly; "I will wait!"

"Wait for what?" thought Beppo. "Waiting won't do any good." And he began to think what he must do. "You lie quite still!" said he to the Cockatrice. "Go to sleep, and I will still look after you."

"Oh, little master," said the Cockatrice, "but it is difficult to go to sleep when the delicious trouble of spring is in one's tail! How long does this city of yours mean to stay there? I am so alive that I find it hard to shut an eye!"

"I will let the fires that keep you warm go down for a bit," said

Beppo, "and you mustn't eat so much grass; then you will feel better, and your tail will be less of an anxiety."

And presently, when Beppo had let the fires which warmed him get low, and had let time go by without bringing him any fresh fodder, the Cockatrice dozed off into an uneasy, prehistoric slumber.

Then Beppo, weeping bitterly over his treachery to the poor beast which had trusted him, raked open the fires and stamped out the embers; and, leaving the poor Cockatrice to get cold, ran down the hill as fast as he could to the city he had saved—the city of which he meant to be king.

He had been away a good many days, but the boys in the street were still on the watch for him. He told them how he had saved the city from the earthquake; and they beat him from the city gate to his father's door. He told his own father how he had saved the city; and his father beat him from his own door to the city gate. Nobody believed him.

He lay outside the town walls till it was dark, all smarting with his aches and pains; then, when nobody could see him, he got up and very miserably made his way back to the cave on the hill. And all the way he said to himself, "Shall I put fire under the Cockatrice once more, and make him shake the town into ruins? Would not that be fine?"

Inside, the cave was quite still and cold, and when he laid his hand on the Cockatrice he could not feel any stir or warmth in its bones. Yet when he called, the Cockatrice just opened a slit of his green eye and looked at him with trust and affection.

"Dear Cockatrice," cried Beppo, "forgive me for all the wrong I have done you!" And as he clambered his way towards the green light, a great tear rolled from under the heavy lid and flowed past him like a cataract.

"Dear Cockatrice," cried Beppo again when he stood on the margin of the green lake, "take me to sleep with you in the land where the Cockatrices are at play, and keep quite still with your tail!"

Slowly and painfully the Cockatrice opened his eye enough to let Beppo slip through; and Beppo saw the green world with its playful cockatrices waiting to welcome him. Then the great

9

eyelid shut down fast, and the waking days of the Cockatrice were over. And Beppo's native town lay safe, because he had learned from the Cockatrice to be patient and gentle, and had gone to be king of a green world where everything was harmless.

THE BOOK OF MAGGIE OWEN
(chapter 1)
chosen by Honor Arundel

IT is enormously satisfying to be able at long last to introduce Maggie Owen to a wider audience than my nearest friends and relations—for I've never met anyone else who has read her enchanting journal.

I found the book on a second-hand bookstall shortly after the war and the moment I read: "I am a virgin twelve years of age" my attention was riveted and the last page came far too soon.

There is only room for a short extract here and I've had to leave out some of my favourite passages; her lively descriptions of picnics and outings; her ingenuous observations of adult behaviour; her inklings of religious and national tensions:—"Blackstone Race" (the house where she stays) " 'Twas built in old ancient times away back before the English people came over here to tell the Irish what to do with themselves and how to run the country." Her tender conscience: "After me dinner I examined me conscience and wrote down the sins in two rows, the black sins in one and the small sins in the other, there being full and plenty of both. I have a dredful time remembering them and have to take the list along in me glove so I can have a last peep before I go to confess." And her discovery of adolescence: "I have nineteen hairs under one arm and twenty-five under the other."

I have no idea who Maggie Owen was or what happened to her but for me and for you too I am sure she will always remain excitingly and vividly alive.

HONOR ARUNDEL

JANUARY 24, 1908. This is me birthday and I consider me New Year begins this day instead of January first.

Anyways I was given this book for a present and a gold soverign along with it, a prayer book also that I have too many of. I start this book this day and shall put down me best thoughts and all important things that happen to me—if any do—and what I learn at me lessons. I call it a Year Book instead of a Diary. Me name is Margaret Owen, a fine name would anyone call it me. Always they call me Maggie-Ane or Peg, I dont know why Owen is called Ane. I think theres many a thing I'll have to find out.

I am a virgin twelve years of age. Spinster and demoselle and maiden mean the same thing, but not quite. I call meself a virgin and it sounds higher minded and more spiritual. I resolve to be a noble woman but tis hard to be noble in a house along with people not noble. They dont want to be noble and hinder me spiritual effords with teasing. All the well known people you read of have trouble with their families. Look at Joan of Arc and Queen Elizabeth and St. Terese. Their families dident understand them when they started to be noble so they went away from their families. No one understands me either. Some day I will leave Castle Rea and go out in the world and me name will ring down the corridors of time no doubt.

These are me resolves for 1908.

I shall lead a noble life always, am I let.

I shall learn something new each day.

I shall not wrestle with the food caught in me teeth, are there others about that would see me.

I shall be gentle in me mein (this a new word and means how you look when other people look at you.)

I will be more lady like and not get into fights can I help it.

I will be diligent in me tasks and not fall asleep when I say me prayers.

It snowed last night. I looked out the window and there was not a track anywhere and the snow was all over the like of a white linen world. I dressed and ran out and nothing was mussed up, it was too early for the men to tend the cattle. There was no one else about so I walked to the long field making tracks. I walked with little steps and betimes made big steps. It was very still and I got to the stream and saw cunning tracks on the far bank, foxes no doubt. When tis bright moonlight I pull me bed across the window and see the foxes run the field and play the like of pups. I like to see them for they are Gods creatures but there are some of Gods creatures I don't care about.

On me way back the cattle were out and everything was spoiled. I got scolded for letting me hood slip back on me shoulders and going without me India-rubbers. Bess said not to mind and gave me breakfast by the kitchen fire. She changed me shoes and gave me hot tea. I'm not supposed to have strong tea but this was the like of physic to take the chill off me.

I took the bellows to the fire this morning and burned a hole in me plaid frock. I was going to ask Bess to put another one on me that twould not be known I burned it but thought conceal-ment not a noble thing. I showed it to Ann—me great-aunt she is—and got three Hail Marys for carelessness. Twasent careless I was, sure the spark jumped right out at me. I said the Hail Marys anyway, it being less bother and more noble.

Me lessons go fine and I had a long talk with Sister Mary-Bernard. She said I have a fine mind and I should train it and use it for the glory of God. I know I have a fine mind and like other people to tell me so. Mostly I'm called Maggie-Flibberty-Gobberty and no one takes me serious. There is great depth to me.

There was a fine party last night and Bess had me sit on the stairs late to watch the ladies and gentlemen come in kerreges. Some gentlemen came on horseback. The doors were open between the parlours and all the candles lighted and two hearth fires burned. Some of the people came and they in love, I always know the people in love. I notice they slip off to themselves and look bothered. Mary is betrothed to a gentleman named Peter.

He brings me sweets and I like him fine but God knows I'd not marry him for his weight in gold. When I marry there will be deep love between the gentleman and me. Peter and Mary mostly think of the fox hunting.

Tonight is a beautiful night and moonlighted. I looked out of the window for long in meditation. Ann sent me here in punishment for losing me temper and getting me eye blacked in a fight. Tis hard to be a noble character when they pick on me. Ann says I'm too big a girl to fight but I doubt if I'd got off with only one black eye had I been smaller.

Ann says tis shamed she is because Vincents mother sent over a note saying Vincent was on the broad of his back with the hurt I put on him and maybe he'll have the doctor to him. Twas Vincent gave me the eye. He sneaked up behind me with a cold pigs tail and dropped it down me back and away with him, and I after him. I caught him up and licked the porrige out of him. I got the eye and me drawers were torn off me almost on a hedge. I larruped him well. He got a bloodied nose and I am glad of it. Nothing can stop me from being glad of it am I kept here forever.

Were I the mother of a lad with twelve and three quarter years over his head and he licked bad by a girl with but twelve years and four days to her name, I'd keep it like a secret of the dead and not go and annoy the neighbours with notes written about it and trouble made for the innocent. A black imp of hell is Vincent and it not a lie that I write. Tim, me great-uncle, says if ever a lad had a licking coming to him tis the same Vincent and nothing should be made of it. But Ann sent me up here anyway with the rosary to say. Bess brought up me supper though I'm supposed to fast with penance on me for the fight. Had I been a truly noble woman I'd sent it back with her. Twas hungry I was and sore with misfortune and there was a sweet pudding to it. I ate it and hope the good Lord will forgive me lack of nobility.

Today was bright and fair. I walked a long way over till I could see the water. One wouldent know there was a storm at all. I had me long cloak and hood about me and was not cold. There was a strong breeze blowing. I sat and tried to meditate on me sins. I was not given leave to go so far alone. I thought maybe I could make good come of me disobedience but could not meditate because twas like singing I felt. I gave it up and let the songs come. I was back before tea and no one the wiser but Bess, and she hung me cloak up to dry. It was spray wet. Tis a great sin to disobey but I cant be noble all of the time.

I wish I was fourteen. I think tis going to school I'll be when I'm fourteen. I will be a growen woman. My mother was married at fourteen, I was born when she was but fifteen. She's dead. My father is dead too, God rest them.

This is February first. Tis leap year. Leap year is when a lady can ask the hand of a gentleman in marriage without being forward the like of some people all of the time. Bess says can she not be married this year she'll give up hope. She says she wants to marry James the tavern keeper in the town but theres many a one after him and she has but ten pounds saved. I think it no romantic way to think of marriage. I think marriage should be beautiful and fancy all over. I used to think a knight in armour would ride up on a white horse and bear me off in marriage to an enchanted castle. No one wears armour these days and a knight is but a gentleman with a title. Tim is knighted and he says small use its been to him. He got it done to please Ann, she sets store by such things. I know quite a few knights and dont believe I'd want any of them in marriage.

I'd like to marry a tall handsome man that had jet black hair and a kindly nature. He should have a moustache no doubt and they stylish, though I dont like the taste much. Tims tastes always of whiskey. Ann doesent mind, she likes whiskey herself. I'd like me husband to know about poetry and have really good hunters in his stable. I dont think money special but I'd like him to be a landed gentleman and have a lake with white swans and a boat that I could sit in under a lace parasole and drag me hands in the water. Some lilies in it too. There is a beautiful picture the like of that in the morning room.

I'd like to have nine children. Girls with fine blond curls and boys with dark black hair the like of their father. Not many boys, I dont like boys much. I'd like to have plenty of colonge water on me dressing table to use every day and not just for special. I'd like to have a pink silk gowen the like of Norahs and bright pins in me hair. I shall be a very dignified wife and not let the gentlemen crowd about me like Norah. Bess says if Norahs husband would take a gad to her he'd soon put a stop to her galivanting.

There is a new boy in the town visiting his uncle. He is an English boy. His name is Edward. He wears golf breeches with tassels to them at the knees, and fancy stockings. He has skinny legs. He was long sick, it well may be tis the sickness made him skinny. His father is a British soldier in India. Edward was sent home to England because of the sickness on him. He is a fine boy but he talks funny. Bess says he talks as if he'd a mouthfull of buttermilk and she doesent like him at all. I think him fine. His uncle brought him to call and Ann says he has beautiful manners. I am poor mannered, I slopped me tea on me good wool frock and was scolded afterwards. Ann says tis no wonder the British think us barberryians.

I think it well may be this book will fall to the hands of me grandchildren or me great-grandchildren and they'll wonder what I was like. I will set down what I am like for them. I have red hair with curls to it and wish Ann would let me thrust it up. Twelve years is almost a woman growen, Standing with reluctant feet where the brook and river meet (by Alfred Lord Tenneyson I think). It means the time when a girl begins to be a woman and not a girl any more. I have great grey eyes and a nose that turns up but looks all right. Ann says I have a good skin, did I take care of it and not run wild and get burned the like of a red Indian. Me ears are not excellent but you cant see them with all the hair I have. No one will ever see them, not even when I'm married to me husband, if I get one. Bess says husbands are getting scarcer every day. I am four feet in heighth and weigh six stone. I am not beautiful now as when a child, me photografs show me very beautiful then though simpering. I am good at me lessons when I put me mind to them. I am a sensitive child and no wonder with the affliction I had on me. Thanks be to God tis gone and I speak well as the next and hear too much for me own good Ann says. It was a long bad time and made me sensitive in me feelings.

This was a long day. Before tea Edward came over with his uncle. We played at jack straws, that was good fun. I like Edward fine. It well maybe that I'll marry him do his legs fill out. As he gets to the age of proper breeches they'll not show. I expect it well may be we could each keep our dire secrets from the other.

Edward thinks it would be nice to be married to me but says I'd have to go to live in India as he's to be an army officer the like of his father. I am an adventurous child and would like to go off all of the time. I would like to come back to visit with a long gowen I'd have to hold up when I got out of the kerrege, and with a fine silk petticoat that would rustle, and a veil. I'd like to have four of me children along with me, girls with big hats and streamers down their backs and a dark Ayah to mind them the like of the one that raised Edward up. Wouldent I cut a dash just!

I asked Edward would he like to have some children with me and he acted odd and did not answer me. Edwards fifteen. He has a tutor and studies at home the like of meself.

This was a fine bright day. Crofty brought the horses and I rode forth with Crofty and Ann. A grand ride could I be by meself. Ann catches me up about me riding manners. She says God knows why I dont ride better as I come from horse people that rode when they were diapered. Ann called Crofty up to ride on one side of me and she on the other and all of the time they spoke of me ill riding and told me to do this and do that till twas muddled I was.

I suppose tis fitten I should have manners for the hunt not to disgrace a riding family but God knows tis a lot of bother. I like to go to the paddock by meself and take along sugar, can I get it, or a handful of oats and the first horse that comes for it is the horse I take. I like to have the lads saddle the horse, not Crofty who always talks too much, and then up and away with me. I like to thrust up me skirt till I can feel the wind blow on me legs and let me hands do what they feel like doing. I like a fine gallop on a stretch with the wind tossing me hair and I like to take a hedge clean and not bother about how I do it so long as I'm well over it.

Today I was off to Edwards for tea. His uncle is a full fleshed man and gay. I've been there oft before but today was different because of Edward. I had on me green silk frock and Bess said for Gods sake be careful, did I mess it she'd have the blame of it. She put wool drawers on me because the silk frock is thinner than the wool frocks I wear, and she's fearsome of a cold for me as she'd be blamed for that also. I wish she hadent put the drawers on me. It dident feel so much the like of a party as they itched me. I bore the itching with Christian fortitude.

Edward took me for a long walk by the water before our tea and we talked of serious matters. Edward would like to marry me but he is a Prodestand and I a Catholic and we cant see how it can be come over. Neither of us will budge an inch.

Theres a rise in the land where we stood and looked at the water and the wind blew me cloak about me and me hair in me eyes and I had a fine feeling of wanting to shout and run but it was not manners to do so. We turned back and breasted the wind and Edward held me and helped me to walk or we'd never come home at all. Their Catherine put me to rights before tea, combing me hair and washing me up. She is pretty and has hair the like of me own. Her cap and her apron have fine lace to them. There is talk about her living at the Majors. I dont know what the talk is. Edwards uncle, the Major, is a batchelor retired with an illness on him but it doesent show at all.

There were two kinds of cake to our tea and hot toast with butter and jam, and we could put on as much of it as ever we liked with no one to hum at us and raise eyebrows. We had real china tea in great English cups and the Major held his cup with both hands. I did it also and found it was easier to drink. I like Edwards uncle. He said Your to be a beauty, Marget. Ged! you are a beauty right now.

19

Ladies like to be called beautiful no doubt. There was a long glass on the wall and I went to see had I changed because no one ever told me I had beauty on me. Ann says I'm clumsy, and Sister Mary-Bernard says beauty is having a good soul and your looks are not important, and Bess says I'm over young to bother me head with such nonsense. So it was fine to be told I am beautiful. I'll say naught of it least Ann will say I'm not to have nonsense put in me head. Am I quiet maybe he'll say it again some time. I wish I knew what Edward thinks of me.

Today I rode alone with Crofty, Ann was busy. We had a good gallop and not so much was said of me manners, but enough. We met Edward and his uncle near to home and they rode back along with us for tea. It was very exciting. Two days running I've seen Edward. I think I have deep love for Edward. I dont know have I or not but there is no one that would not laugh me down did I ask them. I told Edward of the journal and he wanted to see it. I'll show him the bits I think best and nothing about himself. Edward appears handsome in his boots. His legs dont show skinny. I was afraid Ann would give me cambric tea and make a child of me but she dident do it for a wonder. Edward and I talked of life. We sat on two stools by the fire apart from the others and they could not laugh at me.

Me tasks are well done again and I get praise which I like. I learned another word. Beatitude—felicity of the highest kind—consummate bliss. I thought beatitude was but a prayer I learned in me catichism. You cant tell what'll be up next. I settled to learn more words and be ahead with me tasks for the morrow that I'd get more praise.

Ann sent word for me to change me frock. We had guests to tea. Bess put me into the brown calico that I dont like much, but tis the first spring dress I've been let to wear and she let me have me pinny with real lace and a great sash behind. I looked fine. I thought Edward had come to tea.

I went down and there was Vincent and his aunt. I was angered and annoyed and hated every bone in his body. Glad enough to see his aunt but that lad! I'd poison him could I and not go to hell for it. Twould be hard to suffer everlasting fire just for getting shut of the likes of him. I had to be polite or I knew Ann would take it out on me later.

Vincent had his best clothing on him and looked odd to me. I dont know as ever I saw him with his best clothing before. He dident say anything. I dident say anything. His aunt kissed me. We had Irish bread which I love with caraway seeds to it and lashings of butter. I hoped Vincent would drip his tea on his best clothing. He wanted that I should sit on the stool by the fire. I would not. I could not but think of me love for Edward and I'd not have the stool made unholy with Vincents behind. I would not sit anywheres but by Ann on a chair. Ann said I was to take Vincent and play. Play with that gawk!

We went into the best parlour and looked at American grasses in the glass dome. Vincent said he could fight Edward and I said well, maybe he could for Edward was a gentleman born and dident go around fighting like an oaf at a fair. Vincent said first class Irishmen were fighters and I said only in war and for their countrys freedom, but not fights with fists which were vulgar. Vincent said the English were oppressors of Irish people and some day he'd be a grown man and take a crack at them and the very first crack he'd take would be at Edward. I sat with me back to him and did not speak to him again. He tried to soothe me with tales of bird nesting he'd take me to. Ann called us and he went home with his aunt and good riddance to them!

I took me fine sewing to the fire and worked at it with me hands clean. Bess looked at me and got up and felt of me head and asked me were I ill. I dont know why she'd think so and me feeling fine. I think I'll pray for Edwards conversion so tis I can marry him. I'll tell him first, tis sneaking to pray behind ones back. I love Edward with all me heart. I want to be a noble woman for him and have him for me nine childrens father. I think nine a fine number. Had I a sister or brother I'd be a happy one. I have no one. Bess thinks tis what makes me an odd child, being lone as I am.

This was a fine day with a wind up and the gulls in from the water. I felt fine when I wakened and took me rosary down to say them out of doors. I think it well may be the prayers went straight up to God and no roof between him and me. Ann looked from the casement and said Glory be to God what is the matter with you, come in before you catch your death.

I went into the big kitchen for me breakfast and Crofty came in and he dressed in his best clothing. They looked badly and wringled on him. He caught Bess up and kissed her and she slapped him hard. The others laughed and Bess told them to take shame to themselves with a child among them. She told Crofty he had the drink in him again and God only knew where he spent the night and along with what company. I like Crofty better with the drink in him than with no drink in him. He's but a crossed, sour old man and he sober. With the drink he's gay as a blackbird. Tis no matter how much of the drink he takes Ann will not send him off. He is the best horseman in the whole county drunk or sober.

I dident learn words this day but made a verse as I walked along with Bess and James and they dident mind me.

> *Help me Lord, Help Maggie-Ane*
> *To keep her conscience free from stain*
> *And guide her feet the long day through*
> *And always turn her thoughts to you.*

When I waked this day I knew there was something amiss with the world. I examined me conscience but there wasent a spot on it. Mostly when I wake troubled tis somewhat done the day before bothers me. Bess came to me her eyes red with weeping and I thought it well might be Ann found she'd taken me to the tavern. I've learned not to ask questions because no one answers them till they feel like it. And do they feel like it they tell you anyway. So I bided me time and said naught but good morning. Bess laid out me clothes and put out the dark black frock that I have for Good Friday and me heart stood still within me. I could stand it no longer and cried out what was it. Bess said I'd know soon enough. I ate me porrige and afterward was taken to Ann and may the good Lord have mercy on us all. Tim was dead and cold with a fall he took as he rode home last night in the dark along with Ann from Glebe House.

Everyone took on and cried save Ann and she sat cold as the corps itself. I think she's dead inside of her. Ann took me that I'd see Tim lying decent in his own bed with his hands crossed and a crusifix in them. It was a dred thing and I puked over me frock and the floor, and the world went dark. I waked in me bed with Ann and the doctor and Bess near to me. I started to cry and lament all over again till Ann lay down by me and soothed me. She said Tim was with his God and I was not to care so hard. She said Tim was an aged man and it was time the both of them thought of going to their reward. I went off to sleep and I waked to find the day far on toward tea time and the doctor with me again. He said I must not stay in the house of death with people coming and going to annoy me. I'm to be off to where I choose for a visit.

Sister Mary-Rose and Mary-Bernard came and said would I like to go to them. I would not. I want to go to Edwards house but I'll say naught for fear there would be shame put on me. Bess said would I go to her mothers and have the children to play with. I would not. There's too many to a bed and they rough children. I'll go nowhere but to Edwards or I'll bide here and they'll not budge me.

23

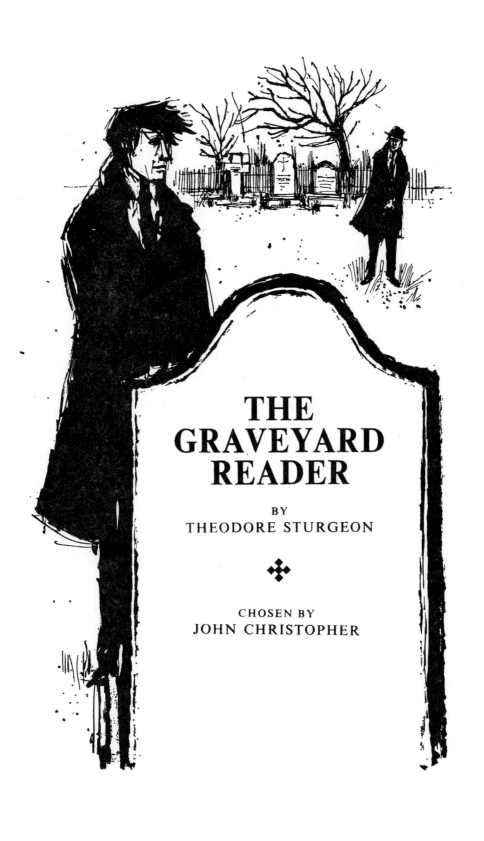

THE GRAVEYARD READER

BY
THEODORE STURGEON

❖

CHOSEN BY
JOHN CHRISTOPHER

As a form of reading fantasy has always attracted the young, and in the last fifty years science fiction has come to join it. Both are excellent as a means of broadening horizons and stimulating the mind, but they share a common weakness—in their concern with ideas and fancies they remove themselves from humanity. The characters they introduce are in general neither real nor memorable; the cardboard of which they are made is sometimes finely painted, but it remains cardboard for all that.

Theodore Sturgeon, who has contributed notably to both fields, proves the rule by exception, and is almost unique in doing so. Sturgeon is always concerned with people. The characters who move through his wonderful speculations are men and women who live and breathe, suffer and rejoice.

Harlan Ellison, introducing a story by Sturgeon in his notable science fiction anthology, DANGEROUS VISIONS, speaks of a personal contact he had with Sturgeon and goes on to say: "I knew virtually nothing about love but was totally familiar with hate, while Ted knew almost nothing about hate, yet was completely conversant with love in almost all its manifestations."

Mr. Ellison, I am sure, was doing himself an injustice there, but his comment on Sturgeon rings true. Every one of his stories is informed with compassion; with love in its purest sense, which is charity.

The Graveyard Reader, in my view, is Sturgeon's finest story, for fantasy and humanity and what one must call wisdom, and I am immensely grateful for the opportunity of giving it a wider audience. As fantasy it is breath-taking, with a marvellous sting in the tail. As counsel for the sore, self-wounded heart, it is superb.

JOHN CHRISTOPHER

THE stone was included in the price of the plot; I hadn't known. I hadn't wanted a stone because stones have to say something, and what can you say in a case like this? but unwittingly I'd bought the thing and because I had, the man had put it up—what else? I had anger enough to scatter around heart-deep, but, reasonably, not a flake for the men who had put up the stone.

It was a right and proper stone, I supposed, if one must have one of the things at all: bigger than many of the cheating, bargain sort of stones that stood nearby, and tastefully smaller than the hulking ostentatious ones. *Here lies my wife between poverty and vulgarity.* Now there you go. Have a single elevating thought about that woman and it comes out sounding like that. Soils everything she touches.

The stone called me a liar for that. It was of a whitish granite that would weather whiter still. It had edges of that crinkly texture like matted hair that nothing would stick to because nothing could possibly want to, and a glassy face that nothing would stick to if it wanted nothing else. Whited sepulchre, that's what the hell. The stone is its own epitaph, because look: it's white forever, white and clean, and it has no words—which is to say, nothing. Nothing, and clean, ergo, *Here lies nothing clean.*

What I always say is, there's a way to say anything in the world if you can only think of the way to say it, and I had. I liked this epitaph just fine. There would be no words on this stone, and it had its epitaph.

Laughing out loud is bad form in a graveyard, and stepping down hard on a man's instep is bad form anywhere. This was the moment when, backing off for some perspective on this my masterpiece, I did both these things. The man, apparently, had been standing behind me watching. I whirled and looked him up and down, hoping sincerely that he was offended. There are times in a man's life when he wouldn't want even his friends to like him, and such a time is not time to pay court to the esteem of a stranger.

He wasn't offended. All I got out of him (just then) was a pleasant smile. He had a sort of anybody's face, the like of which you might encounter anywhere, which is to say he had the kind of face you wouldn't be surprised to see visiting a cemetery. I'll say this for him: he was harmonious; his voice and clothing exactly suited his face, and though he wasn't an old man, the things he said weren't hard to figure, coming from a man like that. You could tell he was experienced.

Neither of us said anything right away when I bumped him. He sort of put his hands on my shoulders for a second either to hold one of us up or to keep the other from falling, which gave the gesture a full fifty per cent chance of being selfish, and I am not about to give away a thank-you in the face of those odds. As for an excuse-me, I didn't want to be excused, I wanted to be blamed. So I glared at first, while he smiled, and after those things got used up there was nothing for it but to stand where we were, side by side, looking at my wife's grave because that was straight ahead and we couldn't just go on looking at each other. It was while we were doing this that he said, "Mind if I read it?"

I looked at him. Even if this had been the perfect time and place for joking, a face that looked the way his face looked contained no jests. I looked from him to the bland, uncommunicative sheet of stone and the raw mound with its neat planes still unslumped by wind or water, and I looked back at him. It occurred to me then that maybe his eyes weren't so good, and he honestly didn't know there was nothing on the stone. "Yes," I said as offensively as I could, "I mind."

He put up his hands placatingly, and said in that same good-natured way, "All right, all *right!* I won't." And he gave me a sort of friendly half-wave and started off.

I looked at the grave and at his retreating back and "Hey!" I called before I realized I wanted to.

He came back, smiling. "Yes?"

I felt robbed, that's why I had called him back. I'd realized I wanted to see his face when he got close enough to squint at that unmarked stone. I said, "What I mean is, I'd mind if anyone read anything off that. It would give me the creeps."

He didn't even glance toward the grave, but said patiently, "It's all right. I promised you I wouldn't."

I said, "Oh for God's sake," disgustedly, and with an angry motion beckoned him to follow me. I had that oafish feeling you get when you tell a joke and somebody doesn't get it, so instead of letting the matter drop you lay your ears back and start explaining, knowing perfectly well that when you finally get the point across it isn't going to be funny, either to your victim or to yourself. I ranged up on one side of the grave and he came up and crossed over and stood at the other side, not four feet away from the headstone. He was looking right at it, but didn't say anything, so I barked, "Well?"

"Well," he asked politely, "what?"

The oafish feeling intensified. "Don't you find the language of that epitaph a little on the terse side?" I said sarcastically.

He glanced at it. "There's never very much on the stone," he said, and added, as if to himself, "while it's new."

"New or old," I said, and I guess I showed something of the anger I felt, "the way it is is the way it stays. Anything that gets written on that rock is not going to be written by me."

"Naturally not," he said.

To make it quite clear, I said, "Or by anyone I hire."

"Well," he said comfortingly, "don't worry. I won't read it, now or later."

"You can say that again," I growled. I was finally coming to a certainty about this grave. "The less said about this whole thing, including her *and* her slab, the better. That was her strong point anyway; keeping her mouth shut. At long last, anything she's hiding, she can keep. I won't want to hear it."

"Then you won't," he said peacefully, "and neither will I, because I've promised." After a sort of pause, he added, "I think I ought to warn you, though, that somebody else might come along and read it, not knowing of your objections."

"What are you talking about?"

"I'm not the only one in the world who can read graves."

"I told you—I'm not putting any inscription on. Not a

monogram. Not so much as *Hers,* or even—hey, this would be cute: *Her lies.* Not that she was really ever a liar. She just wouldn't *say.*"

"The inscriptions never say very much by themselves," he said in his patient voice, "taken out of context."

"What do you mean, context?"

"I don't think you quite understood me. I didn't say I read gravestones. I said I read graves."

I looked blankly at that tidy, tamped-down mound and the virgin stone, and back at the shovel-patted yellow earth turning grainy in the late warm sunlight, and a more uncommunicative arrangement I had never laid eyes on. It conveyed nothing about her and, for that matter, nothing about anyone else. Me, for instance. No flowers.

"Not this one, you can't," I said finally.

"I wouldn't."

"That promise of yours," I said with a certain amount of smug enmity, "comes in pretty handy, doesn't it? I think I see what you're driving at, and I don't think it's any too funny. You've spent a lot of time ghouling around places like this until you can tell to a dime what the planting cost, how much the survivors give a damn, if any, how long the box has been buried, and how good a job the crew did on the detail. But any time there's a little more than readily meets the eye, like a guy who says he won't have an inscription after paying for a stone, you don't have to risk a wrong guess. You just make a gentlemanly promise, casual-like." I snorted through my nostrils.

He still wouldn't let me annoy him. He simply explained where I was wrong. He said, "It isn't like that at all. There's nothing to deduce, or to guess at. It's all there," he said, nodding at but not looking at the grave, "to be read. I'll admit that it's a little harder to do on a very new grave; you might say that it's all in very fine print and a little hard to see unless you read well. But in time it all comes clear—very clear. As to the promise, it's very obvious that you wouldn't want a stranger like myself to know everything about her."

"Everything?" I laughed bitterly. "Nobody knows everything about *her.*"

"Well, it's all there."

"You know what's happened to me," I said a little too loudly and a little too fast, "I'm a little bit out of my head from all that's happened the last week or so, which makes me stand here listening to you as if you made sense."

He didn't say anything.

"By God," I mumbled, not talking to him or to anyone special at the moment, "it wasn't too long ago I'd given anything you like to know some things about that woman. Only since I made up my mind I don't want to know, I feel much better," I said, feeling miserable. "You know what she did, she wasn't home when I got there that night, we'd had a little sort of fight the morning before, and that night she was just gone. No note and she didn't pack anything or take anything but that one green tweed suit and that stupid hat she used to wear with it. If she had any money it wasn't much. Then, nothing for three whole days and nights, until that phone call." My hands got all knotted up and then seemed to get too heavy, pulling my shoulders into a slump. I sat down on the edge of an iron-pipe railing at the edge of the next grave and let the heavy hands dangle down between my thighs. I hung my head down so I could watch them while I talked. Watching them didn't tell me anything. "Phone call from the police who found her driver's license in her handbag, the one that matched that stupid hat."

I raised my head and looked across the grave at the man. I couldn't see him too clearly until I hit myself across the eyes with my sleeve. The cuff buttons had got themselves turned around, and it hurt. "Eight hundred miles from home with some guy in a sports car, and all she had on was one of those fancified bath-robes, you know, hostess gown, a good one, I never saw it before. Don't know where the green suit got to or the stupid hat either. Bag was in the car. Car was in an oak tree. No kidding. Upside down in an oak tree fifteen feet off the ground. The police said he had to be going a hundred and twenty to hit as hard as that. I never heard of him before. I don't know how she got there. I don't know why. Well," I said after I thought about it for a minute, "I guess I do know more or less why, but not *exactly* why; not exactly what was in her mind when she did whatever it was she did to get herself into that. I never knew exactly what was in her mind. I could never get her to say. She would—"

I guess at that point I stopped talking out loud, because it all turned into a series of swift pictures, one after the other, inside my head, too fast for words, and too detailed. *What's the matter?* I'd be saying, and her, kissing my hands, looking up at me with tears in her eyes: *Can't you see?* And again: me yelling at her, *Well if what I do makes you unhappy, why don't you tell me what you want? Go ahead, write the script, I'll play it.* And the way she'd turn her back when I talked like that, and I'd hear her voice softly: *If you'd only*—and *I just*—and then she'd stall, inarticulate, shake her head. She never talked enough. She never *said* the things that . . . that . . . World of feeling, spectrum of sensitivity, and no words, no dammit dammit words. Picture of her smiling, looking off, out, a little up; I say *What are you so happy about?* Oh, she says, coming back into the world, *Oh* . . . and whispers my name four times, smiling. Now what is that—communication?

"I got so there was nothing in the world for me, sleeping or waking or working or mixing a drink," I said aloud to the man, "but *Why won't she tell me?* And right to the end, she did that to me. Wondering why she does this or that, why she wears one particular kind of look instead of another, maybe, after all, these things don't matter. But look how she winds up, dead in that new housecoat I didn't buy for her, eight hundred miles from home with a guy I don't know; all in the world I have now is *why? why?* and the idea that she wound it up in the one way where I'd never find out. I mean," I added as soberly as I could, because I was unaccountably out of breath, just from talking to a man, imagine? "I mean, not that I want to find out. Because I don't give a damn any more."

"Well, that's good then," he said, "because you'll save yourself a lot of trouble."

"What trouble?"

"Learning to read graves."

I got enormously tired of this conversation suddenly. "Now what good would it do me to learn a thing like that?"

"None," he said in that pleasant way of his. "You have just

finished saying that you don't want to know anything about her, any more."

"It finally sinks in," I said sarcastically, "that what you're trying to tell me is that a person who can read graves can stand in front of one and read it like a book."

"A biography." He nodded.

"And get out of it everything that person ever did."

"Or said, or thought," he agreed.

I looked at the grave, its empty crumbling bare planes, its empty-faced headstone. I looked again, but briefly, at the events that had made it be here just where it was, when it was, containing what, and I wet my lips and said, "You're kidding."

He never seemed to answer what deserved no answer, that man.

I asked him, "Even things nobody ever knew before?"

"Especially those things," he said. "What you can see of a human being is only the outside of the top part of the surface. Now if everything—is there—" he pointed—"to be read— *everything*—then it follows that you can read far more than the most penetrating analysis of anything living." When I had no response to this, he said, "Living things aren't finished, you see. Everything they have ever been in contact with, each thought they have had, each person they have known—these things are still at work in them; nothing's finished."

"And when they're buried, they . . . do something to the grave? There's a real difference between one grave and another, or . . . a grave would be different if one person or another was buried in it?"

"It has to be that way," he said. Again one of those odd, waiting pauses, which I refused to take for myself. He said, "Surely you've had that feeling that a human being is too much, has too much, means too much just to go out like a light, or be eroded away like the soil of a dust bowl."

I looked at the grave. So new, so raw, so . . . blank. In a low voice, I asked, "What do you read?"

He understood what I meant: what are the "letters," the "words," the "grammar"?

He said, "A lot of things. The curve of the mound, the encroachment of growth on it—grass, weeds, mosses. The kind of vegetation that grows there, and the shape of each stem and leaf, even the veining in them. The flight of insects over it, the shadows they cast, the contours of rain-rivulets as they form, as they fill, as they dry." He laughed deprecatingly. "It sounds like more than a man could learn, doesn't it?"

I thought it did.

He said, "You are so completely familiar with the act of reading that it never occurs to you how complex an act it is, or how vast is your accomplishment. You take in stride a variety of alphabets—upper case and lower case are very nearly two separate ones, and then upper and lower case in script are quite different from printing or typing. Old English and black-letter faces might slow you down but they won't stop you. Your eye measures light intensities between ink and paper: green letters on a yellow page wouldn't stop you. You select, without effort, just what you read on a page and what you do not. For example, every page of a book might have the book title at the top and a page-number at the bottom, and you don't even know they're there. In a magazine or a newspaper, blocks of type might be broken up, carried over, interrupted by pictures or advertisements, and you sail right along reading what you are interested in and nothing else. You might notice a misprint or a misspelling, or even an out-of-context line of type lost in the middle of your paragraph, but in most cases it doesn't bother you much. In addition, you're reading in English—one of the richest of all languages, but also one of the most difficult, with irregular structure, spelling, and some pretty far-fetched semantic shorthand and shortcuts. But all these are the rarefied complications; to get back to basics, what about the letters themselves? The letter 'a' doesn't look like the sound—or several sounds—of 'a.' It's only a most arbitrary symbol, chosen by custom and usage to mean what it means."

"But . . . at least there's a system. I mean, an established alphabet. Accepted spelling. And—for all their exceptions, there are rules of grammar and syntax."

Again he said nothing, just waiting for me to come up with something or other. To think, perhaps.

I did, and said, "Oh. You mean—there *is* some such system?"
I laughed suddenly. "A crooked thorn for the letter 'b,' and a
line of mud for past tense?"

He smiled and nodded. "Not those, but things like those. Yes,
that's the idea."

"Not as hard as it seems at first, hm?"

"The thing you try to put over to every first-grader," he
agreed. "But—it *is* hard. As hard as anything else you can study.
Just as hopeless-looking at times, too, when the over-all pattern
just won't emerge and all your work seems useless. Then—it
comes clear, and you go on."

I looked at him and said, "I don't know why I believe
you."

He waited until I said, "—but I'd like to learn that trick."

"Why?"

I glanced at the bare new grave. "You said . . . '*everything.*'
You said I could find out what she did, with whom. And—why."

"That's right."

"So . . . let's go. Where do we start?" I went down on one
knee and made an across-the-board gesture at my wife's grave.

"Not here." He smiled. "You don't use Dostoevsky as a first
reader."

"Dostoevsky? *Her?*"

"They're all Dostoevskys. They can all express every shade of
meaning of every event, and through what they think and feel
one can see the meaning of all their world. Isn't that what makes
a great writer?"

"I guess it is . . . but . . . great writer? *Her?*"

"She lived," he said. "Now what she was is . . . graven here.
Living and feeling are things done by everybody. Writing on
their graves is done by everybody. Dostoevsky, now, had what
you might term a *previous* skill. He could do it while he was alive.
Dead, they can all do it."

This guy made my head spin. I got up slowly and followed
him to the . . . "first reader." Like most such volumes, it was a
very little one.

I went back every evening, after work, for nearly a year. I

learned the meaning of the curl of a leaf and the glisten of wet pebbles, and the special significance of curves and angles. A great deal of the writing was unwritten. Plot three dots on a graph and join them; you now have a curve with certain characteristics. Extend that curve while maintaining the characteristics, and it has meaning, up where no dots are plotted. In just this way I learned to extend the curve of a grass-blade and of a protruding root, of the bent edges of wetness on a drying headstone.

I quit smoking so I could sharpen my sense of smell, because the scent of earth after a rain has a clarifying effect on graveyard reading, as if the page were made whiter and the ink darker. I began to listen to the wind, and to the voices of birds and small animals, insects and people; because to the educated ear, every sound is filtered through the story written on graves, and becomes a part of it.

The man met me every day; early or late, he was around. I never asked him anything about himself. Somehow that never came up. He never read anything to me. He would point out the "letters" and occasionally the "letter-groups" like (analogously) "-ing" and "-ous" and "un-," and would correct me where I read it wrong. But when I got to where I could read whole sentences, he stopped me. He told me that the one thing I must never do is to read off what I read on a grave, aloud. Not even to him. Those who could read it, would, if they cared to. Those who could not must learn as I was learning, or not know what was written there. "There are reasons enough for not wanting to die," he told me, "without adding the fear that someone like you will go around abusing this privilege."

I would go home at night filled with a gray hope, that at last all the mysteries of that woman would be solved for me, and every sordid, rotten thing she had done and kept secret would be illuminated for me. I didn't sleep very well—I hadn't, since the day she left—and I had lots of time to think over the things she had done to me, and the things she probably had done to me, and the things she was doubtless capable of doing. Maybe this long period of insufficient sleep did something to me; I don't know, but I didn't mind it. I did my work at the office, enough to get along saving my strength and my brain for the evening; and then I worked at my lessons. I worked.

We went from the "first readers" into more complicated stuff. You can have no idea how complicated a thing like a three-year-old is when you first start. The only thing that took me through this stage was his promise that however hopeless it looked, sooner or later the pattern would emerge and I'd understand and could go on. He was right. He was always right.

I began to learn about people. I began to find out how many were afraid of the same things—afraid of being shut out, of being found out, of being unloved, unwanted, or—worst of all—unneeded. I learned how flimsy were the bases of so many of their fears, and how unimportant, in the long run, were the things on which so many of them pitifully spent their lives. More than anything else, I learned how uncharacteristic of most of them were their cruelties, how excusable their stupidities; in short, how damned decent they were.

I found out the difference between "the truth" and "all the truth." You can know some pretty terrible things about a person, and you can know they're true. But sometimes it makes a huge difference if you know what else is true too. I read something in a book once about an old lady who was walking along the street minding her own business when a young guy came charging along, knocked her down, rolled her in a mud-puddle, slapped her head and smeared handsful of wet mud all over her hair. Now what should you do with a guy like that?

But then if you find out that someone had got careless with a drum of gasoline and it ignited and the old lady was splashed with it, and the guy had presence of mind enough to do what he did as fast as he did, and severely burn his hands in the doing of it, then what should you do with him?

Yet everything reported about him is true. The only difference is the amount of truth you tell.

Reading a grave, you read it all. All of the truth makes a difference—but what a difference—in the way you feel about people.

One day the man said to me, "I would say that there are only a half-dozen graves here that are beyond you. I think you're a pretty remarkable student."

I said thanks, but I'd blame the quality of the teaching. "You've taken an awful lot of trouble over me."

He shrugged. "It's what I do," he said inclusively. Then he waited.

I wondered what he was waiting for, and so searched back through what he had been saying. "Oh," I said, and with him, looked up at the north corner of the cemetery where my wife's grave lay. It wasn't sharp-planed any more, or bare. Everything about it had changed . . . been changed . . . except, of course, that unsoilable headstone. So, "Oh," I said. "I could read it."

"Easily," he said.

I went up there. I don't know if he followed me. I wasn't thinking about him any more. I came to the grave and stood looking at it for a long time. I thought about her, and about the facts I had. Truths. The truth about her. The time I pried her out of a dark corner at a party with a drunk named Wilfred. The time she snatched a letter off the mantel when I came in and threw it into the fire. The time that guy on the boat laughed when her name was mentioned and then shut up when he found I was married to her. More than anything else, the fact of her death in the sports car, the fact of that housecoat, of the missing tweed suit and stupid hat. Now I could know. Now I could know what, where, and how many times. Now I could know why.

I guess I was up there for longer than I realized. When I came to myself it was almost dark, and growing cold. I almost fell when I started to walk. I walked slowly until my legs woke up and, seeing a light in the caretaker's building, went in to talk to the old fellow for a minute. I didn't see the graveyard reader around anywhere.

I was back the next morning. It was Saturday. The stone-cutter was there already, crouched in front of my plot, tick-ticking away. I'd had to agree to time-and-a-half to get him, but I was willing. When at last I decided on an epitaph for that stone, I wanted it put there, and right *now*.

I walked up there to watch the man work. He knew his trade, that stone-cutter, and he had almost finished. After a few minutes I was aware of someone standing next to me, and sure enough, it was the graveyard reader. "Hi."

"How are you?" he asked—not the way anyone else might ask, but meaning it: how was I? what had happened? how did I feel about it? was I all right?

"I'm all right," I said. Also, not the way you'd say it to just anybody.

Silently we watched the man finish up. I nodded to him and said it was fine. He grinned and gathered up his tools and the tarpaulin with the chips in it, and waved and went away. The reader and I stood looking at the inscription.

I said, a little embarrassed, "Not very original."

"But very effective," he answered.

"You think so? You really think so?"

He nodded, and that made me very, very glad. I hadn't meant to tell him, but it slipped out in one great big blurt: "I didn't read it."

"No?"

"No," I said. "I came up here and stood for a long time, thinking about . . . all the work I'd done to be able to read it, and about—the truth, what kind of a difference *all* the truth makes. And I thought a lot about people, and about . . . *her*."

"Yes," he said, interested and . . . non-prying.

"Yes, about her, the things she'd done, the things she could have done. The way she used to talk to me. Do you know, people like her, who aren't so hot with words—they have ways of talking, if you can read them, almost like a grave has?"

"I think you're right."

"Well, I thought about that too. And my own illiteracy . . ." I laughed in some sort of embarrassment and said, "Anyway, the way it wound up, I didn't read it. I went and ordered this epitaph instead."

"Why that particular one?"

We read it over together, and I said, "It's taken me over a year, and a pretty tough year at that, but this is what I wanted to say to her. This is what I want her to know, now and from now on, from me."

He laughed.

39

I confess to being a little annoyed at that, even after all I had gone through with this fellow. "What's funny?"

"*You're* saying that, to *her?*"

"Something wrong with that?"

"Sure is," he said. And he walked off, and when I called, he just waved, but kept on walking.

I turned to look back at the headstone, with its clean new inscription. I'd put it there because I wanted to say something to her that——

Me? say something to *her?*

No wonder he had laughed. A guy spends more than a year learning to read a grave, and then gets the silly notion that it's reading him.

So I read it again—not the grave; I would never read that—I read just the inscription. I read what she said to me, now, this morning, new and crisp for the very first time: *Rest in peace.*

"Thanks, honey," I whispered, "I will," and I went on home and got the first real sleep I'd had since she'd left me.

The Purple Moccasin
by MacKinlay Kantor

chosen by Vera & Bill Cleaver

ONE must be thankful to MacKinlay Kantor for *The Purple Moccasin*. From a little scene of early American wilderness it speaks to us of a deeper, stronger, more worthy life pattern that is sought by most men. It contains all the necessary ingredients for greatness: humor, simplicity, narrative vigor, the pursuit of grand purpose, an enlarging look at one life-enhancing way.

While holding in mind that the situation presented in this short tale is of another, perhaps richer era, still we know there are people like Dr. Sickles and Flora Katherine and Jesse who, today, arm themselves with spades and shovels and buckets and travel our back roads in search of wild, green gold. For we have done a little of this kind of traveling ourselves and have observed and I tell you it is a thrilling thing.

Surely this story was written for us and for you, for all who would keep safe the pigeons and the lordly bison and the purple moccasin.

VERA AND BILL CLEAVER

ONCE upon a time there was a boy who had run away from home, and he said that he was going up into northern Missouri to find Jesse James.

The runaway traveled all day on unfamiliar roads, and his legs grew powerful weary; but still he kept on traveling, because he was in anger with his pappy. The bunting birds sang constantly, and I reckon they were surprised to see him loping down the rocky twists and turns that led into valleys he had never walked before.

It seemed as if the devil himself was pursuing, and nagging, and saying, "Hasten up, bubby. You've got a long ways to go, and you don't want Jesse James to be vanished when you get there."

And at sunset the boy came to a secret place beside a brown river. It was cool there, and you could smell the sweet marsh that neighbored the stream. A hot day's journey had brought that boy nigh the point where he was ready to fling himself down and cry his heart empty and dry. I have knowledge how he was feeling, for I was that boy.

I sat me down on an old log bridge across the stream; I let my sore feet swing close to the water, and I put my little bundle of possessions beside me. I wondered if my sisters were crying, because I hadn't come back to take supper at home.

And then, the next moment, I was standing square erect as any cat—for the sound of a shotgun takes an exhausted person by surprise.

Over in those woods I had just passed was where the shot came from. And now I could hear voices, a clear, high-pitched voice, and one that was deeper, but more threatening. I legged it across the bridge, because I was plumb certain that the Pinkerton men had sighted me, and that somehow they had got wind of my intentions about Jesse James.

But by the time I got to the far shore, my curious nature

43

had come alive; I couldn't have stirred another step until I saw just what was in those woods, and who had fired the shotgun, and who was roaring like the bull of Bashan.

Then they came out of the brush, moving mighty quick. The first was a little girl, and she went through the rails of that old fence like a garter snake. The second was a man, a tall one, with a shabby coat flapping about his thighs. He'd lost his hat sure enough, for his hair shone white and silvery in the dusk. He crossed the fence, but more dignified than the little girl. At first I thought he was toting a rifle along with him, but in the next moment, even through the gloom, I could see that it was only a spade.

There were firearms abroad, though; I hadn't mistrusted my ears. The bushes began to wave, and a strong-built man stepped into the open space behind the fence. He carried his weapon so that the muzzle was aimed threateningly at those two figures in the road. I scrooched low, but I was mighty near all eyes and ears.

"This is the second offense," said the man with the gun. "I warn you, mister, that the third offense will prove fatal."

The white-haired gentleman in the road kind of pulled himself together and straightened his coattails. "My friend," he said, "your boast is hollow unless you improve your marksmanship."

"The goodness of my aim hain't never been questioned," replied he who held the shotgun. "That time I fired into a buttonball tree, so as not to orphan this kid of yourn."

"Orphan or not," the older man told him, kind of loftily, "she'll acquit herself skillfully in the world. But I insist that you listen to reason, my good sir! I have only one purpose in visiting your property, and. . . ."

The armed man swung back into the bushes. "Good enough purpose, too, I'll be bound!" he yelled over his shoulder. "You want that gold and you want that silverware. But if there's any digging to be done on this property, I reckon I'll hoist the shovel myself!" Then, before there could be a reply, he had gone crackling through the bushes.

I heard that tall bareheaded man say distinctly, "Flower of My Life, I shall yet lift the purple moccasin from alien soil!"

The little girl laughed with a terrified voice. Then the two of them came toward me, and they were halfway across the bridge before they saw the kind of lump I made, squatting there in the twilight.

He pulled up right smart, and the girl with him. They eyed me for a spell, and I managed to stand erect, though me knees were palsied. "Another wayfarer is present," cried the old man. "Kitty Cat, do you think he intends to dispute our crossing?"

The little girl made a few steps forward and peered at me. The sunset was far distant beyond that valley and the trees that rimmed it, but I swear it was reflected in the mane of hair that dressed her head, and I'll think about her every time I see embers glowing in the night.

"Why, Daddy," she yelped, "he's just a little boy!"

I was jealous of my age and didn't admire to be called a little boy. "Howdy," I said, but my voice did sound mighty piping.

He came closer, until he could look down into my face. "My son," he said, "you seem to be unhappy about something."

"No," I whispered, "I've just been traveling."

"Where from?"

An idea snapped into my head, quick as lightning. "Arkansas," I told him.

"Arkansas," repeated the stranger. He took note of my bare feet and the bundle in my hand, and he kind of chuckled. "My young friend, I assume from your demeanor and from the state of your attire, that you are a wanderer drifting abroad like the tumbleweed blown from its native heath."

Well, I was flabbergasted by his speech, because folks didn't talk that way in our neighborhood. But I did manage to mumble out something about how I was going to attach myself to Jesse James, and Cole Younger, too, as soon as he got out of Stillwater.

"Ah," said this man, "Jesse James indeed! A ruthless man, no doubt, and given to incursions and forays."

"Mister," I said, "he robs banks and trains, and he don't give a hoot about Pinkerton men."

The little girl said, kind of pert, "I bet, little boy, he'd eat you up in one bite, if you came nigh to him."

45

"*Near*, Kitty Cat," cried the tall man. "The word is *near*. I resent your adoption of the colloquial phrase." He kept fondling that spade, with the dusk growing thicker at every breath. He seemed powerful old, to have a daughter smaller than me.

The girl called Kitty Cat or Flower of My Life, as the case may be, came real close and poked her finger at my chest. "Boy," she said, "how old are you?"

"Mighty nigh onto thirteen," said I, kind of fuming, "and I'm no little boy, either."

"Oh," said Kitty Cat, "you're scarcely older than I, because I'm just twelve myself! Daddy, I guess he's the dirtiest boy I've ever seen."

The old man shook his head at her, and his long locks danced about his ears. "Impolite, Flora Katherine, highly impolite. Your own appearance is scarcely impeccable."

"Boy," she demanded to know, "what's your name?"

"Jesse," I said, "same as Jesse James. And I've got a weapon too. It's a pepperbox revolver that my Uncle Andrew gave me last year, and I've got it right here in this bundle." And then I added, in proud manner, "I'll show it to you, if you want me to."

"No," she said, "I don't like guns. That old man Travis just fired off his shotgun to scare us. And I was scared, and I bet you'd be scared too."

"I wager I wouldn't," I said. We glared at each other, though the gloom was getting so thick you could cut it with a knife.

All this time her father had been dreaming to himself— sighing, and saying over and over again, "Alien soil. Alien soil." But now he shook his head and clucked like a hen coming off her nest, and he poked his finger at me. "Jesse," he said, "fellow traveler of the unfriendly byways, have you broken bread of late?"

Though folks didn't talk that way in our neck of the woods, my father used to read aloud out of books; I wasn't the ignorant little hillbilly that I looked to be. "Mister," I said, "I reckon I could eat a polecat."

"Inedible," he cried. "Absolutely inedible! Carnivorous

mammal. *Mephitis mephitica*, wholly unfit for food. But, to return to my invitation, our stores are ample for our simple needs. I can sup very eagerly myself, despite my disappointment," and then he went to mumbling, uttering again that strange remark about the purple moccasin.

He led the way along the road past the bridge, and the little girl and I scampered after him. A kind of cavern opened up beside us, and it was a lane leading down to a forgotten ford by the brookside. The man went ahead, tall and straight and dreamy, with his silvery hair shaking in a little breeze that had sprung up with the falling of night.

But now it was dark in that tunnel through the trees, and I stumbled in all directions. Next thing I knew, Flora Katherine had reached out her hand; she pulled me along, because she knew the way over these roots and boulders, and it was kind of comforting to have her holding on to me. I thought of my sisters Melissa and Algy, and I kept blinking my eyes.

When I had blinked the wetness out of them, I could see a fire burning low, as if it hadn't been tended for an hour or two. There was a wagon with a canvas top, like movers rode in when they passed our house, but smaller, and there was an old white horse that nickered his head off when he heard us.

They had camped here for days and days. The grass was all tromped down, and there was a scattering of little things underfoot, and there was a tent set up beside the wagon. Not far away, the river chattered among its rocks and told a good and comforting message about the black bass and the little nibbling suckers that lived there.

"Kitty Cat," said the man, "do you put that skillet on the coals. And possibly our young visitor can fetch some wood from the pile. Unless I am gravely mistaken, a reluctant visitor or two may be quivering on our line."

So he vanished toward the river, and I went smelling around for wood. As for Flora Kitty Cat, she spread herself high, wide, and handsome around that clearing. She scooped the coals together and set the frying pan level and true; next minute she had dropped in some bacon. And after that, she was getting out a sack of fodder and shaking some loose for the old white horse,

47

though anybody could see that he was fat as a pig already. And she called him Linnaeus, which was a mighty strange name for a horse.

"Why do you call him Linnaeus?" I demanded to know.

"Because that's his name."

"It's a crazy variety of name, if you ask me," I told her.

Kitty Cat said, "Well, I didn't ask you," and went right on feeding him.

"At home," I made bold to say, "a horse critter is named Dobbin or Maud or Betsy or Bill, or some decent-sounding name."

She snapped at me, "At home—where's that?" I came close to saying "Rosy Ridge," but I thought twice and gulped out "Arkansas."

"Linnaeus was a great man," she said. "He defined genera and species. He deserves to have a horse named after him."

I tell you she made me boil, because I didn't admire having any girl fling that variety of language at me. But I swallowed my pride and went on building one side of the fire, while the bacon stewed and smoked and frizzled on the other side. Next moment we heard a kind of yell, which I reckoned was happiness, from the direction of the river. It was plumb certain that we wouldn't have to content ourselves with side meat.

"What's his name?" I asked.

"Who?"

"Your pappy."

"He's Doctor Samuel Sickles, Mister Jesse, and I'll thank you not to push those coals into the bacon."

Well, I got the coals out, but burned my fingers doing it. And I wanted to know whether he doctored horses or people, for those were the only two kinds of doctors that I knew anything about; no other kind had ever come a-visiting us.

"He's a doctor of science," she chirped, "and I guess that's what I'll be, too, when I grow up. You're very clumsy, boy. Will you please get your legs out of the way, so that I can put this corn pone to get hot?"

Her manner was driving me wild; but Doctor Samuel Sickles came back, and he had two catfish, not big enough to be coarse and strong, but big enough to be worth eating. And that supper which we ate—there was a jar of pickles to go with it, and some apples, and peach preserves that had never been stewed over that fire—was something to remember. I reckon I'll remember it until I give up the ghost, no matter how tart and ornery Flora Katherine acted.

There are strange miseries that enter the heads and hearts of older folks, which young'uns know nothing about. Doctor Samuel Sickles was now besieged by an ailment of that kind. For he did not eat sufficient to keep him alive. Soon he was silent and melancholy, over by his side of the fire, and the little girl undertook to nurse him. She offered him the finest morsels of catfish and pone and pickles, but he didn't pay heed. He hunched down lower and lower, with the points of his shoulders going up against his ears, and every now and then his voice would exclaim in sadness or contempt.

"What ails him anyway?" I managed to whisper to Kitty Cat, when she gave me my last slab of fish.

"He's feeling bad about the purple moccasin."

"Can't he make one for his own self?" I wanted to know.

She looked reproving, and she told me that God had made this purple moccasin, and it was the only one in the world, so far as she knew.

I asked, "Is it a snake?"

"Oh, no!" she said shivering. "I don't like snakes a bit. But this is beautiful."

By this time she was talking as loud as you please. Still, Doctor Sickles gave us no attention. He looked moody as a ghost that couldn't get back to his tomb, and when he stood up, he walked right into the frying pan, and he had no swear word to utter about it. The fire was low again, so it was hard to make out the figure of this old man, once he had wandered away from the embers. Though I could follow the red glow on his gleaming hair, and I saw him go to the tail of the wagon; then, from somewhere, he had drug out a tin lamp and a watering pot.

He lighted the lamp and clumb up over the tailboard. For a while we could watch his tall shape shadowing around inside

49

the canvas, all lit up, like a big black spook, by the lamp glow. He was doing strange things inside that wagon, and I reckoned I'd die of curiosity.

"Is your pap going to bed?" I asked Kitty Cat.

"We don't sleep there," she said. "He's just seeing after things."

"People always sleep in wagons," I told her, for plenty of movers had gone by our house, bound for Texas and the Indian country, and I knew their habits.

But Flora Katherine Sickles was as sharp as her name, and she told me to be more polite. She said that she wasn't allowed to sleep in the wagon, nor did Doctor Sickles allow himself to do it, and there wasn't room for them anyway.

We were fussing and fuming at each other again, and our angriness got the better of us both, and then we didn't talk again for a long time.

I sat there cross-legged by the fire, and thought how many miles away my home was lying and how badly I had been mistreated. And finally I was feeling lonesome and bereft, and I couldn't see the fire at all because my eyes were so blurry. Then, just when the spasms were rising and I thought they'd slay me in my throat, I felt a hard little hand take hold of mine, and there was Kitty Cat kneeling beside me.

In the low firelight, her hair seemed too wonderful to adorn any living head, and it overcome my breath. For she did look like a kind of angel, although one that had been running loose in the woods and tearing her dress when she did it.

"Jesse," she said, "you seem to be feeling miserable. I feel sorry for you, Jesse."

I contrived to tell her that she didn't need to and that pretty soon I'd go on looking for Jesse James.

"I'll bet you ran away from home," she murmured. But I said it wasn't none of her business if I had.

She asked, "Haven't you got a mother or a sister?"

I told her that I had two sisters and a mighty handsome mother, but that my father had been meaner than Satan, and he had whipped me out, though it was only the third time in my life I had ever been licked. He whipped me because I hit the red cow with a wagon spoke, and he said it wasn't her fault that the milk pail was upset, though I reckoned it was.

"I won't stay around home to be whipped on account of red cows," I cried to Flora Katherine. "And they're all going to feel mighty discontented if I get caught by the Pinkerton men and get shut up in Stillwater Penitentiary."

But all this time she was looking at me, and her eyes, which had seemed like the eyes of a deer when first I saw her, and like the eyes of an angry tomcat sometime later, were now pitying and motherly; and I let her hang onto my hand as much as she liked, and I wondered what it would feel like to kiss a girl who wasn't your sister.

"You can't go wandering off after Jesse James tonight," she said. "Daddy wouldn't let you. You might get caught by robbers, or something."

"No, I wouldn't," I said. "I'd shoot them quick as scat," and I forgot my sadness in opening up my bundle, to show her the pepperbox revolver that Uncle Andrew had given me.

"Why," said Flora Katherine, "it's all rusty! You couldn't shoot any robbers."

I was on the point of telling her that someday I'd get the revolver fixed up, and have caps and cartridges for it, when Doctor Samuel Sickles came back to the fire and kicked some ends of charred logs onto the coals. The flames shot up immediately, and then we could see his face, grave and furrowed and imposing in the red light, and his thin mane of hair curling around his neck.

"Kitty Cat," he said, "Torrey and Gray make no mention whatsoever of the purple moccasin." He had a thick book in his hands, but it didn't look like any Bible I ever saw.

"The ecologists do not suspect its existence," the old man continued, ruffling the pages with his hand. "They list many others, but none resembles it." He closed the book with a bang and went back to the wagon and put the book inside. He blew out the tin lamp, too, which he had left standing on the tailboard with little betty-millers flittering around it. Then he returned to us, and I was standing up by this time, for I had never seen such goings-on in all my born days.

51

Doctor Sickles planted his shabby boots wide apart, and he slid one hand inside his coat like a lawyer in court. "Our woodlands have been raped," he said. "The fairest flowers have been plucked from full many a tree, until the branches hang withered and barren. God's creatures have been scourged out of the underbrush and slaughtered without discrimination. With my own eyes I have seen the wild pigeons dashed to the ground, an acre at a time. They tell me, too, that the lordly bison are fading before the hunters' guns. Do you remember those stacks of hides we saw in St. Jo, Kitty Cat?"

Kitty Cat nodded and clapped her hands, and I thought I ought to clap, because this was marvellous speechifying.

The old man kind of nodded, as if we had pleased him. He picked up the spade, which was lying on the ground. "The Lord himself only knows," he said. "I may be an instrument of regeneration, and I may be holding one of the very tools in my hand! Who am I to be balked by a mere Travis and a mere shotgun?"

Flora Katherine was dancing up and down with excitement; I tell you, he shed excitement like a sunset sheds paint, the way he stood there so gaunt and grand. "He said he'd shoot you next time, Daddy," the girl cried. "Do you really think he would? Do you really think he'll shoot?"

"He had murder in his eyes," said Doctor Sickles solemnly.

Her red hair fairly curled with the flames in it. She gasped, "He'll think you came after all that gold, and after the silver spoons. Maybe. . . ."

Her father declared, "Stealth, Kitty Cat! We can circumvent murder by stealth. We will go by night, now, this very night, when the ignorant are slumbering and their guns are behind the doors."

Well, she screamed with joy, and then she said, "Can Jesse come along with us?" and my heart was heated in my mouth.

"Jesse can come, if he will." He came around the fire and put his long bony hand under my chin and turned my face up until it looked square into his. "My son," he said, and I had the ague down into my toes, "my son, your ambition is to become an outlaw. Will you be content with this strange outlawry of ours?"

I mumbled that I'd like to go with them.

"We'll need the spade," Doctor Sickles decided, "and the bucket and the lantern, and we'll need three pairs of hands to manage the deed with due safety and dispatch. Come along," he said, "both of you, and we'll prepare ourselves."

Sometimes it seems as if the deepest shades of night are those in the earliest hours, with the horn calls of whippoorwills sounding mournful in every brake, and the air fuzzy with June bugs and flying beetles and the plump gray moths that come to the kitchen window when a lamp is there. This is no occasion for ghosts, but a time for human beings to be faring abroad on most mysterious errands.

The bridge sounded like a hollow drum under our feet, no matter how dainty we walked. We went into Mr. Travis's timber at about the point where he had chased the Sickleses out with his shotgun; Doctor Sickles led the way, with a sooty lantern in his hand, and little daggers of light pointed hot into the under-brush on every side. Kitty Cat and I stayed to hand, but still we were behind him, and there was chance for me to question her about Mr. Travis again, and about all the excitement he had bespoken when he talked of silverware and gold.

What she told me set the skin to puckering over my shoulder blades. They had questioned some folks in the neighbourhood, and they knew why Mr. Travis hated to have other people step upon his soil. Because it was a soil that he believed to be filled with fortunes, and folks declared him to be a no-account farmer, but a savage man with a gun. During the war, that land had belonged to somebody else, and the somebody else who owned it was rich, and all his money and the costly silver-ware from his house were hidden away when the Yankees came nigh. It still lay, the story said, buried, unknown, and neglected, in some corner of the farm. And Mr. Travis demanded to be left in peace to dig it up, and then he'd be rich himself and beholden to no one.

It wasn't disturbing of rabbits and muskrats that dwelt in his underbrush, which he dreaded, but the prowling foot, and the

53

hand reaching out for money; and most of all he hated anybody who carried a spade. Already he had dug a hundred holes around his farm, and he concluded that he might have to dig the whole place up, but he was more than willing to do it.

Like enough, he never knew that the purple moccasin was there until the day when Doctor Sickles saw it with his own eyes, and Flora Katherine saw it with hers. And maybe he wasn't even aware of it now. He had ordered them off his property with his gun ready cocked, and the second time, as I knew, he plotted to scare them by firing.

I kept imagining how the purple moccasin would look, as we circulated through the thickets. I wondered why it hadn't rotted away long before. Probably the Indians had left it behind them when they were persecuted down into the Ouachita Mountains; I had never heard of anybody finding one of their moccasins before. But I had found arrowheads myself, and Uncle Andrew dug up part of a stone axe when he was punching post holes for his new gate. So it was plumb sensible to consider that a purple moccasin might be important, and with my own ears I had heard Mr. Yeary offer Uncle Andrew thirty cents for the axe. Still, Doctor Sickles wasn't one to go hog-wild over money; the whole thing had me perplexed to death.

We went astray a dozen times. The hazel brush scratched our faces, and the berry vines did things to our clothes. "We're off the track, Kitty Cat," the old man would whisper. "We've gone far afield. Stand by until I survey the route again." And then he'd prowl ahead, holding the lantern in front of him and bending his shoulders low, until he thought he saw a familiar trunk or a combination of trees to guide him.

"Are you fearful?" he'd want to know, time and again. "My children, keep your ears receptive for the approach of Mr. Travis."

So we'd listen, and all we could hear was the fluttering of catbirds that we disturbed off their roosts, and the buzzing of unknown critters in the air; and our frightened eyes would start out of our heads whenever we walked into webs of the big black-and-gold spiders that lived there. All the time, we were going deeper and deeper into the hollows; once a fox yapped on the hill above, and I jumped out of my skin.

Then, when at last the talking of the river had faded plumb into the past, we found ourselves at the rim of a twisting gully, and Kitty Cat's hand was perspiring instead of cold, when it clutched mine. "We're here," she whispered. "This is the place, Jesse. This is where we found the purple moccasin." Doctor Sickles was breathing hard as he tumbled down the steepness ahead of us. We brought up amongst basswood trunks that shone pearl-gray in the lantern light, and I felt my feet go deeper and deeper into the mold of forgotten leaves.

Doctor Sickles was squatting now. His hand shook so that he seemed ready to upset the lantern and maybe burn those woods to ash, and the purple moccasin too. For there it was directly under our eyes, and at the first second I felt a shiver of disappointment inside me. But the next minute I reckoned that here was something kind of holy, if it could make Doctor Sickles cry the way he was doing.

It was a flower, and it grew tall and straight in its solitary little pocket of wilderness. It was like the lady's slippers I had picked so many times, but instead of being yellow or being pinkish or white, the swollen petals of this flower were as purple as the purplest dress that any lady ever wore. They seemed fashioned of silk and velvet, and numerous fabrics out of fairy tales; the color was as rich as a crow's-foot violet, and when a little wind came down the hollow, the long pointed leaves seemed to sway with pride.

Doctor Sickles sucked in his breath until it made a steamy sound through his teeth. "*Cypripedium*," he said. I reckoned that was a new kind of prayer, like the French Catholic said who came to work for my pap one time. "*Cypripedium* most certainly, Kitty Cat. And I would have said *hirsutum* from the beginning, but I had no chance to observe the corolla before Travis was upon us. Look! Look!" He was fair shouting with delight and astonishment, and the noise he made would have tweaked a dozen Mr. Travises out of their slumbers.

"*Acaule*," he said, "*Cypripedium acaule*. Certainly there must be a close alliance. Winthrop may say that this is aberration,

55

Kitty Cat, and he may be correct. But I believe that here is treasure of the rarest tincture."

And then he sort of sighed and lifted up his head and surveyed the barrier of darkness. "If I only knew, my children, what other beauties lie buried in yonder fastnesses. . . . Young Jesse, give me the spade."

He cut deep into the rich, clinging soil, and he took out a generous circle all around that plant. He worked carefully with fingers and blade, and I saw that he had intention of filling the wooden bucket we had brought, with all the earth that had nourished that most peculiar flower. And maybe that same earth would nourish it in the future and let it grow to be a joy forever.

It seemed hours. My throat was dry, a-watching and a-waiting, but there wasn't much that Kitty Cat and I could do, except to hold the lantern and fetch the bucket close when he wanted it. He brought up the whole enormous beauty of the soil in one cake, and it couldn't have been more than the passage of a few moments before the purple moccasin was growing from the bucket as if it had always grown there. Then we crept out of the gully, and this time Kitty Cat was carrying the lantern and I had the spade, and Doctor Samuel Sickles nursed the bucket like it was a cradle with a two days' babe inside.

But the fortune that had attended us began to slip and yield; far away we caught a flicker of light, and a dog barked even closer.

"Daddy," asked Flora Katherine, in a weak little voice, "shall I blow out the lantern?"

The old man stood stock-still. He didn't seem to breathe. "Heaven forgive me," I heard him murmur, "if my avarice has brought harm to you." And then he whispered sharply, "No! We must run. The dog would find us, even if we lay in the dark."

We went through that brush as hard as we could pelt. The vines harried us, and I reckon we weren't following the path by which we had come in, for it was no path at all. But we did know our directions; we could catch sight of the Big Dipper high ahead of us, and other stars that anybody might know. The dog bayed and barked, and once he was silent for a long time, so long that he seemed lost in the brambles. But he came forth again, nearer at hand, and we heard the voice of Mr. Travis, urging him on.

It wasn't rapid fleeing that we did. The bucket hung heavy in the old man's hands, and he had to shield the tall flower from dead limbs that reached out and tried to smash it. I tripped twice and went flat, but was on my feet spunky enough thereafter; and Kitty Cat was the fastest runaway ever I saw, to escape through unfamiliar forests in this fashion. But the dog and the man were coming closer behind us.

I reckon some kind of angels opened up the underbrush, for it's certain we made more rapid journeying coming out than we had made going in. . . . Rays of the lantern flew helter-skelter across the rail fence that lined the road. Horses were gallivanting beyond; the light caught their legs; and in all our breathlessness and fear, we could seek dark forms of riders atop them.

By this time Mr. Travis's dog was close amongst us, and though he didn't snap or bite, he outcried in a way to drive us distracted; and Mr. Travis himself was crashing through the final thicket, and I wondered in my agony why he didn't shoot.

A rail scraped my shin. Another took a bite out of my shoulder, and then I was through the fence, and so was Kitty Cat. But poor Doctor Sickles couldn't fly through any fence— not with that bucket, and all the stiffness of his limbs, and his intention of guarding the purple moccasin that nodded and swayed under the bucket's bail.

He swung around to face his pursuer, and he held up one hand. "Mr. Travis," he cried, "be wary with your shotgun! Don't stain your hands with the blood of these innocent young!"

"They're no more innocent than you be!" yelled Mr. Travis, bursting from the hazel brush like a bear from his den. "I see you've got a bucket full, but you'll never cross that fence with it!" The barrel of the shotgun poked out long and vicious in the dull light.

Those horses in the road had the bits drawn tight in their

57

mouths, and they were rearing with astonishment, and the men who rode them were mighty well astonished too.

"Stop that!" came a voice. "Put down that gun, or I'll drill you quick!" and the rider who had spoken talked as if he had a revolver in his hand.

Slow and uncertain, the barrel of the shotgun went down; I heard Mr. Travis a-growling.

Doctor Sickles stood there, facing him steadily, with the bucket handle gripped tight. Then a horse crowded against me so close that I could smell his hair, and a wonderful voice cried out, "Jesse! What in time are you doing here!" My knees turned to dough all on a sudden for I knew that voice, it was my pap, and he was close to hand.

They got down from their horses—three men—and they took the lantern from Flora Katherine. Sure enough, here was Pap, and he took hold of my arm, and I liked to feel him doing it.

And nigh to him was Uncle Andrew, and a third man that I couldn't recognize for a moment, as I'd never seen him frequent. He was tall and dark and young, and he had a handsome black mustache that hung low on either side of his mouth. And then I knew him for Mr. Charley Gaffney. Even with the frail light making patterns on his face, I should have been able to recognize him before this: he was sheriff of Barbary County, and a right mean man to come against.

"Ben Travis," he said, "you won't commit murder in my presence."

"He's got the gold off of my land!" cried Mr. Travis, pointing at the bucket. "They've been coming after it for days, and they'll only carry it off over my dead body!"

The sheriff chuckled, and then he climbed over the fence most speedily and bent down to glimpse the burden that Doctor Sickles was carrying. "He's got a plant, Ben Travis. Some kind of flower. And that's all he seems to have, and a lot of dirt with it. . . . I reckon it's mighty lucky we happened by here a-searching for this young'un of Henry Bohun's."

Well, the explaining started up, and for a while they couldn't make much out of Doctor Sickles's talk, with all his praise and wonderment about the purple moccasin; and through the whole rigmarole, Ben Travis was still demanding Doctor Sickles's blood, but the sheriff took his shotgun away.

Sheriff Gaffney laughed his head off, and he said that it was astonishing how crazy Mr. Travis acted about that land of his, and he had better look out or they'd lock him up for a lunatic. "Who owned this land during the war, Ben Travis?" he kept demanding.

"Your pappy!" said Travis. "But everybody knows that his slaves buried the treasure at a point unknown to him, and then they skun out when the Yankees rode up, and they never come back. And with my own ears I heard your pap say that there was gold and silver in this soil, long before he died and long before I ever bought this farm."

But Mr. Sheriff Gaffney just put his arm on Ben's shoulder and begged him to consider reason. "It may be," he said, "that there's a dozen or two teaspoons and a hundred dollars in gold stowed under a stump somewhere. But there's no great wealth, Ben Travis. If my father spoke of gold and silver in this earth, he meant the kind that comes from grain and hogs and apple trees, from toil well performed and duties done honest. That's what he meant, and you'd better put in some crops instead of raring around with a shooting iron."

They had to hear all about Doctor Sickles, too, and whence he came. He told them his wagon was filled with plants, but none so wonderful as the purple moccasin, and he reckoned folks wouldn't believe he had it, when sometime he wandered back to the cities with his little girl and stopped at the dooryards of men who took interest in such things. He wanted all of us to come to his camp, and we did have to go for my bundle. Doctor Sickles wanted us to see his herbs and posies, and others that were squashed flat in big books, and I guess he had written a few books himself. And most of all, when they could pull him away from his plants, he marveled at how my pap had ridden from Arkansas to find me.

"Arkansas!" cried out Uncle Andrew, and I had to hang my head. "Why this boy ain't no more than fourteen mile from home this minute. He was born right here in Barbary County, and we all live on Rosy Ridge, and we'd admire to have you

59

come a-visiting us." He put his hands down and played with Flora Katherine's hair, though I was annoyed with him for doing so.

But Doctor Sickles made another wonderful speech in which he talked about the pigeons and the lordly bison, and the flora that had been despoiled. He said that he had right smart of journeying to do this season, and many more flowers to stow away in his wagon, and that there might be wondrous things as pleasurable to find as a purple moccasin.

So now the time was come when I must say good-bye to the purple moccasin and to Doctor Sickles, and, most of all, to Flora Katherine. I sort of mumbled around; then, quick, I thought how I'd like to kiss her. And I did it, too, before my pap took me up on his horse to ride home through the night.

A
WHITE HERON

by Sarah Orne Jewett
chosen by
Elizabeth Coatsworth.

SARAH ORNE JEWETT was born in 1849, the daughter of a country doctor who was glad to have his daughter's company as he drove on his rounds. At the leisurely pace of a doctor's horse he told her of the people he had been visiting and their lonely and courageous lives. It was of this world that she later wrote, adding her own insights to her father's earlier ones. She lived at a time when many of the old homesteads had not yet been abandoned. Often her stories are of women living with frugal dignity in their weather-beaten and solitary houses. The fields have run out, the farming is all but gone, soon there will be only cellar holes with a chimney for monument and a clump of lilacs clinging to the foundations. But Miss Jewett wrote of a world dying, indeed, but not yet dead. Her people do not pity themselves. They still show humor and gusto. They keep to their traditions and to their pride.

Such are the grandmother and the little girl in *A White Heron*, and such is the little house almost, but not quite, lost in the woods. Theirs is a poor life but filled with self-respect and feeling. When *A White Heron* was written, there was no talk of conservation. Audubon himself shot numberless birds so that he might study them at close quarters. The young stranger in the story sees no contradiction in loving birds and killing them. His interest is in the species.

But women and children are different. They think and feel in terms of individuals. So for the child in this tale, there arises a moral question.

This story is considered one of the classics of New England writing. It is thin but pure as a spring of waters.

ELIZABETH COATSWORTH

THE woods were already filled with shadows one June evening, just before eight o'clock, though a bright sunset still glimmered faintly among the trunks of the trees. A little girl was driving home her cow, a plodding, dilatory, provoking creature in her behavior, but a valued companion for all that. They were going away from whatever light there was, and striking deep into the woods, but their feet were familiar with the path, and it was no matter whether their eyes could see it or not.

There was hardly a night the summer through when the old cow could be found waiting at the pasture bars; on the contrary, it was her greatest pleasure to hide herself away among the huckleberry bushes, and though she wore a loud bell she had made the discovery that if one stood perfectly still it would not ring. So Sylvia had to hunt for her until she found her, and call Co'! Co'! with never an answering Moo, until her childish patience was quite spent. If the creature had not given good milk and plenty of it, the case would have seemed very different to her owners. Besides, Sylvia had all the time there was, and very little use to make of it. Sometimes in pleasant weather it was a consolation to look upon the cow's pranks as an intelligent attempt to play hide and seek, and as the child had no playmates she lent herself to this amusement with a good deal of zest. Though this chase had been so long that the wary animal herself had given an unusual signal of her whereabouts, Sylvia had only laughed when she came upon Mistress Moolly at the swamp-side, and urged her affectionately homeward with a twig of birch leaves. The old cow was not inclined to wander farther, she even turned in the right direction for once as they left the pasture, and stepped along the road at a good pace. She was quite ready to be milked now, and seldom stopped to browse. Sylvia wondered what her grandmother would say because they were so late. It was a great while since she had left home at half-past five o'clock, but everybody knew the difficulty of making this errand a short one. Mrs. Tilley had chased the hornéd torment too many summer evenings herself to blame any one else for lingering, and was only thankful as she waited that she had Sylvia, nowadays, to give such valuable assistance. The good woman suspected that Sylvia loitered occasionally on her own account; there never was such a child for straying about out-of-doors since the world was made! Everybody said that it was a good change for a little maid who had tried to grow for eight years in a crowded manufacturing town, but, as for Sylvia herself, it seemed as if she never had been alive at all before she came to live at the farm. She thought often with a wistful compassion of a wretched geranium that belonged to a town neighbor.

" 'Afraid of folks,' " old Mrs. Tilley said to herself, with a smile, after she had made the unlikely choice of Sylvia from her daughter's houseful of children, and was returning to the farm. " 'Afraid of folks,' they said! I guess she won't be troubled no great with 'em up to the old place!" When they reached the door of the lonely house and stopped to unlock it, and the cat came to purr loudly, and rub against them, a deserted pussy, indeed, but fat with young robins, Sylvia whispered that this was a beautiful place to live in, and she never should wish to go home.

The companions followed the shady woodroad, the cow taking slow steps and the child very fast ones. The cow stopped long at the brook to drink, as if the pasture were not half a swamp, and Sylvia stood still and waited, letting her bare feet cool themselves in the shoal water, while the great twilight moths struck softly against her. She waded on through the brook as the cow moved away, and listened to the thrushes with a heart that beat fast with pleasure. There was a stirring in the great boughs overhead. They were full of little birds and beasts that seemed to be wide awake, and going about their world, or else saying good-night to each other in sleepy twitters. Sylvia herself felt sleepy as she walked along. However, it was not much farther to the house, and the air was soft and sweet. She was not often in the woods so late as this, and it made her feel as if she were a part of the gray shadows and the moving leaves. She was just thinking how long it seemed since she first came to the farm a year ago, and wondering if everything went on in the noisy town just the same as when she was there; the thought of the great red-faced boy who used to chase and frighten her made her hurry along the path to escape from the shadow of the trees.

Suddenly this little woods-girl is horror-stricken to hear a clear whistle not very far away. Not a bird's whistle, which would have a sort of friendliness, but a boy's whistle, determined, and somewhat aggressive. Sylvia left the cow to whatever sad fate might await her, and stepped discreetly aside into the bushes, but she was just too late. The enemy had discovered her, and called out in a very cheerful and persuasive tone, "Halloa, little girl, how far is it to the road?" and trembling Sylvia answered almost inaudibly, "A good ways."

She did not dare to look boldly at the tall young man, who carried a gun over his shoulder, but she came out of her bush and again followed the cow, while he walked alongside.

"I have been hunting for some birds," the stranger said kindly, "and I have lost my way, and need a friend very much. Don't be afraid," he added gallantly. "Speak up and tell me what your name is, and whether you think I can spend the night at your house, and go out gunning early in the morning."

Sylvia was more alarmed than before. Would not her grandmother consider her much to blame? But who could have foreseen such an accident as this? It did not seem to be her fault, and she hung her head as if the stem of it were broken, but managed to answer "Sylvy," with much effort when her companion again asked her name.

Mrs. Tilley was standing in the doorway when the trio came into view. The cow gave a loud moo by way of explanation.

"Yes, you'd better speak up for yourself, you old trial! Where'd she tucked herself away this time, Sylvy?" But Sylvia kept an awed silence; she knew by instinct that her grandmother did not comprehend the gravity of the situation. She must be mistaking the stranger for one of the farmer-lads of the region.

The young man stood his gun beside the door, and dropped

a lumpy game-bag beside it; then he bade Mrs. Tilley good-evening, and repeated his wayfarer's story, and asked if he could have a night's lodging.

"Put me anywhere you like," he said. "I must be off early in the morning, before day; but I am very hungry, indeed. You can give me some milk at any rate, that's plain."

"Dear sakes, yes," responded the hostess, whose long slumbering hospitality seemed to be easily awakened. "You might fare better if you went out to the main road a mile or so, but you're welcome to what we've got. I'll milk right off, and you make yourself at home. You can sleep on husks or feathers," she proffered graciously. "I raised them all myself. There's good pasturing for geese just below here towards the ma'sh. Now step round and set a plate for the gentleman, Sylvy!" And Sylvia promptly stepped. She was glad to have something to do, and she was hungry herself.

It was a surprise to find so clean and comfortable a little dwelling in this New England wilderness. The young man had known the horrors of its most primitive housekeeping, and the dreary squalor of that level of society which does not rebel at the companionship of hens. This was the best thrift of an old-fashioned farmstead, though on such a small scale that it seemed like a hermitage. He listened eagerly to the old woman's quaint talk, he watched Sylvia's pale face and shining gray eyes with ever growing enthusiasm, and insisted that this was the best supper he had eaten for a month, and afterward the new-made friends sat down in the door-way together while the moon came up.

Soon it would be berry-time, and Sylvia was a great help at picking. The cow was a good milker, though a plaguy thing to keep track of, the hostess gossiped frankly, adding presently that she had buried four children, so Sylvia's mother, and a son (who might be dead) in California were all the children she had left. "Dan, my boy, was a great hand to go gunning," she explained sadly. "I never wanted for pa'tridges or gray squer'ls while he was to home. He's been a great wand'rer, I expect, and he's no hand to write letters. There, I don't blame him, I'd ha' seen the world myself if it had been so I could."

"Sylvy takes after him," the grandmother continued affectionately, after a minute's pause. "There ain't a foot o' ground she don't know her way over, and the wild creaturs counts her one o' themselves. Squer'ls she'll tame to come an' feed right out o' her hands, and all sorts o' birds. Last winter she got the jay-birds to bangeing here, and I believe she'd 'a' scanted herself of her own meals to have plenty to throw out amongst 'em, if I had n't kep' watch. Anything but crows, I tell her, I'm willin' to help support—though Dan he had a tamed one o' them that did seem to have reason same as folks. It was round here a good spell after he went away. Dan an' his father they did n't hitch,—but he never held up his head ag'in after Dan had dared him an' gone off."

The guest did not notice this hint of family sorrows in his eager interest in something else.

"So Sylvy knows all about birds, does she?" he exclaimed, as he looked round at the little girl who sat, very demure but increasingly sleepy, in the moonlight. "I am making a collection of birds myself. I have been at it ever since I was a boy." (Mrs. Tilley smiled.) "There are two or three very rare ones I have been hunting for these five years. I mean to get them on my own ground if they can be found."

"Do you cage 'em up?" asked Mrs. Tilley doubtfully, in response to this enthusiastic announcement.

"Oh no, they're stuffed and preserved, dozens and dozens of them," said the ornithologist, "and I have shot or snared every one myself. I caught a glimpse of a white heron a few miles from here on Saturday, and I have followed it in this direction. They have never been found in this district at all. The little white heron, it is," and he turned again to look at Sylvia with the hope of discovering that the rare bird was one of her acquaintances.

But Sylvia was watching a hop-toad in the narrow footpath.

"You would know the heron if you saw it," the stranger continued eagerly. "A queer tall white bird with soft feathers and long thin legs. And it would have a nest perhaps in the top of a high tree, made of sticks, something like a hawk's nest."

Sylvia's heart gave a wild beat; she knew that strange white bird, and had once stolen softly near where it stood in some

67

bright green swamp grass, away over at the other side of the woods. There was an open place where the sunshine always seemed strangely yellow and hot, where tall, nodding rushes grew, and her grandmother had warned her that she might sink in the soft black mud underneath and never be heard of more. Not far beyond were the salt marshes just this side the sea itself, which Sylvia wondered and dreamed much about, but never had seen, whose great voice could sometimes be heard above the noise of the woods on stormy nights.

"I can't think of anything I should like so much as to find that heron's nest," the handsome stranger was saying. "I would give ten dollars to anybody who could show it to me," he added desperately, "and I mean to spend my whole vacation hunting for it if need be. Perhaps it was only migrating, or had been chased out of its own region by some bird of prey."

Mrs. Tilley gave amazed attention to all this, but Sylvia still watched the toad, not divining, as she might have done at some calmer time, that the creature wished to get to its hole under the doorstep, and was much hindered by the unusual spectators at that hour of the evening. No amount of thought, that night, could decide how many wished-for treasures the ten dollars, so lightly spoken of, would buy.

The next day the young sportsman hovered about the woods, and Sylvia kept him company, having lost her first fear of the friendly lad, who proved to be most kind and sympathetic. He told her many things about the birds and what they knew and where they lived and what they did with themselves. And he gave her a jack-knife, which she thought as great a treasure as if she were a desert-islander. All day long he did not once make her troubled or afraid except when he brought down some unsuspecting singing creature from its bough. Sylvia would have liked him vastly better without his gun; she could not understand why he killed the very birds he seemed to like so much. But as the day waned, Sylvia still watched the young man with loving admiration. She had never seen anybody so charming and delightful; the woman's heart, asleep in the child, was vaguely thrilled by a dream of love. Some premonition of that great power stirred and swayed these young creatures who traversed the solemn woodlands with soft-footed silent care. They stopped to listen to a bird's song; they pressed forward again eagerly, parting the branches—speaking to each other rarely and in whispers; the young man going first and Sylvia following, fascinated, a few steps behind, with her grey eyes dark with excitement.

She grieved because the longed-for white heron was elusive, but she did not lead the guest, she only followed, and there was no such thing as speaking first. The sound of her own un-questioned voice would have terrified her—it was hard enough to answer yes or no when there was need of that. At last evening began to fall, and they drove the cow home together, and Sylvia smiled with pleasure when they came to the place where she heard the whistle and was afraid only the night before.

II

Half a mile from home, at the farther edge of the woods, where the land was highest, a great pine-tree stood, the last of its generation. Whether it was left for a boundary mark, or for what reason, no one could say; the woodchoppers who had felled its mates were dead and gone long ago, and a whole forest of sturdy trees, pines and oaks and maples, had grown again. But the stately head of this old pine towered above them all and made a landmark for sea and shore miles and miles away. Sylvia knew it well. She had always believed that whoever climbed to the top of it could see the ocean; and the little girl had often laid her hand on the great rough trunk and looked up wistfully at those dark boughs that the wind always stirred, no matter how hot and still the air might be below. Now she thought of the tree with a new excitement, for why, if one climbed it at break of day, could not one see all the world, and easily discover from whence the white heron flew, and mark the place, and find the hidden nest?

What a spirit of adventure, what wild ambition! What fancied triumph and delight and glory for the later morning when she could make known the secret! It was almost too real and too great for the childish heart to bear.

All night the door of the little house stood open and the whippoorwills came and sang upon the very step. The young sportsman and his old hostess were sound asleep, but Sylvia's great design kept her broad awake and watching. She forgot to think of sleep. The short summer night seemed as long as the winter darkness, and at last when the whippoorwills ceased, and she was afraid the morning would after all come too soon, she stole out of the house and followed the pasture path through the woods, hastening toward the open ground beyond, listening with a sense of comfort and companionship to the drowsy twitter of a half-awakened bird, whose perch she had jarred in passing. Alas, if the great wave of human interest which flooded for the first time this dull little life should sweep away the satisfactions of an existence heart to heart with nature and the dumb life of the forest!

There was the huge tree asleep yet in the paling moonlight, and small and silly Sylvia began with utmost bravery to mount to the top of it, with tingling, eager blood coursing the channels of her whole frame, with her bare feet and fingers, that pinched and held like bird's claws to the monstrous ladder reaching up, up, almost to the sky itself. First she must mount the white-oak tree that grew alongside, where she was almost lost among the dark branches and the green leaves heavy and wet with dew; a bird fluttered off its nest, and a red squirrel ran to and fro and scolded pettishly at the harmless housebreaker. Sylvia felt her way easily. She had often climbed there, and knew that higher still one of the oak's upper branches chafed against the pine trunk, just where its lower boughs were set close together. There, when she made the dangerous pass from one tree to the other, the great enterprise would really begin.

She crept out along the swaying oak limb at last, and took the daring step across into the old pine-tree. The way was harder than she thought; she must reach far and hold fast, the sharp dry twigs caught and held her and scratched her like angry talons, the pitch made her thin little fingers clumsy and stiff as she went round and round the tree's great stem, higher and higher upward. The sparrows and robins in the woods below were beginning to wake and twitter to the dawn, yet it seemed much lighter there aloft in the pine-tree, and the child knew she must hurry if her project were to be of any use.

The tree seemed to lengthen itself out as she went up, and to reach farther and farther upward. It was like a great main-mast to the voyaging earth; it must truly have been amazed that morning through all its ponderous frame as it felt this determined spark of human spirit wending its way from higher branch to branch. Who knows how steadily the least twigs held themselves to advantage this light, weak creature on her way! The old pine must have loved his new dependent. More than all the hawks, and bats, and moths, and even the sweet-voiced thrushes, was the brave, beating heart of the solitary grey-eyed child. And the tree stood still and frowned away the winds that June morning while the dawn grew bright in the east.

Sylvia's face was like a pale star, if one had seen it from the ground, when the last thorny bough was past, and she stood trembling and tired but wholly triumphant, high in the tree-top. Yes, there was the sea with the dawning sun making a golden dazzle over it, and toward that glorious east flew two hawks with slow-moving pinions. How low they looked in the air from that height when one had only seen them before far up, and dark against the blue sky. Their gray feathers were as soft as moths; they seemed only a little way from the tree, and Sylvia felt as if she too could go flying away among the clouds. Westward, the woodlands and farms reached miles and miles into the distance; here and there were church steeples, and white villages, truly it was a vast and awesome world!

The birds sang louder and louder. At last the sun came up bewilderingly bright. Sylvia could see the white sails of ships out at sea, and the clouds that were purple and rose-colored and yellow at first began to fade away. Where was the white heron's nest in the sea of green branches, and was this wonderful sight and pageant of the world the only reward for having climbed to such a giddy height? Now look down again, Sylvia, where the green marsh is set among the shining birches and dark hemlocks; there where you saw the white heron once you will see him again; look, look! a white spot of him like a single floating feather comes up from the dead hemlock and grows larger, and rises, and comes close at last, and goes by the landmark pine with steady sweep of wing and outstretched slender neck and crested head. And wait! wait! do not move a foot or a finger, little girl, do not send an arrow of light and consciousness from your two eager eyes, for the heron has perched on a pine bough not far beyond yours, and cries back to his mate on the nest and plumes his feathers for the new day!

The child gives a long sigh a minute later when a company of shouting cat-birds comes also to the tree, and vexed by their fluttering and lawlessness the solemn heron goes away. She knows his secret now, the wild, light, slender bird that floats and wavers, and goes back like an arrow presently to his home in the green world beneath. Then Sylvia, well satisfied, makes her perilous way down again, not daring to look far below the branch she stands on, ready to cry sometimes because her fingers ache and her lamed feet slip; wondering over and over again what the stranger would say to her, and what he would think when she told him how to find his way straight to the heron's nest.

"Sylvy, Sylvy!" called the busy old grandmother again and again, but nobody answered, and the small husk bed was empty and Sylvia had disappeared.

The guest waked from a dream, and remembering his day's pleasure hurried to dress himself that it might sooner begin. He was sure from the way the shy little girl looked once or twice yesterday that she had at least seen the white heron, and now she must really be made to tell. Here she comes now, paler than ever, and her worn old frock is torn and tattered, and smeared with pine pitch. The grandmother and the sportsman stand in the door together and question her, and the splendid moment has come to speak of the dead hemlock-tree by the green marsh.

But Sylvia does not speak after all, though the old grandmother fretfully rebukes her, and the young man's kind, appealing eyes are looking straight in her own. He can make them rich with money; he has promised it, and they are poor now. He is so well worth making happy, and he waits to hear the story she can tell.

No, she must keep silence! What is it that suddenly forbids her and makes her dumb? Has she been nine years growing and now, when the great world for the first time puts out a hand to her, must she thrust it aside for a bird's sake? The murmur of the pine's green branches is in her ears, she remembers how the white heron came flying through the golden air and how they watched the sea and the morning together, and Sylvia cannot speak; she cannot tell the heron's secret and give its life away.

Dear loyalty, that suffered a sharp pang as the guest went away disappointed later in the day, that could have served and followed him and loved him as a dog loves! Many a night Sylvia heard the echo of his whistle haunting the pasture path as she came home with the loitering cow. She forgot even her sorrow at the sharp report of his gun and the sight of thrushes and sparrows dropping silent to the ground, their songs hushed and their pretty feathers stained and wet with blood. Were the birds better friends than their hunter might have been,—who can tell? Whatever treasures were lost to her, woodlands and summer-time, remember! Bring your gifts and graces and tell your secrets to this lonely country child!

Visitors

BY WALTER DE LA MARE

chosen by

HELEN CRESSWELL

I HAVE chosen *Visitors* because I fell in love with it at first sight. I only discovered it recently, quite by chance (though chance is something I do not quite believe in).

I am not sure whether it is a very good short story as short stories go—by the rule book. I love it because, for me, it contains nearly everything there is to be said about everything, and because it is beautiful. So there is not very much that I can add. In any case it says, almost as nearly as poetry can, what *can't* be said.

Walter de la Mare was always doing this in his own poetry, and in this story he is well aware of the near impossibility of what he is trying to do:

"And what you don't actually see, you can't put a name to."

But often the things you can't put a name to are the only ones really worth trying to say. (Work *that* one out!)

I should read this story more than once, or you might fall into the trap of thinking it a little lop-sided, instead of a marvellous balancing act between two kinds of reality. You might miss the fact that the author has his tongue in his cheek when he says that Tom is "odd". You might miss things like,

"Surely, he thought to himself, nothing could be so ugly as all that if it were just the truth."

There's no *end* to what you might miss. So read it twenty times, as I have, or thirty, just to make sure.

HELEN CRESSWELL

ONE of the very last things that Tom Nevis was to think about in this world was a sight he had seen when he was a child of about ten. Years and years were to pass by after that March morning; and at the last Tom was far away from home and England in the heat and glare of the tropics. Yet this one far-away memory floated up into his imagination to rest there in its peace and strangeness as serenely as a planet shining in its silver above the snows of remote hills. It had just stayed on in the quiet depths of his mind—like the small insects that may be seen imprisoned in lumps of amber, their wings still glistening ages after they were used in flitting hither-thither in their world as it was then.

Most human beings have little experiences similar to Tom's. But they come more frequently to rather solitary people— people who enjoy being alone, and who have daydreams. If they occur at other times, they may leave little impression, because perhaps one is talking or laughing or busy, working away at what has to be done, or perhaps reading or thinking. And then they may pass unnoticed.

But Tom had always been a funny solitary creature. Even as a child he enjoyed being alone. He would sit on a gate or a stile for an hour at a time just staring idly into a field, following with his eyes the shadows of the clouds as they swept silently over its greenness, or the wandering wind, now here, now there, stooping upon the taller weeds and grasses. It was a pleasure to him merely even to watch a cow browsing her way among the buttercups, swinging the tuft of her tail and occasionally rubbing her cinnamon-coloured shoulder with her soft nose. It seemed to Tom at such times—though he never actually put the feeling into words—almost as if the world were only in his mind; almost as if it were the panorama of a dream.

So too Tom particularly enjoyed looking out of his window when the moon was shining. Not only in winter when there is snow on the ground, and clotting hoar-frost, but in May and summer too, the light the moon sheds in her quiet rests on the trees and the grass and the fields like a silver tissue. And she is for ever changing: now a crescent slenderly shining—a loop of silver or copper wire in the western after-glow of sunset; and now a mere ghost of herself, lingering in the blue of morning like a lantern burning long after the party is over which it was meant to make gay.

Tom was more likely to be left alone than most boys, owing to a fall he had had when he was three. He had a nurse then, named Alice Jenkins. One morning she sat him up as usual close to the nursery table and his bowl of bread and milk; and had then turned round an instant at the sound of something heard at the window. And he, in that instant, to see perhaps what she was looking at, had jumped up in his chair, the bar had slipped out, and he had fallen sprawling on to the floor.

The fall had injured his left arm. And try as the doctors might, they had never been able to make it grow like his right arm. It was lean and shrunken and almost useless, and the fingers of the hand were drawn up a little so that it could be used only for simple easy things. He was very little good at games in consequence, and didn't see much of other boys of his own age. Alice had cried half the night after that miserable hour; but the two of them loved each other the more dearly for it ever afterwards. Even now that she was married and kept a small greengrocer's shop in a neighbouring town, Tom went to see her whenever he could, and munched her apples and pears and talked about everything under the sun.

This accident had happened so long ago that he had almost forgotten he had ever at all had the full use of his arm. He grew as much accustomed to its hanging limply from his shoulder as one may become accustomed to having a crooked nose, prominent ears or a squint. And though he realized that it kept him out of things like climbing trees or playing such games as other boys could do with ease, though it had made a kind of scarecrow of him, it was simply because of this that he was left more to himself and his own devices than most boys. And though he never confessed it to himself, and certainly not to anybody else, he immensely enjoyed being in his own company. It was not a bit

—as it well might be—like being in an empty house, but rather in an enchanted one; wherein you never knew what might not happen next, even though everything was still and quiet—the sun at the windows, the faint shadows in the corridors, the water in the green fishpond and the tangled branches in the orchard.

Tom, too, beside being for this reason rather odd in his body —small for his age, with narrow shoulders, a bony face, light grey-blue eyes and a stiff shock of yellow hair standing up on his high head—was also a little odd in mind. He was continually making up stories, even when there was no one to listen to them. For his black-eyebrowed elder sister very seldom had time to do so; and the nurse he had after Alice was married had not much patience with such things. But he almost as much enjoyed telling them to himself. And when his sister Emily died he seemed to get into the habit of mooning and daydreaming more than ever.

He had other queer little habits too. Whenever he went downstairs from his bedroom—unless he was in a violent hurry or his father had called him—he always sat down for a few moments on a narrow stair from which he looked out from a tall landing window over the garden. It seemed to him you could never tell what you might *not* see at such a moment; though as a matter of fact he never saw anything very unusual: just the grass and the lawn and the currant-bushes and the monkey-puzzle; perhaps a cat walking gingerly on its errand, and the usual thrushes and blackbirds, tits and robins, and the light of the sun on the red-brick wall. And what you don't actually see you cannot put a name to.

Another fancy of his was, whenever he passed it, to stoop down and peer through the keyhole of a cellar that spread out underneath the old Parsonage. He might just as well have looked up a chimney for there was even less light to be seen through the keyhole. And nothing was stowed away in the cellar except a few old discarded pieces of furniture, some bottles of wine, empty hampers, an old broken rocking-horse and such things as that. None the less, whenever he passed that door, Tom almost invariably stooped on his knees, puckered up one eye and peered through its keyhole with the other, and smelt the fusty smell.

There was no end to his cranky comicalities. Long ago, for example, he had made a rule of always doing certain things on certain days. He cared no more for washing in those early days than most boys: but he always had a "thorough good wash" on Fridays; even though it was "bath night" on Saturdays. He went certain walks on certain evenings, that is, evenings after it had been raining, or maybe when some flower or tree was just out. And he always went to see his sister Emily's grave once a month.

She had died on the twelfth of April; and apart from her birthday, he always kept her month day—all the twelfths throughout the year. If he could, and if he had time, he would take a bunch of flowers along with him, choosing those which Emily had liked the best or those he liked the best, or both together. The churchyard was not far away, as the crow flies, but it was yet another of his odd habits not to go there direct—as if that might be too easy—but to go round by a meadow path that was at least three-quarters of a mile further than the way by the village lane.

Except when he happened to be by himself at evenings just after the sun was set, Tom always felt more alone on these monthly journeys than at any other time. And for as long a time as he could spare he would sit on an old bench under the church-yard yew. At first he had been exceedingly wretched and miserable on these visits. The whole Parsonage, his father and his sister and the maids—it was just as if a kind of thick cold mist had come over them all when Emily died. Everything that was familiar in the house had suddenly stood up strange and exclamatory, as if to remind them something was gone that would never come back again. And though none of the others, of course, really forgot what had happened, though he often actually noticed his father desisting from what he was just about to say simply because he could not bear the grief of mentioning Emily's name, as time went on, things began to be much as ever again.

In the early days Tom's black-haired elder sister, Esther, used to come with him to the churchyard now and then; but she soon had so many things to think about and to amuse herself with that there was very little time to spend with him. Besides, they agreed about nothing and spent most of the time arguing and wrangling. So for a good many months Tom had gone alone.

He knew his own particular monthly walk to the churchyard as well as he knew his own clothes or anything else in the world. He never set out on it without wishing he could see his sister Emily again, and he never came home again to the Parsonage without thinking to himself that it was better perhaps he could *not* bring her back. For he was somehow sure, wherever her body might be, that she herself was perfectly happy, and, as it were, always to be young. Now and then, indeed, it seemed as if some wraith of herself had actually whispered this into his ear as he sat on his bench looking out across the tombstones, and sometimes wondering how long it would be before he was dead too. But then Tom's little moperies came very near at times to being a little mad.

That was another odd thing about Tom. He enjoyed thinking and puzzling over everything that came into his head, whereas most people will not allow hard or disagreeable thoughts to stay in their minds. They drive them out like strange dogs out of a garden, or wasps out of a sunny room. Tom thought of them, however, in the most practical way possible. He knew, for example, as much about grave-digging when he was ten as the old sexton could tell him at sixty. The thought of the bones beneath the turf did not frighten him a bit. Surely, he thought to himself, nothing could be as ugly as all that if it were just the truth. And if it was, why, then it *was*.

Not that he did not enjoy being alive in this world. He fairly ached sometimes with delight in it. He had talked to Alice about it, and to Emily too, sitting on a green bank in the sunshine or in the hayfields, or by the banks of their secret pond in the woods. He loved also to brood on what might happen to him in the future; though he never had the faintest notion in those days that he was going to travel, that he was going to leave England when he was still a young man, for good and all, and never come back. He had no notion of that at all until there came a talk one afternoon in her husband's shop with his nurse Alice. After that he knew he had been born to be a traveller in spite of his arm and his cranky meagre body. And what led up to the talk was what happened to him that March morning as he came back from his customary visit to the churchyard.

A faint but bleak east wind was blowing. Except for a light silvery ridge of cloud in the south the sky was blue all over, and the sunlight was as bright as if a huge crystal reflector behind it were casting back its beams from the heavens upon the earth. A few daffodils were out in the fields, and the celandine with its shovel-shaped glossy leaves too; and the hedges were beginning to quicken, looking from a distance as if a faint green mist hung over them. The grass was already growing after its winter's rest, and the birds of the countryside were busy flying hither and thither as if time were something that melted in the sun. Instead of returning from the churchyard to the house by the way he had come, Tom had turned in through a wicket gate into a straggling wood of birch and hazel, and so came out at the corner of a large meadow which lay over against the Old Farm.

There had been heavy rains during the previous week, and as Tom—absent-minded as ever—came edging along the path of the meadow, he lifted his eyes and was astonished to see a pool of water in the green hollow of the meadow beneath him, where none had lain before. Its waters were evidently of the rains that had fallen in the past few days. They stretched there grey and sparkling, glassing the sky, and the budding trees which grew not far from their margin. And floating upon this new wild water he saw two strange birds. Never had he seen their like before, though he guessed they might be straying sea-birds. They were white as snow, and were disporting themselves gently in this chance pool, as if it were a haven of refuge or meeting-place which they had been seeking from the first moment they had come out of their shells.

Tom watched them, fixed motionless where he stood, afraid almost to blink lest he should disturb their happy play. But at last he took courage, and gradually, inch by inch, he approached stealthily nearer until at last he could see their very eyes shining in their heads, and the marvellous snow of their wings and their coral beaks reflected in the shallow wind-rippled pool. They appeared to be companions of all time. They preened their feathers, uttering faint cries as if of delight, as if they were telling secrets one to the other. And now and again they would desist from their preening and float there quietly together on the surface of the water, in the silvery sunshine. And still Tom continued to gaze at them with such greedy eagerness it was a marvel this alone did not scare the wild creatures away. It seemed to Tom as if he had been looking at them for ages and ages under the huge shallow bowl of the March sky. He dreaded every instant they would lift their wings and fly away. That would be as if something had gone out of his own inmost self.

He was whispering too under his breath, as if to persuade them to remain there always, and let there be no change. Indeed they might be human creatures, they floated there on the water so naturally and happily in their devotion to one another's company. And it seemed once more to Tom as if the whole world and his own small life had floated off in to a dream, and that he had stood watching their movements and their beauty for as many centuries as the huge oak that towered above the farm had stood with outflung boughs, bearing its flowers and its acorns from spring on to spring, and from autumn to autumn until this very morning.

What was curious too, the two strange birds seemed at last to have no fear of his being there, even though the bright shallow basin of rain on which they rested in the meadow was not more than eleven paces wide. They eyed him indeed with a curious sharp brightness, almost as if they wished to be sharing their secret with him, one brought from the remote haunts from which they had set out over-night; as if this was the end of their journey. The drops they flung with their bills over their snowy plumage gleamed like little balls of changing silver or crystal, though not brighter than their eyes. The red of their webbed feet showed vividly beneath the grey clear water. And the faint soft cries uttered in their throats rather than with open bills, were not sweet or shrill as a peewit or a linnet singing, but were yet wonderfully gentle and tender to listen to.

And Tom's odd mind slipped once more into a deep daydream as he stood there—in his buttoned-up jacket, with his cap over his short springy hair—in the light but bleak east wind that swept out of the clouds across the meadow and the roof and chimneys of the old red-brick farm. . . . In the middle of that

83

night he woke up: as suddenly almost as if a voice had called him. And the scene was still as sharp and fresh in his imagination as if he were looking at it again spread out in actuality in the morning light before his very eyes.

It was just like ridiculous Tom not to visit the meadow again for many days afterwards. Once or twice he actually set out in that direction, but turned off before the farmyard came into view. And when at last he did go back again, towards evening, the whole scene had changed. No longer was the wind from the east, but from the south. Lofty clouds towered up into the intense blue of the sky, like snow-topped mountains. The air was sweet with spring. The tight dark buds had burst in the hedges into their first pale-green leaf; thrushes were singing among the higher branches of the elms. But the pool of rainwater had sunk out of sight in its hollow, had been carried up by the wind and sun into the heavens, leaving only the greener and fresher grass behind it. The birds were flown. . . .

One day in the following July, Tom went off to see his old nurse, Alice Hubbard. She had grown a good deal stouter after her marriage, and Tom sat with her in the cramped parlour behind the shop, looking out into the street across the bins of green peas and potatoes, carrots and turnips, lettuces and cabbages and mint, the baskets of gooseberries and currants and strawberries and the last cherries. And while Alice was picking out for him a saucerful of strawberries, he told her all about himself: what he had been doing and thinking, and about the new maid, and about the Parsonage. And she would say as she paused with finger and thumb over her basket, "Lor, Master Tom," or "Did you ever, now, Master Tom!" or "There now, Master Tom!" And all of a sudden the memory of the pool of water and the two strange birds flitted back into his mind and he fell silent. Alice put down before him the saucer of strawberries, with a little blue-and-white jug of cream, and she glanced a little curiously into his narrow, ugly face.

"And what might you be thinking of now, I wonder?" she said.

An old woman in a black bonnet and shawl who had been peering about at the fruit from the pavement close to the window

84

outside, at this moment came into the shop, and Alice went out to serve her with what she wanted. Tom watched the two of them; watched the potatoes weighed and the sprig of mint thrown into the scale; watched a huge dapple-grey cart-horse go by, dragging its cartload of bricks, with its snuff-coloured driver sitting on a sack on top. And then Alice had come back into the little parlour again, and he was telling her all about the birds and the pool.

"Lor now, that *was* queer, Master Tom," said Alice. "And where might you have been that morning?"

And Tom told her he had been to the churchyard.

"Now you know, my dear soul," she said in a hushed voice as if somebody might be listening; "you know you didn't ought to go there too often. It isn't good for you. You think too much already. And Joe says—and you wouldn't believe how happy I am, Master Tom, living here in this little shop, though I never never forget the old Parsonage and the kindness of your dear mother—but Joe, he says that one didn't ought to keep on thinking about such things. Not keep on, he means. How would the world go round, he says, if we was all of us up in the clouds all day. It looks to me as if you were more a bag of bones than ever, though p'raps you have been growing—sprouting up a good deal."

"But wasn't it funny about the birds?" said Tom.

"Why," said Alice, "what was funny?"

"Why," said Tom, "they weren't just ordinary birds. I am not sure now they were even quite live birds—real birds I mean, though they might have come from the sea. And why didn't they fly away when I got near? They saw me right enough. And why, do you think, do I keep on thinking about them?"

"Lor bless me," said Alice. "The questions he asks! And all them whys! You ain't much changed at that, Master Tom."

"Yes, but why?" Tom persisted, spoon in hand, looking up at her over his saucer of strawberries and cream.

Alice stood on the other side of the table, resting the knuckles of one hand upon it, and as she looked out across the shop a vacancy came into her blue eyes, just as if, like Tom himself, she too at times fell into daydreams. "Well, I suppose—I suppose," she said at last in a low far-away voice, "you keep on thinking about them because you can't get them out of your head."

"Oh that's all right," said Tom a little impatiently; "but what I want to know is why they stay there?"

"Well," said Alice, "some things do. I can see those birds meself. And of course they were real, Master Tom. Of course they were real. Or else"—she gave a little gentle laugh—"or else, why you and me would be just talking about ghost birds. What I mean is that it doesn't follow even if they *was* real that they didn't mean something else too. I don't mean exactly that such things do mean anything else, but only, so to speak, it *seems* that they do. All depends, I suppose, in a manner of speaking, on what they are to us, Master Tom. Bless me, when I stand here in this shop sometimes, looking out at the people in the street and seeing customers come in—even serving them, too—I sometimes wonder if the whole *thing* mayn't mean something else. How was I to know that I was ever going to get married to my Joe and keep a greengrocer's shop too? And yet, believe *me*, Master Tom, it seems just as ordinary and natural now as if I had been meant to do it from my very cradle."

Tom looked at her curiously. "Then what do you think the birds *mean?*" he repeated.

The soft lids with their light lashes closed down a little further over her blue eyes as Alice stood pondering over the same old question. "Why," she whispered almost as if she were talking in her sleep, "if you ask me, it means that you are going to travel. That's what *I* think the birds mean. But then I couldn't say where."

And suddenly she came back again, as it were—came out of her momentary reverie or daydream, and looked sharply round at him as if he might be in danger of something. She was frowning, as though she were frightened. "You know, Master Tom," she went on in a solemn voice, "I can never forgive myself for that poor arm of yours. Why you might by now. . . . But there! life *is* a mystery, isn't it? I suppose in a sort of a way—though Joe would say we oughtn't to brood on it—life itself is a kind of a journey. That goes on too."

"Goes on where?" said Tom.

"Ah, that we can't rightly say," said Alice, smiling at him. "But I expect if them birds of yours could find their way from over the sea, there is no particular reason why human beings should not find theirs."

"You mean Emily found hers?" said Tom.

Alice nodded two or three times. "That I do," she said.

"Well, all I can say is," said Tom, "I wish they'd come back, and the water too. They were more—more—well, I don't know *what*, than anything I have ever seen in the whole of my life."

"And that's a tidy-sized one too!" said Alice, smiling at him again. And they exchanged a long still look.

And what she had said about his travelling came perfectly true. Quite early in his twenties Tom had pushed on up the gangway and into the bowels of the ship that was to take him across the sea to that far-away country from which he was never to come back. And though green peas and mint and the last of the cherries may not be quite such magical things in the memory as the sight of two strange sea-birds disporting themselves in a pool of rain-water on a bleak silvery March morning far from their natural haunts, these too when they came round each year always reminded Alice of that talk with Tom. Indeed she loved him very dearly, for Tom was of course—and especially after his accident—a kind of foster son. And when she heard of his going abroad she remembered the birds as well.

THE RUUM

BY ARTHUR PORGES
CHOSEN BY PETER DICKINSON

OCCASIONALLY you read something which does not seem at the time to be any more than pretty good, but which then—though perhaps you never read it again—haunts you. When I first read *The Ruum*, about fifteen years ago, I doubt if I thought more than "That's an exciting one—and what a cunning end!" But since then I have remembered it often. Partly this is because the ruum itself is such a well-made nightmare, a silent and indestructible blob which follows its victim however it may hide or flee; partly for the excitement of the chase itself; and partly for the neat ending which harks back so beautifully to an unnoticed point in the first dozen lines.

It's curious how certain ideas recur again and again in science fiction; some of them are obvious echoes of our own worries, such as what would a civilisation be like when it was running down, and people had forgotten our hard-won knowledge, and how to use the machines that rusted round them. But others don't seem to say anything to us—the ones about the mad, super-human collector, for instance. *The Ruum* is one of the best of those.

PETER DICKINSON

THE cruiser *Ilkor* had just gone into her interstellar over-drive beyond the orbit of Pluto when a worried officer reported to the Commander.

"Excellency," he said uneasily, "I regret to inform you that because of a technician's carelessness a Type H-9 Ruum has been left behind on the third planet, together with anything it may have collected."

The Commander's triangular eyes hooded momentarily, but when he spoke his voice was level.

"How was the ruum set?"

"For a maximum radius of 30 miles, and 160 pounds plus or minus 15."

There was silence for several seconds; then the Commander said: "We cannot reverse course now. In a few weeks we'll be returning, and can pick up the ruum then. I do not care to have one of those costly, self-energizing models charged against my ship. You will see," he ordered coldly, "that the individual responsible is severely punished."

But at the end of its run, in the neighborhood of Rigel, the cruiser met a flat, ring-shaped raider; and when the inevitable fire-fight was over, both ships, semi-molten, radio-active, and laden with dead, were starting a billion-year orbit around the star.

And on the earth, it was the age of reptiles.

When the two men had unloaded the last of the supplies, Jim Irwin watched his partner climb into the little seaplane. He waved at Walt.

"Don't forget to mail that letter to my wife," Jim shouted.

"The minute I land," Walt Leonard called back, starting to rev the engine. "And you find us some uranium—a strike is just what Cele needs. A fortune for your son and her, hey?" His white teeth flashed in a grin. "Don't rub noses with any grizzlies—shoot 'em, but don't scare 'em to death!"

Jim thumbed his nose as the seaplane speeded up, leaving a frothy wake. He felt a queer chill as the amphibian took off. For three weeks he would be isolated in this remote valley of the Canadian Rockies. If for any reason the plane failed to return to the icy blue lake, he would surely die. Even with enough food, no man could surmount the frozen peaks and make his way on foot over hundreds of miles of almost virgin wilderness. But, of course, Walt Leonard would return on schedule, and it was up to Jim whether or not they lost their stake. If there was any uranium in the valley, he had twenty-one days to find it. To work then, and no gloomy forebodings.

Moving with the unhurried precision of an experienced woodsman, he built a lean-to in the shelter of a rocky overhang. For this three weeks of summer, nothing more permanent was needed. Perspiring in the strong morning sun, he piled his supplies back under the ledge, well covered by a waterproof tarpaulin, and protected from the larger animal prowlers. All but the dynamite; that he cached, also carefully wrapped against moisture, two hundred yards away. Only a fool shares his quarters with a box of high explosives.

The first two weeks went by all too swiftly, without any encouraging finds. There was only one good possibility left, and just enough time to explore it. So early one morning towards the end of his third week, Jim Irwin prepared for a last-ditch foray into the north-east part of the valley, a region he had not yet visited.

He took the Geiger counter, slipping on the earphones, reversed to keep the normal rattle from dulling his hearing, and reaching for the rifle, set out, telling himself it was now or never so far as this particular expedition was concerned. The bulky .30-06 was a nuisance and he had no enthusiasm for its weight, but the huge grizzlies of Canada are not intruded upon with impunity, and take a lot of killing. He'd already had to dispose of two, a hateful chore, since the big bears were vanishing all too fast. And the rifle had proved a great comfort on several ticklish occasions when actual firing had been avoided. The .22 pistol he left in its sheepskin holster in the lean-to.

THE RUUM

He was whistling at the start, for the clear, frosty air, the bright sun on blue-white ice fields, and the heady smell of summer, all delighted his heart despite his bad luck as a prospector. He planned to go one day's journey to the new region, spend about thirty-six hours exploring it intensively, and be back in time to meet the plane at noon. Except for his emergency packet, he took no food or water. It would be easy enough to knock over a rabbit, and the streams were alive with firm-fleshed rainbow trout of the kind no longer common in the States.

All morning Jim walked, feeling an occasional surge of hope as the counter chattered. But its clatter always died down. The valley had nothing radioactive of value, only traces. Apparently they'd made a bad choice. His cheerfulness faded. They needed a strike badly, especially Walt. And his own wife, Cele, with a kid on the way. But there was still a chance. These last thirty-six hours—he'd snoop at night, if necessary—might be the pay-off. He reflected a little bitterly that it would help quite a bit if some of those birds he'd staked would make a strike and return his dough. Right this minute there were close to eight thousand bucks owing to him.

A wry smile touched his lips, and he abandoned unprofitable speculations for plans about lunch. The sun, as well as his stomach, said it was time. He had just decided to take out his line and fish a foaming brook, when he rounded a grassy knoll to come upon a sight that made him stiffen to a halt, his jaw dropping.

It was like some enterprising giant's outdoor butcher shop: a great assortment of animal bodies, neatly lined up in a triple row that extended almost as far as the eye could see. And what animals! To be sure, those nearest him were ordinary deer, bear, cougars, and mountain sheep—one of each, apparently—but down the line were strange, uncouth, half-formed, hairy beasts; and beyond them a nightmare conglomeration of reptiles. One of the latter, at the extreme end of the remarkable display, he recognized at once. There had been a much larger specimen, fabricated about an incomplete skeleton, of course, in the museum at home.

93

No doubt about it—it was a small stegosaur, no bigger than a pony!

Fascinated, Jim walked down the line, glancing back over the immense array. Peering more closely at one scaly, dirty-yellow lizard, he saw an eyelid tremble. Then he realized the truth. The animals were not dead, but paralysed and miraculously preserved. Perspiration prickled his forehead. How long since stegosaurs had roamed this valley?

All at once he noticed another curious circumstance: the victims were roughly of a size. Nowhere, for example, was there a really large saurian. No tyrannosaurus. For that matter, no mammoth. Each specimen was about the size of a large sheep. He was pondering this odd fact, when the underbrush rustled a warning behind him.

Jim Irwin had once worked with mercury, and for a second it seemed to him that a half-filled leather sack of the liquid-metal had rolled into the clearing. For the quasispherical object moved with just such a weighty, fluid motion. But it was not leather; and what appeared at first a disgusting wartiness turned out on closer scrutiny to be more like the functional projections of some outlandish mechanism. Whatever the thing was, he had little time to study it, for after the spheroid had whipped out and retracted a number of metal rods with bulbous, lens-like structures at their tips, it rolled towards him at a speed of about five miles an hour. And from its purposeful advance, the man had no doubts that it meant to add him to the pathetic heap of living-dead specimens.

Uttering an incoherent exclamation, Jim sprang back a number of paces, unslinging his rifle. The ruum that had been left behind was still some thirty yards off, approaching at that moderate but invariable velocity, an advance more terrifying in its regularity than the headlong charge of a mere brute beast.

Jim's hand flew to the bolt, and with practised deftness he slammed a cartridge into the chamber. He snuggled the battered stock against his cheek, and using the peep sight, aimed squarely at the leathery bulk—a perfect target in the bright afternoon sun. A grim little smile touched his lips as he squeezed the trigger. He knew what one of those 180-grain, metal-jacketed, boat-tail slugs could do at 2700 feet per second. Probably at this close range it would keyhole and blow the foul thing into a mush.

Wham! The familiar kick against his shoulder. E-e-e-e! The whining screech of a ricochet. He sucked in his breath. There could be no doubt whatever. At a mere twenty yards, a bullet from this hard-hitting rifle had glanced from the ruum's surface.

Frantically Jim worked the bolt. He blasted two more rounds, then realized the utter futility of such tactics. When the ruum was six feet away, he saw gleaming finger-hooks flick from warty knobs, and a hollow, sting-like probe, dripping greenish liquid, poised snakily between them. The man turned and fled.

Jim Irwin weighed exactly 149 pounds.

It was easy enough to pull ahead. The ruum seemed incapable of increasing its speed. But Jim had no illusions on that score. The steady five-mile-an-hour pace was something no organism on earth could maintain for more than a few hours. Before long, Jim guessed, the hunted animal had either turned on its implacable pursuer, or, in the case of more timid creatures, run itself to exhaustion in a circle out of sheer panic. Only the winged were safe. But for anything on the ground the result was inevitable: another specimen for the awesome array. And for whom the whole collection? Why? Why?

Coolly, as he ran, Jim began to shed all surplus weight. He glanced at the reddening sun, wondering about the coming night. He hesitated over the rifle; it had proved useless against the ruum, but his military training impelled him to keep the weapon to the last. Still, every pound raised the odds against him in the gruelling race he foresaw clearly. Logic told him that military reasoning did not apply to a contest like this; there would be no disgrace in abandoning a worthless rifle. And when weight became really vital, the .30-06 would go. But meanwhile he slung it over one shoulder. The Geiger counter he placed as gently as possible on a flat rock, hardly breaking his stride.

One thing was certain. This would be no rabbit run, a blind, panicky flight until exhausted, ending in squealing submission. This would be a fighting retreat, and he'd use every trick of survival he'd learned in his hazard-filled lifetime.

95

Taking deep, measured breaths, he loped along, watching with shrewd eyes for anything that might be used for his advantage in the weird contest. Luckily the valley was sparsely wooded; in brush or forest his straightway speed would be almost useless.

Suddenly he came upon a sight that made him pause. It was a point where a huge boulder overhung the trail, and Jim saw possibilities in the situation. He grinned as he remembered a Malay mantrap that had once saved his life. Springing to a hillock, he looked back over the grassy plain. The afternoon sun cast long shadows, but it was easy enough to spot the pursuing ruum, still oozing along on Jim's trail. He watched the thing with painful anxiety. Everything hinged upon this brief survey. He was right! Yes, although at most places the man's trail was neither the only route nor the best one, the ruum dogged the footsteps of his prey. The significance of that fact was immense, but Irwin had no more than twelve minutes to implement the knowledge.

Deliberately dragging his feet, Irwin made it a clear trail directly under the boulder. After going past it for about ten yards, he walk backwards in his own prints until just short of the overhang, and then jumped up clear of the track to a point behind the balanced rock.

Whipping out his heavy-duty belt knife, he began to dig, scientifically, but with furious haste, about the base of the boulder. Every few moments, sweating with apprehension and effort, he rammed it with one shoulder. At last, it teetered a little. He had just jammed the knife back into his sheath, and was crouching there, panting, when the ruum rolled into sight over a small ridge on his back trail.

He watched the gray spheroid moving towards him and fought to quiet his sobbing breath. There was no telling what other senses it might bring into play, even though the ruum seemed to prefer just to follow in his prints. But it certainly had a whole battery of instruments at its disposal. He crouched low behind the rock, every nerve a charged wire.

But there was no change of technique by the ruum; seemingly intent on the footprints of its prey, the strange sphere rippled along, passing directly under the great boulder. As it did so, Irwin gave a savage yell, and thrusting his whole muscular weight against the balanced mass, toppled it squarely on the ruum. Five tons of stone fell from a height of twelve feet.

Jim scrambled down. He stood there, staring at the huge lump and shaking his head dazedly. He gave the boulder a kick. "Hah! Walt and I might clear a buck or two yet from your little meat market. Maybe this expedition won't be a total loss. Enjoy yourself in hell where you came from!"

Then he leaped back, his eyes wild. The giant rock was shifting! Slowly its five-ton bulk was sliding off the trail, raising a ridge of soil as it grated along. Even as he stared, the boulder tilted, and a gray protuberance appeared under the nearest edge. With a choked cry, Jim Irwin broke into a lurching run.

He ran a full mile down the trail. Then, finally, he stopped and looked back. He could just make out a dark dot moving away from the fallen rock. It progressed as slowly and as regularly and as inexorably as before, and in his direction. Jim sat down heavily, putting his head in his scratched, grimy hands.

But that despairing mood did not last. After all, he had gained a twenty-minute respite. Lying down, trying to relax as much as possible, he took the flat packet of emergency rations from his jacket, and eating quickly but without bolting, disposed of some pemmican, biscuit, and chocolate. A few sips of icy water from a streamlet, and he was almost ready to continue his fantastic struggle. But first he swallowed one of the three benzedrine pills he carried for physical crises. When the ruum was still an estimated ten minutes away, Jim Irwin trotted off, much of his wiry strength back, and fresh courage to counter bone-deep weariness.

After running for fifteen minutes, he came to a sheer face of rock about thirty feet high. The terrain on either side was barely passable, consisting of choked gullies, spiky brush, and knife-edged rocks. If Jim could make the top of this little cliff, the ruum sure would have to detour, a circumstance that might put it many minutes behind him.

He looked up at the sun. Huge and crimson, it was almost touching the horizon. He would have to move fast. Irwin was no rock-climber but he did know the fundamentals. Using every crevice, roughness, and minute ledge, he fought his way up the cliff. Somehow—unconsciously—he used that flowing climb of a natural mountaineer, which takes each foothold very briefly as an unstressed pivot-point in a series of rhythmic advances.

He had just reached the top when the ruum rolled up to the base of the cliff.

Jim knew very well that he ought to leave at once, taking advantage of the few precious remaining moments of daylight. Every second gained was of tremendous value; but curiosity and hope made him wait. He told himself that the instant his pursuer detoured he would get out of there all the faster. Besides, the thing might even give up and he could sleep right here.

Sleep! His body lusted for it.

But the ruum would not detour. It hesitated only a few seconds at the foot of the barrier. Then a number of knobs opened to extrude metallic wands. One of these, topped with lenses, waved in the air. Jim drew back too late—their uncanny gaze had found him as he lay atop the cliff, peering down. He cursed his idiocy.

Immediately all the wands retracted, and from a different knob a slender rod, blood-red in the setting sun, began to shoot straight up to the man. As he watched, frozen in place, its barbed tip gripped the cliff's edge almost under his nose.

Jim leaped to his feet. Already the rod was shortening as the ruum reabsorbed its shining length. And the leathery sphere was rising off the ground. Swearing loudly, Jim fixed his eyes on the tenacious hook, drawing back one heavy foot.

But experience restrained him. The mighty kick was never launched. He had seen too many rough-and-tumbles lost by an injudicious attempt at the boot. It wouldn't do at all to let any part of his body get within reach of the ruum's superb tools. Instead he seized a length of dry branch, and inserting one end under the metal hook, began to pry.

There was a sputtering flash, white and lacy, and even

through the dry wood he felt the potent surge of power that splintered the end. He dropped the smouldering stick with a gasp of pain, and wringing his numb fingers, backed off several steps, full of impotent rage. For a moment he paused, half inclined to run again, but then his upper lip drew back and, snarling, he unslung his rifle. He knew he had been right to lug the damned thing all this way—even if it had beat a tattoo on his ribs. Now he had the ruum right where he wanted it!

Kneeling to steady his aim in the failing light Jim sighted at the hook and fired. There was a soggy thud as the ruum fell. Jim shouted. The heavy slug had done a lot more than he expected. Not only had it blasted the metal claw loose, but it had smashed a big gap in the cliff's edge. It would be pretty damned hard for the ruum to use that part of the rock again!

He looked down. Sure enough, the ruum was back at the bottom. Jim Irwin grinned. Every time the thing clamped a hook over the bluff, he'd blow that hook loose. There was plenty of ammunition in his pocket and, until the moon rose, bringing a good light for shooting with it, he'd stick the gun's muzzle inches away if necessary. Besides, the thing—whatever it might be—was obviously too intelligent to keep up a hopeless struggle. Sooner or later it would accept the detour. And then, maybe the night would help to hide his trail.

Then—he choked and, for a brief moment, tears came to his eyes. Down below, in the dimness, the squat, phlegmatic spheroid was extruding three hooked rods simultaneously in a fanlike spread. In a perfectly co-ordinated movement, the rods snagged the cliff's edge at intervals of about four feet.

Jim Irwin whipped the rifle to his shoulder. All right—this was going to be just like the rapid fire for record back at Benning. Only, at Benning, they didn't expect good shooting in the dark!

But the first shot was a bull's-eye, smacking the left-hand hook loose in a puff of rock dust. His second shot did almost as well, knocking the gritty stuff loose so the center barb slipped off. But even as he whirled to level at number three, Jim saw it was hopeless.

The first hook was back in place. No matter how well he

shot, at least one rod would always be in position, pulling the ruum to the top.

Jim hung the useless rifle muzzle down from a stunted tree and ran into the deepening dark. The toughening of his body, a process of years, was paying off now. So what? Where was he going? What could he do now? Was there anything that could stop that damned thing behind him?

Then he remembered the dynamite.

Gradully changing his course, the weary man cut back towards his camp by the lake. Overhead the stars brightened, pointing the way. Jim lost all sense of time. He must have eaten as he wobbled along, for he wasn't hungry. Maybe he could eat at the lean-to . . . no, there wouldn't be time . . . take a benzedrine pill. No, the pills were all gone and the moon was up and he could hear the ruum close behind. Close.

Quite often phosphorescent eyes peered at him from the underbrush and once, just at dawn, a grizzly whoofed with displeasure at his passage.

Sometimes during the night his wife, Cele, stood before him with outstretched arms. "Go away!" he rasped, "Go away! You can make it! It can't chase both of us!" So she turned and ran lightly alongside of him. But when Irwin panted across a tiny glade, Cele faded away into the moonlight and he realized she hadn't been there at all.

Shortly after sunrise Jim Irwin reached the lake. The ruum was close enough for him to hear the dull sounds of its passage. Jim staggered, his eyes closed. He hit himself feebly on the nose, his eyes jerked open and he saw the explosive. The sight of the greasy sticks of dynamite snapped Irwin wide awake.

He forced himself to calmness and carefully considered what to do. Fuse? No. It would be impossible to leave fused dynamite in the trail and time the detonation with the absolute precision he needed. Sweat poured down his body, his clothes were sodden with it. It was hard to think. The explosion *must* be set off from a distance and at the exact moment the ruum was passing over it. But Irwin dared not use a long fuse. The rate of burning was not constant enough. Couldn't calibrate it perfectly with the ruum's advance. Jim Irwin's body sagged all over, his chin sank toward his heaving chest. He jerked his head up, stepped back—and saw the .22 pistol where he had left it in the lean-to.

His sunken eyes flashed.

Moving with frenetic haste, he took the half-filled case, piled all the remaining percussion caps among the loose sticks in a devil's mixture. Weaving out to the trail, he carefully placed box and contents directly on his earlier tracks some twenty yards from a rocky ledge. It was a risk—the stuff might go any time— but that didn't matter. He would far rather be blown to rags than end up living but paralysed in the ruum's outdoor butcher's stall.

The exhausted Irwin had barely hunched down behind the thin ledge of rock before his inexorable pursuer appeared over a slight rise five hundred yards away. Jim scrunched deeper into the hollow, then saw a vertical gap, a narrow crack between rocks. That was it, he thought vaguely. He could sight through the gap at the dynamite and still be shielded from the blast. If it was a shield . . . when that half-caste blew only twenty yards away. . . .

He stretched out on his belly, watching the ruum roll forward. A hammer of exhaustion pounded his ballooning skull. When had he slept last? This was the first time he had lain down in hours. Hours? Ha! it was days. His muscles stiffened, locked into throbbing, burning knots. Then he felt the morning sun on his back, soothing, warming, easing. . . . No! If he let go, if he slept now, it was the ruum's macabre collection for Jim Irwin! Stiff fingers tightened around the pistol. He'd stay awake! If he lost—if the ruum survived the blast—there'd still be time to put a bullet through his brain.

He looked down at the sleek pistol, then out at the innocent-seeming booby trap. If he timed this right—and he would—the ruum wouldn't survive. No. He relaxed a little, yielding just a bit to the gently insistent sun. A bird whistled softly somewhere above him and a fish splashed in the lake.

Suddenly he was wrenched to full awareness. Damn! Of all times for a grizzly to come snooping about! With the whole of Irwin's camp ready for greedy looting, a fool bear had to come

sniffing around the dynamite! The furred monster smelled carefully at the box, nosed around, rumbled deep displeasure at the
alien scent of man. Irwin held his breath. Just a touch would
blow a cap. A single cap meant . . .

The grizzly lifted his head from the box and growled hoarsely.
The box was ignored, the offensive odor of man was forgotten.
Its feral little eyes focused on a plodding spheroid that was now
only forty yards away. Jim Irwin snickered. Until he had met
the ruum the grizzly bear of the North American continent was
the only thing in the world he had ever feared. And now—why
the hell was he so calm about it?—the two terrors of his existence
were meeting head on and he was laughing. He shook his head
and the great side muscles in his neck hurt abominably. He
looked down at his pistol, then out at the dynamite. *These* were
the only real things in his world.

About six feet from the bear, the ruum paused. Still in the
grip of that almost idiotic detachment, Jim Irwin found himself wondering again what it was, where it had come from.
The grizzly arose on its haunches, the embodiment of utter
ferocity. Terrible teeth flashed white against red lips. The
business-like ruum started to roll past. The bear closed in,
roaring. It cuffed at the ruum. A mighty paw, armed with
black claws sharper and stronger than scythes, made that cuff.
It would have disembowelled a rhinoceros. Irwin cringed as
that side-swipe knocked dust from the leathery sphere. The
ruum was hurled back several inches. It paused, recovered, and
with the same dreadful casualness it rippled on, making a wider
circle, ignoring the bear.

But the lord of the woods wasn't settling for any draw.
Moving with that incredible agility which has terrified Indians,
Spanish, French and Anglo-Americans since the first encounter
of any of them with his species, the grizzly whirled, side-stepped
beautifully and hugged the ruum. The terrible, shaggy forearms
tightened, the slavering jaws champed at the gray surface.
Irwin half rose. "Go it!" he croaked. Even as he cheered the
clumsy emperor of the wild, Jim thought it was an insane
tableau: the village idiot wrestling with a beach ball.

Then silver metal gleamed bright against gray. There was

a flash, swift and deadly. The roar of the king abruptly became a whimper, a gurgle and then there was nearly a ton of terror wallowing in death—its throat slashed open. Jim Irwin saw the bloody blade retract into the gray spheroid, leaving a bright-red smear on the thing's dusty hide.

And the ruum rolled forward past the giant corpse, implacable, still intent on the man's spoor, his footprints, his pathway. Okay, baby, Jim giggled at the dead grizzly, this is for you, for Cele, for—lots of poor dumb animals like us—come to, you damned fool, he cursed at himself. And aimed at the dynamite. And very calmly, very carefully, Jim Irwin squeezed the trigger of his pistol.

Briefly, sound first. Then giant hands lifted his body from where he lay, then let go. He came down hard, face in a patch of nettles, but he was sick, he didn't care. He remembered that the birds were quiet. Then there was a fluid thump as something massive struck the grass a few yards away. Then there was quiet.

Irwin lifted his head . . . all men do in such a case. His body still ached. He lifted sore shoulders and saw . . . an enormous, smoking crater in the earth. He also saw, a dozen paces away, gray-white because it was covered now with powdered rock, the ruum.

It was under a tall, handsome pine tree. Even as Jim watched, wondering if the ringing in his ears would ever stop, the ruum rolled toward him.

Irwin fumbled for his pistol. It was gone. It had dropped somewhere, out of reach. He wanted to pray, then, but couldn't get properly started. Instead, he kept thinking, idiotically, "My sister Ethel can't spell Nebuchadnezzar and never could. My sister Ethel——"

The ruum was a foot away now, and Jim closed his eyes. He felt cool, metallic fingers touch, grip, lift. His unresisting body was raised several inches, and juggled oddly. Shuddering, he waited for the terrible syringe with its green liquid, seeing the yellow, shrunken face of a lizard with one eyelid a-tremble.

Then, dispassionately, without either roughness or solicitude, the ruum put him back on the ground. When he opened his

103

eyes, some seconds later, the sphere was rolling away. Watching it go, he sobbed dryly.

It seemed a matter of moments only, before he heard the seaplane's engine, and opened his eyes to see Walt Leonard bending over him.

Later, in the plane, five thousand feet above the valley, Walt grinned suddenly, slapped him on the back, and cried: "Jim, I can get a whirlybird, a four-place job! Why, if we can snatch up just a few of those prehistoric lizards and things while the museum keeper's away, it's like you said—the scientists will pay us plenty."

Jim's hollow eyes lit up. "That's the idea," he agreed. Then, bitterly; "I might just as well have stayed in bed. Evidently the damned thing didn't want me at all. Maybe it wanted to know what I paid for these pants! Barely touched me, then let go. And how I ran!"

"Yeah," Walt said. "That was damned queer. And after that marathon. I admire your guts, boy." He glanced sideways at Jim Irwin's haggard face. "That night's run cost you plenty. I figure you lost over ten pounds."

The Bee-Man of Orn

By Frank R.Stockton

chosen by
Jane Gardam

No one in England had met the Bee-Man of Orn until 1967 though he had been known in America since about 1870 when he first came rambling into Frank R. Stockton's cheerful head. I can't imagine why we didn't meet him sooner.

I found him at Christmastime soon after he'd landed, whilst I was looking for presents, and came to my surroundings again on the last page with pins and needles in my feet and the bookseller pulling my sleeve and saying would I be wanting to buy him (the Bee-Man, not the bookseller). Three Bee-Men and I went home together, two were posted off to godchildren and the third goes about with me most of the time.

It's not a perfect story. It's a bit flabby in the middle. It's not a very conclusive story either for there doesn't seem to be the faintest agreement on what it's about. "Wisdom," says one; "Foolishness," says another; "Religion," says my son. "Psychiatry," (1873?) says my daughter. "A nice old happy man," says my youngest. "Rather a tiresome, silly man," says my aunt.

I don't know why I so adore this story. I kept bees myself for ten years (till they nearly killed my husband) but that's not it. Perhaps I like it because I can't think of anything remotely like it. A faint, faint hint of *Alice* perhaps, a trace of that splendid fellow A. A. Milne's grandfather knew "who did nothing but basking until he was saved". But the Bee-Man *could* stir himself when he felt it was important, and he was much less stuffy and nicer than Alice. In fact I think he was nicer than almost anyone in the world.

JANE GARDAM

IN the ancient country of Orn there lived an old man who was called the Bee-man, because his whole time was spent in the company of bees. He lived in a small hut, which was nothing more than an immense beehive, for these little creatures had built their honeycombs in every corner of the one room it contained, on the shelves, under the little table, all about the rough bench on which the old man sat, and even about the head-board and along the sides of his low bed.

All day the air of the room was thick with buzzing insects, but this did not interfere in any way with the old Bee-man, who walked in among them, ate his meals, and went to sleep without the slightest fear of being stung.

He had lived with the bees so long, they had become so accustomed to him, and his skin was so tough and hard that the bees no more thought of stinging him than they would of stinging a tree or a stone. A swarm of bees had made their hive in a pocket of his old leathern doublet; and when he put on this coat to take one of his long walks in the forest in search of wild bees' nests, he was very glad to have this hive with him, for, if he did not find any wild honey, he would put his hand in his pocket and take out a piece of a comb for a luncheon. The bees in his pocket worked very industriously, and he was always certain of having something to eat with him wherever he went. He lived principally upon honey; and when he needed bread or meat, he carried some fine combs to a village not far away and bartered them for other food. He was ugly, untidy, shriveled, and brown. He was poor, and the bees seemed to be his only friends. But, for all that, he was happy and contented; he had all the honey he wanted, and his bees, whom he considered the best company in the world, were as friendly and sociable as they could be, and seemed to increase in number every day.

One day there stopped at the hut of the Bee-man a Junior Sorcerer. This young person, who was a student of magic, was much interested in the Bee-man, whom he had often noticed in his wanderings, and he considered him an admirable subject for study. He had got a great deal of useful practice by trying to find out, by the various rules and laws of sorcery, exactly why the old Bee-man did not happen to be something that he was not, and why he was what he happened to be. He had studied a long time at this matter, and had found out something.

"Do you know," he said, when the Bee-man came out of his hut, "that you have been transformed?"

"What do you mean by that?" said the other, much surprised.

"You have surely heard of animals and human beings who have been magically transformed into different kinds of creatures?"

"Yes, I have heard of these things," said the Bee-man, "but what have I been transformed from?"

"That is more than I know," said the Junior Sorcerer. "But one thing is certain: you ought to be changed back. If you will find out what you have been transformed from, I will see that you are made all right again. Nothing would please me better than to attend to such a case."

And, having a great many things to study and investigate, the Junior Sorcerer went his way.

This information greatly disturbed the mind of the Bee-man. If he had been changed from something else, he ought to be that other thing, whatever it was. He ran after the young man and overtook him.

"If you know, kind sir," he said, "that I have been transformed, you surely are able to tell me what it is I was."

"No," said the Junior Sorcerer, "my studies have not proceeded far enough for that. When I become a Senior I can tell you all about it. But, in the meantime, it will be well for you to try to find out for yourself your original form; and when you have done that, I will get some of the learned Masters of my art to restore you to it. It will be easy enough to do that, but you could not expect them to take the time and trouble to find out what it was."

And, with these words, he hurried away, and was soon lost to view.

Greatly disturbed, the Bee-man retraced his steps, and went

to his hut. Never before had he heard anything which had so troubled him.

"I wonder what I was transformed from?" he thought, seating himself on his rough bench. "Could it have been a giant, or a powerful prince, or some gorgeous being whom the magicians or the fairies wished to punish? It may be that I was a dog or a horse, or perhaps a fiery dragon or a horrid snake. I hope it was not one of these. But whatever it was, everyone has certainly a right to his original form, and I am resolved to find out mine. I will start early tomorrow morning; and I am sorry now that I have not more pockets to my old doublet so that I might carry more bees and more honey for my journey."

He spent the rest of the day in making a hive of twigs and straw; and, having transferred to this a number of honeycombs and a colony of bees which had just swarmed, he rose before sunrise the next day; and, having put on his leathern doublet and having bound his new hive to his back, he set forth on his quest, the bees who were to accompany him buzzing around him like a cloud.

As the Bee-man pressed through the little village the people greatly wondered at his queer appearance, with the hive upon his back. "The Bee-man is going on a long journey this time," they said; but no one imagined the strange business on which he was bent. About noon he sat down under a tree, near a beautiful meadow covered with blossoms, and ate a little honey. Then he untied his hive and stretched himself out on the grass to rest. As he gazed upon his bees hovering about him, some going out to the blossoms in the sunshine and some returning laden with the sweet pollen, he said to himself, "They know just what they have to do, and they do it, but alas for me! I know not what I may have to do. And yet, whatever it may be, I am determined to do it. In some way or other I will find out what was my original form, and then I will have myself changed back to it."

And now again the thought came to him that perhaps his original form might have been something very disagreeable or even horrid.

"But it does not matter," he said sturdily. "Whatever I was, that I shall be again. It is not right for anyone to keep a form which does not properly belong to him. I have no doubt I shall discover my original form in the same way that I find the trees in which the wild bees hive. When I first catch sight of a bee tree I am drawn toward it, I know not how. Something says to me: 'That is what you are looking for.' In the same way I believe I shall find my original form. When I see it, I shall be drawn toward it. Something will say to me: 'That is it.' "

When the Bee-man was rested, he started off again, and in about an hour he entered a fair domain. Around him were beautiful lawns, grand trees, and lovely gardens; while at a little distance stood the stately palace of the Lord of the Domain. Richly dressed people were walking about or sitting in the shade of the trees and arbors; splendidly equipped horses were waiting for their riders; and everywhere were seen signs of wealth and gaiety.

"I think," said the Bee-man to himself, "that I should like to stop here for a time. If it should happen that I was originally like any of these happy creatures, it would please me much."

He untied his hive and hid it behind some bushes, and, taking off his old doublet, laid that beside it. It would not do to have his bees flying about him if he wished to go among the inhabitants of this fair domain.

For two days the Bee-man wandered about the palace and its grounds, avoiding notice as much as possible but looking at everything. He saw handsome men and lovely ladies; the finest horses, dogs, and cattle that were ever known; beautiful birds in cages, and fishes in crystal globes; and it seemed to him that the best of all living things were here collected.

At the close of the second day the Bee-man said to himself: "There is one being here toward whom I feel very much drawn and that is the Lord of the Domain. I cannot feel certain that I was once like him, but it would be a very fine thing if it were so; and it seems impossible for me to be drawn toward any other being in the domain when I look upon him, so handsome, rich, and powerful. But I must observe him more closely, and feel more sure of the matter, before applying to the sorcerers to change me back into a lord of a fair domain."

The next morning the Bee-man saw the Lord of the Domain walking in his gardens. He slipped along the shady paths and followed him, so as to observe him closely and find out if he were really drawn toward this noble and handsome being. The Lord of the Domain walked on for some time, not noticing that the Bee-man was behind him. But suddenly turning, he saw the little old man.

"What are you doing here, you vile beggar?" he cried, and he gave him a kick that sent him into some bushes that grew by the side of the path.

The Bee-man scrambled to his feet and ran as fast as he could to the place where he had hidden his hive and his old doublet.

"If I am certain of anything," he thought, "it is that I was never a person who would kick a poor old man. I will leave this place. I was transformed from nothing that I see here."

He now traveled for a day or two longer, and then he came to a great black mountain near the bottom of which was an opening like the mouth of a cave.

This mountain, he had heard, was filled with caverns and underground passages, which were the abodes of dragons, evil spirits, horrid creatures of all kinds.

"Ah me!" said the Bee-man with a sigh, "I suppose I ought to visit this place. If I am going to do this thing properly, I should look on all sides of the subject, and I may have been one of those horrid creatures myself."

Thereupon he went to the mountain, and, as he approached the opening of the passage which led into its inmost recesses, he saw, sitting upon the ground and leaning his back against a tree, a Languid Youth.

"Good-day," said this individual when he saw the Bee-man. "Are you going inside?"

"Yes," said the Bee-man, "that is what I intend to do."

"Then," said the Languid Youth, slowly rising to his feet, "I think I will go with you. I was told that if I went in there I should get my energies toned up, and they need it very much; but I did not feel equal to entering by myself, and I thought I would wait until someone came along. I am very glad to see you, and we will go in together."

So the two went into the cave, and they had proceeded but a short distance when they met a very little creature, whom it was easy to recognize as a Very Imp. He was about two feet high and resembled in color a freshly polished pair of boots. He was extremely lively and active, and came bounding toward them.

"What did you two people come here for?" he asked.

"I came," said the Languid Youth, "to have my energies toned up."

"You have come to the right place," said the Very Imp. "We will tone you up. And what does that old Bee-man want?"

"He has been transformed from something and wants to find out what it is. He thinks he may have been one of the things in here."

"I should not wonder if that were so," said the Very Imp, rolling his head on one side and eyeing the Bee-man with a critical gaze.

"All right," said the Very Imp, "he can go around and pick out his previous existence. We have here all sorts of vile creepers, crawlers, hissers, and snorters. I suppose he thinks anything will be better than a Bee-man."

"It is not because I want to be better than I am," said the Bee-man, "that I started out on this search. I have simply an honest desire to become what I originally was."

"Oh! That is it, is it?" said the other. "There is an idiotic moon calf here with a clam head which must be just like what you used to be."

"Nonsense," said the Bee-man. "You have not the least idea what an honest purpose is. I shall go about and see for myself."

"Go ahead," said the Very Imp, "and I will attend to this fellow who wants to be toned up." So saying, he joined the Languid Youth.

"Look here," said the Youth, "do you black and shine yourself every morning?"

"No," said the other, "it is waterproof varnish. You want to be invigorated, don't you? Well, I will tell you a splendid way to begin. You see that Bee-man has put down his hive and his coat with the bees in it. Just wait till he gets out of sight, and then catch a lot of those bees and squeeze them flat. If you spread them on a sticky rag, and make a plaster, and put it on the small of your back, it will invigorate you like everything, especially if some of the bees are not quite dead."

"Yes," said the Languid Youth, looking at him with his mild eyes, "but if I had energy enough to catch a bee I would be satisfied. Suppose you catch a lot for me."

"The subject is changed," said the Very Imp. "We are now about to visit the spacious chamber of the King of the Snap-dragons."

"That is a flower," said the Languid Youth.

"You will find him a gay old blossom," said the other. "When he has chased you round his room, and has blown sparks at you, and has snorted and howled, and cracked his tail, and snapped his jaws like a pair of anvils, your energies will be toned up higher than ever before in your life."

"No doubt of it," said the Languid Youth, "but I think I will begin with something a little milder."

"Well, then," said the other, "there is a flat-tailed Demon of the Gorge in here. He is generally asleep, and, if you say so, you can slip into the farthest corner of his cave and I'll solder his tail to the opposite wall. Then he will rage and roar, but he can't get across his cave; I have measured him. It will tone you up wonderfully to sit there and watch him."

"Very likely," said the Languid Youth, "but I would rather stay outside and let you go up in the corner. The performance in that way will be more interesting to me."

"You are dreadfully hard to please," said the Very Imp. "I have offered them to you loose, and I have offered them fastened to a wall, and now the best thing I can do is to give you a chance at one of them that can't move at all. It is the Ghastly Griffin, and is enchanted. He can't stir so much as the tip of his whiskers for a thousand years. You can go to his cave and examine him just as if he were stuffed, and then you can sit on his back and think how it would be if you should live to be a thousand years old, and he should wake up while you are sitting there. It would be easy to imagine a lot of horrible things he would do to you when you look at his open mouth with its

113

awful fangs, his dreadful claws, and his horrible wings all covered with spikes."

"I think that might suit me," said the Languid Youth. "I would much rather imagine the exercises of these monsters than to see them really going on."

"Come on, then," said the Very Imp, and he led the way to the cave of the Ghastly Griffin.

The Bee-man went by himself through a great part of the mountain, and looked into many of its gloomy caves and recesses, recoiling in horror from most of the dreadful monsters who met his eyes. While he was wandering about, an awful roar was heard resounding through the passages of the mountain, and soon there came flapping along an enormous dragon, with body black as night, and wings and tail of fiery red. In his great fore-claws he bore a little baby.

"Horrible!" exclaimed the Bee-man. "He is taking that little creature to his cave to devour it."

He saw the dragon enter a cave not far away, and, following, looked in. The dragon was crouched upon the ground with the little baby lying before him. It did not seem to be hurt, but was frightened and crying. The monster was looking upon it with delight, as if he intended to make a dainty meal of it as soon as his appetite should be a little stronger.

"It is too bad!" thought the Bee-man. "Somebody ought to do something." And, turning around, he ran away as fast as he could.

He ran through various passages until he came to the spot where he had left his beehive. Picking it up, he hurried back, carrying the hive in his two hands before him. When he reached the cave of the dragon, he looked in and saw the monster still crouched over the weeping child. Without a moment's hesitation, the Bee-man rushed into the cave and threw his hive straight into the face of the dragon. The bees, enraged by the shock, rushed out in an angry crowd and immediately fell upon the head, mouth, eyes, and nose of the dragon. The great monster, astounded by this sudden attack, and driven almost wild by the numberless stings of the bees, sprang back to the farthest corner of his cave, still followed by the bees, at whom he flapped wildly with his great wings and struck with his paws.

While the dragon was thus engaged with the bees, the Bee-man rushed forward, and, seizing the child, he hurried away. He did not stop to pick up his doublet, but kept on until he reached the entrance of the cave. There, he saw the Very Imp hopping along on one leg and rubbing his back and shoulders with his hands, and stopped to inquire what was the matter and what had become of the Languid Youth.

"He is no kind of a fellow," said the Very Imp. "He disappointed me dreadfully. I took him up to the Ghastly Griffin, and told him the thing was enchanted, and that he might sit on its back and think about what it could do if it were awake; and when he came near it the wretched creature opened its eyes, and raised its head, and then you ought to have seen how mad that simpleton was. He made a dash at me and seized me by the ears; he kicked and beat me till I can scarcely move."

"His energies must have been toned up a good deal," said the Bee-man.

"Toned up! I should say so!" cried the other. "I raised a howl, and a Scissor-jawed Clipper came out of his hole and got after him; but that lazy fool ran so fast that he could not be caught."

The Bee-man now ran on and soon overtook the Languid Youth.

"You need not be in a hurry now," said the latter, "for the rules of this institution don't allow creatures inside to come out of this opening or to hang around it. If they did, they would frighten away visitors. They go in and out of holes in the upper part of the mountain."

The two proceeded on their way.

"What are you going to do with that baby?" said the Languid Youth.

"I shall carry it along with me," said the Bee-man, "as I go on with my search, and perhaps I may find its mother. If I do not, I shall give it to somebody in that little village yonder. Anything would be better than leaving it to be devoured by that horrid dragon."

"Let me carry it. I feel quite strong enough now to carry a baby."

"Thank you," said the Bee-man, "but I can take it myself. I like to carry something and I have now neither my hive nor my doublet."

"It is very well that you had to leave them behind," said the Youth, "for bees would have stung the baby."

"My bees never sting babies," said the other.

"They probably never had a chance," remarked his companion.

They soon entered the village, and after walking a short distance, the Youth exclaimed: "Do you see that woman over there sitting at the door of her house? She has beautiful hair, and she is tearing it all to pieces. She should not be allowed to do that."

"No," said the Bee-man. "Her friends should tie her hands."

"Perhaps she is the mother of this child," said the Youth, "and if you give it to her, she will no longer think of tearing her hair."

"But," said the Bee-man, "you don't really think this is her child?"

"Suppose you go over and see," said the other.

The Bee-man hesitated a moment, and then he walked toward the woman. Hearing him coming, she raised her head, and when she saw the child she rushed toward it, snatched it into her arms, and screaming with joy she covered it with kisses. Then, with happy tears, she begged to know the story of the rescue of her child, whom she never expected to see again; and she loaded the Bee-man with thanks and blessings. The friends and neighbors gathered around, and there was great rejoicing. The mother urged the Bee-man and the Youth to stay with her, and rest and refresh themselves, which they were glad to do, as they were tired and hungry.

They remained at the cottage all night, and in the afternoon of the next day the Bee-man said to the Youth: "It may seem an odd thing to you, but never in all my life have I felt myself drawn toward any living being as I am drawn toward this baby. Therefore, I believe that I have been transformed from a baby."

"Good!" cried the Youth. "It is my opinion that you have hit the truth. And now would you like to be changed back to your original form?"

"Indeed I would!" said the Bee-man. "I have the strongest yearning to be what I originally was."

The Youth, who had now lost every trace of languid feeling, took a great interest in the matter, and early the next morning started off to tell the Junior Sorcerer that the Bee-man had discovered what he had been transformed from and desired to be changed back to it.

The Junior Sorcerer and his learned Masters were filled with delight when they heard this report; and they at once set out for the mother's cottage. And there, by magic arts, the Bee-man was changed back into a baby. The mother was so grateful for what the Bee-man had done for her that she agreed to take charge of this baby and to bring it up as her own.

"It will be a grand thing for him," said the Junior Sorcerer, "and I am glad that I studied his case. He will now have a fresh start in life, and will have a chance to become something better than a miserable old man living in a wretched hut with no friends or companions but buzzing bees."

The Junior Sorcerer and his Masters then returned to their homes, happy in the success of their great performance; and the Youth went back to his home anxious to begin a life of activity and energy.

Years and years afterward, when the Junior Sorcerer had become a Senior and was very old indeed, he passed through the country of Orn, and noticed a small hut about which swarms of bees were flying. He approached it, and, looking in at the door, he saw an old man in a leathern doublet, sitting at a table, eating honey. By his magic art he knew this was the baby which had been transformed from the Bee-man.

"Upon my word!" exclaimed the Sorcerer. "He has grown up into the same thing again!"

THE GAY GOSHAWK

BY DOROTHY K. HAYNES

chosen by
MOLLIE HUNTER

I FIRST discovered the short stories of the Scottish writer Dorothy K. Haynes when I was sixteen. I was then and am still enormously impressed by this author's gift of language, and by the versatility of her talent which ranges through the whole subject choice from the gruesome to the light fantastic. Of all the riches she has offered, however, I have chosen *The Gay Goshawk* as the story that has stayed in my mind more than any other I have ever read. The prose of its telling has a spare and strong beauty which makes every word count; yet still there is a dreamlike atmosphere about it which makes it seem that the castle will be for ever deserted, and the yellow dog will be for ever baying the moon while the wounded knight and the hawk for ever patiently wait and watch one another.

The knight is real, however, despite this dreamlike atmosphere; and his tragedy of too little love is also so real that I have often wondered who he was and why his lady failed him at the end. Indeed, he haunts me, this nameless knight, and I think he always will.

MOLLIE HUNTER

THE horse walked under the great beeches, lazily padding by the side of the road. Now and again he stopped to graze, his white head cropping the grass, his tail sweeping the flies away in slow rhythmic switches. Always, after he had eaten, he went on again in the same direction, along the road which led to his stable.

The knight sat with his head drooping, one hand listless on the reins. The wound in his stomach had almost stopped bleeding now, but he could feel its edges pouting like a red mouth. There was no pain, no sensation, but his face was pinched with past agony, the lips and eyes blue shadowed. At last, so quietly, so easily that he hardly realized it, he leaned farther forward, drooped sideways, and slid to the ground. His horse gazed at him sadly, mildly, and went on. Now he lay under a green hedge, with the grasses sweeping his face, and a nettle grinning at him with green teeth. The sky darkened and spun as the pain returned, and his face grew cold in the sunshine.

The horse went on under the beeches, his silken ornaments tawdry and draggled. There was no-one to stop him, to question or harass him with farther journeyings and loud frightened cries. The castle gate swung open, wide and untended, and, unseen, he padded the dusty path, and stopped to graze where the grass was greenest.

They had left the castle two days ago, when they heard that the enemy were coming. A shrill scream had run over the countryside, a cry of alarm, and the women had listened with pale faces. "The enemy! The enemy! Our men are fighting, but they cannot hold them! Give them the castle, give them our homes, our riches, our land—it is easier to part with these than with our honour!" There had been dark rumours, murmured among the matrons. Not only the young, but the old, the mothers and grandmothers, had been used . . . they filled their hands, they grabbed what they could, and, in an hour, the stables were emptied, and the lady of the castle headed the retreat, her robes flowing, her hands grasping the reins like a man's, beating out the words, "Oh, hurry! Hurry!"

Now they were far away, in hiding, waiting for news. They clung together, afraid of what they might hear, and their conscience goaded them to self-justification. "What could we have done? Our knives against their swords, our spades against their battle-axes . . . and they are warriors, well used to fighting! We should have been dragged out, trampled underfoot—best for us to escape with our lives!"

The castle was deserted, inside and out. The battlements jutted sharp into the sky, the flag drooped on its pole. In the kitchen, a yellow dog whined and stretched itself before the hearth. The big black pot was bedded in ashes, and the soup inside had turned sour, a rancid scum mottling the surface, a thin dust sifted over it from the shifting of the fire. Long yellow streaks showed where the broth had boiled over, cooled and congealed. The pitchers of milk on the table had also soured and set, and the bread on the platter was hard as a rock; but the dog's water dish was dry, and the bone he had been gnawing was now white and smooth, kicked into the corner by a hasty foot.

The dog was thirsty. The vermin which trespassed at night had kept him from hunger, but there was no water anywhere. Yawning, his eyes dull, he stretched himself and set off on another search. He could not understand the silence. He thirsted for company even more than for drink. If a man had entered the kitchen, the dog would have leaped on him and overturned him in ecstatic welcome.

Slowly, he nosed around, whining, a high singing plaint. The scrubbed tables and ledges were out of his reach. He reared on his hind legs, paws resting, head craning, but there was nothing to drink, not even a splash of water carelessly spilt. Quietly, patiently, he pattered out, his claws scratching bluntly, his head poked forward in the dust of the passages. Even the cat had gone. He pushed against a door which stood ajar, and found himself in the high dining hall. From habit, he went to his old corner

beside the hearth, where he would wait for his master to throw
him the bones and scraps from his plate. Head erect, ears cocked
he waited, but there was no-one in the high chair, no sound of
laughter, no red faces flaming over the wine-flagon. He sighed,
and his ears drooped, and his tail went limp between his legs.

He could smell his master's presence, faint in the air. He
could smell the scents of women, puzzling, elusive. Where had
they gone, the men who spoke roughly and laughed, the women
who fondled his ears and kissed his yellow head? Up the stairs
he went, round and round, up and up, like a dog on a treadmill.
Here, there were rooms which told the story of flight. He poked
his head into every one, but backed out again, timid, defeated.

In the last room, the largest, something was stirring, a flurry
of sound, a soft metallic jingle. He tiptoed in, whimpering. A
velvet gown was thrown on the floor with satin slippers and a
box of bright silks. The couch where my lady had lain was all
in disorder, and her brushes lay askew on the table. On a perch
by the window, a goshawk rustled its striped feathers, and
stamped angrily, trying to jerk itself free. It looked at the dog,
and the dog leaped forward, yelping and panting and wagging
his tail frantically.

The bird sat still, quieted for the moment. The velvet on the
floor was ruffled under the dog's feet, and the slippers and trin-
kets were scattered as he pranced in joy. Yap! Yap! he went,
and the noise of his breathing filled the pauses between his
barks. The bird's head crouched lower and lower, till at last it
lunged forward with its wings raised and its beak hooked and
vicious. It stabbed twice, and the dog rolled back in dismay,
still yelping, and hurt at the unexpected hostility. Once again,
he tripped up to the perch, his eyes pleading, but the goshawk
glared and beat at him, rattling its fine silver chain, so that he
retreated howling, down the stone stairs to the quiet and the
loneliness.

The white horse stood before his stables in his torn trappings.
Inside was food and shade from the sun, but the door was shut,
and no friendly hand came to open it. Everything was dusty
and dry, no water anywhere. The fountain in the yard had
stopped playing long ago, and though one of the pipes still

trickled, it left only a thick smear of slime, oozing over the stone basin. The horse snuffed at it, and turned away. The sun was very hot, and a bad smell came from the green-coated stone. Patiently, his harness heavy, he waited by the stable, and switched the flies away.

The dog heard the scrape of hooves, and whined at every cranny, every slit where the stone was worn under the oaken doors. He fawned and grovelled, almost insane with longing, and the horse turned mildly and jingled his bridle. At last, the yapping died to a whimper, and faded, as the dog lay with his head on its paws and slept exhausted.

Up in the tower, the goshawk stared coldly at the tumbled finery of my lady's boudoir, and wrenched afresh at its chain.

The knight lay with his knees drawn up to ease the gash in his stomach. His mouth was dry, and though he could feel the stones sharp under him, he had no strength to move. He could not even lift a hand to wipe the dust from his face.

Where was he? The world was all out of focus. There was a rustle of leaves over his head, and grasses waved round him, tickling his ears with their feathery tips. His heel, when he moved it, grated on grit, but he could not puzzle out where he was lying, or which way the road went. When had he come here? Where was his horse? He remembered his wound and the desperate retreat; he remembered being alone, letting the horse take his own way; but after that, there was nothing.

The sky was a deep blue, shading off pale towards the horizon. Against the blueness, the leaves overhead were black, and the grass in which he lay was colourless. It must be night. The moon had not yet risen, but when he tried to calculate the time, his head swam, and he could not think. He lay quiet, almost content, full of a childlike pleasure in being able to stare at the blueness without blinking.

There was no wind, and yet the beech leaves, infinitely more remote than the sky, rustled and trembled miles up in space. The nettle which had grinned in daylight now stood like a spiky sentinel, every leaf rigid and strong. It was too virile, too tense among the delicate grasses. He looked back to the sky, from the farthest turquoise edge to the deep azure above; and then he turned his head and saw the battlemented edge of his castle against the deepest blue of all, and the world swung into focus so suddenly that it dizzied him, and he clung to the ground for safety, forgetting that he could not fall.

His home was just beyond the opposite hedge. A little farther on were the gates, and then the drive curving back in shadow till it reached the castle. His horse must have gone on alone. Why, then, had nobody come to help him? Perhaps they had not guessed he could be so near. Perhaps the horse had gone back to his stable unseen. They were often idle, these hostlers, and, knowing their master to be away, they would be neglecting their duties. Well, any time now, they would come for him . . . .

With an effort, he dug his hands into the grass and levered himself higher, leaning against the bank. Strange how weak his arms were! He felt the wound drag its crusted edges, and drew up his legs again. Now he could watch the tower, and wait for them coming. They would bring lights, and a litter to carry him home. They would have water, and the unguents to salve his wound, wine for his parched throat, and soft linen to lie on. And his lady would weep over him, but smile because he had returned to her.

It was very quiet, as still as death. No voices carried from the castle, no lights winked from the windows. An owl swept past, like a shadow, and a faint glitter of stars was washed up on the deepening tide of blue.

Next time he woke, he thought that day had come. The sky had lightened, and the moon was so bright that he could see everything, the stones in the road, the blood on his clothes, and the colour of the bluebells in the grass, pale beside the crimson of clover. The dead white light poured down, and he was suddenly afraid. Why did they not come? Did his lady not feel, did she not sense that he was here? He turned his head restlessly, but he could not move himself more. It was like lying in a nightmare, pressed down by the knotted covers and the weight of sleep. His head was giddy with too much moonlight. Perhaps he was sleeping now. He would be better in the morning. The dream would pass, and he would rise up rested, and walk into the great hall, and they would flock to welcome him, and *she* would nurse him back to his old strength.

He started. His dog, his little yellow dog, was howling! Far away, it lifted its head and howled at the moon, a long bay dying away in sorrow. The knight was weak, and the sound made the sweat start all over his body. "Hey, Jako!" he tried to call, but the voice stuck in his throat, and his lips were too dry to whistle. When the howling had died away, he watched the tower, ready for all manner of curses to fall on it, witches skimming the coping like bats, flames leaping red from the stone, but the moon shone steady and pale, and nothing moved, not even the dust.

He opened his eyes again, not knowing that he had slept. His head was heavy, the whole world pressing down on him, and his mouth was dry, burned up with fever. The sky was grey, the grasses moist and fresh, and the castle seemed far away now, happed in a white mist. It was cold, so cold that there was hardly any sense in his limbs. It took him a long time to think, to remember who and where he was, and why he was lying in damp grass with nothing to moisten his lips or slake his throat. His mind went wandering in circles, like the bird which hovered above him, round and round, never settling, but never leaving the one spot. . . .

He started when it alighted beside him, pleased at its nearness, the tameness which let it stand unafraid. Idly, he watched its eyes, its strong beak and barred feathers. It was a beautiful bird. . . .

His mind was so slow that, at first, the chain on its leg meant nothing to him. It was a delicate chain, broken off raggedly, and round the leg was a silver ring, the coat of arms graven finely, so that it stood out clear for all it was so minute. When at last the meaning seeped into him, a faint flush of warmth ran into his body. Strength came back to his hands and his fingers fretted and tore at the torn silk of his cloak, but all he could wrench off was one thread. He held out his arm, and the bird came nearer, as it was used to do when he called. Fumbling with weakness, he looped the stuff inside the looseness of the ring, till the bird protested and flapped its wings. It was done, though. It was accomplished. Now, as it had been taught, it would fly to its mistress, and soon, soon . . .

It would not move. Sinister, it raked its beak along its claws, and ruffled its soft feathers. Its eyes were cold, but expectant. And suddenly, the knight knew that there was no one for it to fly to, and that it would watch beside him now till the last. Beyond that, he did not care to think.

The Wild Goat's Kid *by Liam O'Flaherty*

chosen by Joan Lingard

I HAVE two favourite stories about goats. This is not because I am in any way addicted to goats or, in fact, have had any dealings with them in the flesh; it is merely a matter of coincidence that two writers I admire each happened to write a haunting and beautiful little story about a goat. One is French and should be read in that language to be enjoyed fully. It is *La Petite Chevre de Monsieur Seguin* by Alphonse Daudet. Monsieur Seguin is a poor man who has difficulty in keeping goats: they always want their freedom and once they get it, they go up into the mountain and there, the wolf always eats them. "La petite chevre" is a little white goat called Blanquette. She is Monsieur Seguin's last hope but she, like all the others, looks longingly at the mountain and will not listen to her master's warnings. The other story, *The Wild Goat's Kid*, is also about a white goat. She has found freedom and roams the cliff tops above the sea. She gives birth to a kid. Like Blanquette, she encounters an enemy; hers is a savage black dog who wants to kill not only her, but her exquisite little grey-black kid as well. Here, as in most of his stories, whether they are about people or animals, Liam O'Flaherty writes about the basic things of life: birth and death, love, joy in living, and the urge to survive. It is a story full of poetry, emotion and excitement. I have only to read the first line to feel that I am on a cliff top in Ireland with the birds wheeling overhead and the sea surging below.

JOAN LINGARD

HER nimble hoofs made music on the crags all winter, as she roamed along the cliff-tops over the sea.

During the previous autumn, when goats were mating, she had wandered away, one of a small herd that trotted gaily after a handsome fellow, with a splendid grey-black hide and winding horns. It was her first mating. Then, with the end of autumn, peasant boys came looking for their goats. The herd was broken up. The gallant buck was captured and slain by two hungry dogs from the village of Drumranny. The white goat alone remained. She had wandered too far away from her master's village. He couldn't find her. She was given up as lost.

So that she became a wild one of the cliffs, where the sea-gulls and the cormorants were lords, and the great eagle of Mohur soared high over the thundering sea. Her big, soft, yellow eyes became wild from looking down often at the sea, with her long chin whiskers swaying gracefully in the wind. She was a long, slender thing, with short, straight horns and ringlets of matted hair trailing far down on either haunch.

With her tail in the air, snorting, tossing her horns, she fled when anybody approached. Her hoofs would patter over the crags until she was far away. Then she would stand on some eminence and turn about to survey the person who had disturbed her, calmly, confident in the power of her slender legs to carry her beyond pursuit.

She roamed at will. No stone fence, however high, could resist her long leap, as she sprang on muscular thighs that bent like silk. She was so supple that she could trot on the top of a thin fence, carelessly, without a sound except the gentle tapping of her delicate hoofs. She hardly ever left the cliff-tops. There was plenty of food there, for the winter was mild, and the leaves and grasses that grew between the crevices of the crags were flavoured by the strong, salt taste of the brine carried up on the wind. She grew sleek and comely.

Towards the end of winter a subtle change came over her.

131

Her hearing became more acute. She took fright at the least sound. She began to shun the sea except on very calm days, when it did not roar. She ate less. She grew very particular about what she ate. She hunted around a long time before she chose a morsel. She often went on her knees, reaching down into the bottom of a crevice to nibble at a briar that was inferior to the more accessible ones. She became corpulent. Her udder increased.

Winter passed. Green leaves began to sprout. Larks sang in the morning. There was sweetness in the air and a great urge of life. The white goat, one morning a little after dawn, gave birth to a grey-black kid.

The kid was born in a tiny, green glen under an over-hanging ledge of low rock that sheltered it from the wind. It was a male kid, an exquisite, fragile thing, tinted delicately with many colours. His slender belly was milky white. The insides of his thighs were of the same colour. He had deep rings of grey, like bracelets, above his hoofs. He had black knee-caps on his forelegs, like pads, to protect him when he knelt to take his mother's teats into his silky, black mouth. His back and sides were grey-black. His ears were black, long, and drooping with the weakness of infancy.

The white goat bleated over him, with soft eyes and shivering flanks, gloating over the exquisite thing that had been created within her by the miraculous power of life. And she had this delicate creature all to herself, in the wild solitude of the beautiful little glen, within earshot of the murmuring sea, with little birds whistling their spring songs around about her, and the winds coming with their slow murmurs over the crags. The first tender hours of her first motherhood were undisturbed by any restraint, not even by the restraint of a mate's presence. In absolute freedom and quiet, she watched with her young.

How she manoeuvred to make him stand! She breathed on him to warm him. She raised him gently with her forehead, uttering strange, soft sounds to encourage him. Then he stood up, trembling, staggering, swaying on his curiously long legs. She became very excited, rushing around him, bleating ner- vously, afraid that he should fall again. He fell. She was in agony. Bitter wails came from her distended jaws and she crunched her teeth. But she renewed her efforts, urging the kid to rise, to rise and live . . . to live, live, live.

He rose again. Now he was steadier. He shook his head. He wagged his long ears as his mother breathed into them. He took a few staggering steps, came to his padded knees, and rose again immediately. Slowly, gently, gradually, she pushed him towards her udder with her horns. At last he took the teat within his mouth, he pushed joyously, sank to his knees and began to drink.

She stayed with him all day in the tiny glen, just nibbling a few mouthfuls of the short grass that grew around. Most of the time she spent exercising her kid. With a great show of anxiety and importance, she brought him on little expeditions across the glen to the opposite rock, three yards away and back again. At first he staggered clumsily against her sides, and his tiny hoofs often lost their balance on tufts of grass, such was his weakness. But he gained strength with amazing speed, and the goat's joy and pride increased. She suckled and caressed him after each tiny journey.

When the sun had set he was able to walk steadily, to take little short runs, to toss his head. They lay all night beneath the shelter of the ledge, with the kid between his mother's legs, against her warm udder.

Next morning she hid him securely in a crevice of the neighbouring crag, in a small groove between two flags that were covered with a withered growth of wild grass and ferns. The kid crawled instinctively into the warm hole without any resistance to the gentle push of his mother's horns. He lay down with his head towards his doubled hind legs, and closed his eyes. Then the goat scraped the grass and fern-stalks over the entrance hole with her fore feet, and she hurried away to graze, as carelessly as if she had no kid hidden.

All the morning, as she grazed hurriedly and fiercely around the crag, she took great pains to pretend that she was not aware of her kid's nearness. Even when she grazed almost beside the hiding-place, she never noticed him, by look or by cry. But still, she pricked her little ears at every distant sound.

At noon she took him out and gave him suck. She played with him on a grassy knoll and watched him prance about. She taught him how to rear on his hind legs and fight the air with his forehead. Then she put him back into his hiding-place and returned to graze. She continued to graze until nightfall.

Just when she was about to fetch him from his hole and take him to the overhanging ledge to rest for the night, a startling sound reached her ears. It came from afar, from the south, from beyond a low fence that ran across the crag on the skyline. It was indistinct, barely audible, a deep, purring sound. But to the ears of the mother-goat, it was loud and ominous as a thunder-clap. It was the heavy breathing of a dog sniffing the wind.

She listened stock-still, with her head in the air and her short tail lying stiff along her back, twitching one ear. The sound came again. It was nearer. Then there was a patter of feet. Then a clumsy, black figure hurtled over the fence and dropped on to the crag, with awkward secrecy. The goat saw a black dog, a large, curly fellow, standing by the fence in the dim twilight, with his fore paw raised and his long, red tongue hanging. Then he shut his mouth suddenly, and raising his snout upwards sniffed several times, contracting his nostrils as he did so, as if in pain. Then he whined savagely, and trotted towards the goat sideways.

She snorted. It was a sharp, dull thud, like a blow from a rubber sledge. Then she rapped the crag three times with her left fore foot, loudly and sharply. The dog stood still and raised his fore paw again. He bent down his head and looked at her with narrowed eyes. Then he licked his breast and began to run swiftly to the left. He was running towards the kid's hiding-place, with his tail stretched out straight and his snout to the wind.

With another fierce snort the goat charged him at full speed, in order to cut him off from his advance on the kid's hiding-place. He stopped immediately when she charged. The goat halted too, five yards from the hiding-place, facing the dog.

The dog stood still. His eyes wandered around in all directions, with the bashfulness of a sly brute, caught suddenly in an awkward position. Then slowly he raised his bloodshot eyes to the goat. He bared his fangs. His mane rose like a fan. His tail shot out. Picking his steps like a lazy cat, he approached her without a sound. The goat shivered along her left flank, and she snorted twice in rapid succession.

When he was within six yards of her he uttered a ferocious roar—a deep, rumbling sound in his throat. He raced towards her, and leaped clean into the air, as if she were a fence that he was trying to vault. She parried him subtly with her horns, like a swordthrust, without moving her fore feet. Her sharp horns just grazed his belly as he whizzed past her head. But the slight blow deflected his course. Instead of falling on his feet, as he had intended cunningly to do, between the goat and the kid, he was thrown to the left and fell on his side, with a thud. The goat whirled about and charged him.

But he had arisen immediately and jerked himself away, with his haunches low down, making a devilish scraping and yelping and growling noise. He wanted to terrify the kid out of his hiding-place. Then it would be easy to overpower the goat, hampered by the task of hiding the kid between her legs.

The kid uttered a faint, querulous cry, but the goat immediately replied with a sharp, low cry. The kid mumbled something indistinct, and then remained silent. There was a brushing sound among the ferns that covered him. He was settling himself down farther. The goat trotted rigidly to the opposite side of the hiding-place to face the dog again.

The dog had run away some distance, and lay on his belly, licking his paws. Now he meant to settle himself down properly to the prolonged attack, after the failure of his first onslaught. He yawned lazily and made peculiar mournful noises, thrusting his head into the air and twitching his snout. The goat watched every single movement and sound, with her ears thrust forward past her horns. Her great, soft eyes were very wild and timorous in spite of the valiant posture of her body, and the terrific force of the blows she delivered occasionally on the hard crag with her little hoofs.

The dog remained lying for half an hour or so, continuing his weird pantomime. The night fell completely. Everything became unreal and ghostly under the light of the distant myriads of stars. An infant moon had arisen. The sharp rushing wind and the thunder of the sea only made the silent loneliness of the night more menacing to the white goat, as she stood bravely on the limestone crag defending her newborn young. On all sides the horizon was a tumultuous line of barren crag, dented with shallow glens and seamed with low, stone fences that hung like tattered curtains against the rim of the sky.

Then the dog attacked again. Rising suddenly, he set off at a long, swinging gallop, with his head turned sideways towards the goat, whining as he ran. He ran around the goat in a wide circle, gradually increasing his speed. A white spot on his breast flashed and vanished as he rose and fell in the undulating stretches of his flight. The goat watched him, fiercely rigid from tail to snout. She pawed the crag methodically, turning around on her own ground slowly to face him.

When he passed his starting-point, he was flying at full speed, a black ball shooting along the gloomy surface of the crag, with a sharp rattle of claws. The rattle of his claws, his whining and the sharp tapping of the goat's fore feet as she turned about, were the only sounds that rose into the night from this sinister engagement.

He sped round and round the goat, approaching her imperceptibly each round, until he was so close that she could see his glittering eyes and the white lather of rage on his half-open jaws. She became slightly dizzy and confused, turning about so methodically in a confined space, confused and amazed by the subtle strategy of the horrid beast. His whining grew louder and more savage. The rattle of his claws was like the clamour of hailstones driven by a wind. He was upon her.

He came in a whirl on her flank. He came with a savage roar that deafened her. She shivered and then stiffened in rigid silence to receive him. The kid uttered a shrill cry. Then the black bulk hurtled through the air, close up, with hot breathing, snarling, with reddened fangs and . . . smash.

He had dived for her left flank. But as he went past her head she turned like lightning and met him again with her horns. This time she grazed his side, to the rear of the shoulder. He yelped and tumbled sideways, rolling over twice. With a savage snort she was upon him. He was on his haunches, rising, when

136

her horns thudded into his head. He went down again with another yelp. He rolled over and then suddenly, with amazing speed, swept to his feet, whirled about on swinging tail and dived for her flank once more. The goat uttered a shriek of terror. He had passed her horns. His fangs had embedded themselves in the matted ringlet that trailed along her right flank. The dog's flying weight, swinging on to the ringlet as he fell, brought her to her haunches.

But she was ferocious now. As she wriggled to her feet beside the rolling dog that gripped her flank, she wrenched herself around and gored him savagely in the belly. He yelled and loosed his hold. She rose on her hind legs in a flash, and with a snort she gored him again. Her sharp, pointed horns penetrated his side between the ribs. He gasped and shook his four feet in the air. Then she pounded on him with her fore feet, beating his prostrate body furiously. Her little hoofs pattered with tremendous speed for almost a minute. She beat him blindly, without looking at him.

Then she suddenly stopped. She snorted. The dog was still. She shivered and looked down at him curiously. He was dead. Her terror was passed. She lifted her right fore foot and shook it with a curious movement. Then she uttered a wild, joyous cry and ran towards her kid's hiding-place.

Night passed into a glorious dawn that came over a rippling sea from the east. A wild, sweet dawn, scented with dew and the many perfumes of the germinating earth. The sleepy sun rose brooding from the sea, golden and soft, searching far horizons with its concave shafts of light. The dawn was still. Still and soft and pure.

The white goat and her kid were travelling eastwards along the cliff-tops over the sea. They had travelled all night, flying from the horrid carcass of the beast that lay stretched on the crag beside the little glen. Now they were far away, on the summit of the giant white Precipice of Cahir. The white goat rested to give suck to her kid, and to look out over the cliff-top at the rising sun.

Then she continued her flight eastwards, pushing her tired kid gently before her with her horns.

THE STAR BEAST

BY NICHOLAS STUART GRAY

CHOSEN BY ANDRE NORTON

SOME years ago very fortunate chance brought me a copy of Nicholas Stuart Gray's THE SEVENTH SWAN. With the result that thereafter I ordered from my London bookseller everything appearing under his name. In due time a collection of short stories, MAINLY IN MOONLIGHT, arrived, to be most eagerly read. There are stories which continued to haunt one long after the volume in which they have appeared has been laid away. One can not put aside the memory of such. And usually they are tales which stab below the surface which protects us from strong emotion we would rather did not trouble us.

The Star Beast is such a goad, being especially pertinent to the space minded age in which we live. It is a rebuke to our own species' general smug attitude of superiority, as well as a warning that perhaps somewhere beyond our own solar system man is not as all important as he cries to the heavens he is. This is a tale to make one look both outward at the civilization about one, and inward at one's own prejudices and blindness; so simply told with the art of a master of fantasy that its lesson can not be avoided, no matter how the reader may try to evade the mirror held up to reflect our whole arrogant kind.

ANDRE NORTON

SOON upon a time, and not so far ahead, there was a long streak of light down the night sky, a flicker of fire, and a terrible bang that startled all who heard it, even those who were normally inured to noise. When day came, the matter was discussed, argued, and finally dismissed. For no one could discover any cause at all for the disturbance.

Shortly afterwards, at a farm, there was heard a scrabbling at the door, and a crying. When the people went to see what was there, they found a creature. It was not easy to tell what sort of creature, but far too easy to tell that it was hurt and hungry and afraid. Only its pain and hunger had brought it to the door for help.

Being used to beasts, the farmer and his wife tended the thing. They put it in a loose-box and tended it. They brought water in a big basin and it drank thirstily, but with some difficulty—for it seemed to want to lift it to its mouth instead of lapping, and the basin was too big, and it was too weak. So it lapped. The farmer dressed the great burn that seared its thigh and shoulder and arm. He was kind enough, in a rough way, but the creature moaned, and set its teeth, and muttered strange sounds, and clenched its front paws. . . .

Those front paws . . . ! They were so like human hands that it was quite startling to see them. Even with their soft covering of grey fur they were slender, long-fingered, with the fine nails of a girl. And its body was like that of a boy—a half-grown lad—though it was as tall as a man. Its head was man-shaped. The long and slanting eyes were as yellow as topaz, and shone from inside with their own light. And the lashes were thick and silvery.

"It's a monkey of some kind," decided the farmer.

"But so beautiful," said his wife. "I've never heard of a monkey like this. They're charming—pretty—amusing—all in their own way. But not beautiful, as a real person might be."

They were concerned when the creature refused to eat. It turned away its furry face, with those wonderful eyes, the straight nose, and curving fine lips, and would not touch the best of the season's hay. It would not touch the dog biscuits or the bones. Even the boiled cod-head that was meant for the cats' supper, it refused. In the end, it settled for milk. It lapped it delicately out of the big basin, making small movements of its hands—its forepaws—as though it would have preferred some smaller utensil that it could lift to its mouth.

Word went round. People came to look at the strange and injured creature in the barn. Many people came. From the village, the town, and the city. They prodded it, and examined it, turning it this way and that. But no one could decide just what it was. A beast for sure. A monkey, most likely. Escaped from a circus or menagerie. Yet whoever had lost it made no attempt to retrieve it, made no offer of reward for its return.

Its injuries healed. The soft fur grew again over the bare grey skin. Experts from the city came and took it away for more detailed examination. The wife of the farmer was sad to see it go. She had grown quite attached to it.

"It was getting to know me," said she. "And it talked to me— in its fashion."

The farmer nodded slowly and thoughtfully.

"It was odd," he said, "the way it would imitate what one said. You know, like a parrot does. Not real talking, of course, just imitation."

"Of course," said his wife. "I never thought it was real talk. I'm not so silly."

It was good at imitating speech, the creature. Very soon, it had learned many words and phrases, and began to string them together quite quickly, and with surprising sense. One might have thought it knew what it meant—if one was silly.

The professors and elders and priests who now took the creature in hand were far from silly. They were puzzled, and amused, and interested—at first. They looked at it, in the dis- used monkey-cage at the city's menagerie, where it was kept. And it stood upright, on finely-furred feet as arched and perfect as the feet of an ancient statue.

"It is oddly human," said the learned men.

They amused themselves by bringing it a chair and watching

it sit down gracefully, though not very comfortably, as if it was used to furniture of better shape and construction. They gave it a plate and a cup, and it ate with its hands most daintily, looking round as though for some sort of cutlery. But it was not thought safe to trust it with a knife.

"It is only a beast," said everyone. "However clever at imitation."

"It's so quick to learn," said some.

"But not in any way human."

"No," said the creature, "I am not human. But, in my own place, I am a man."

"Parrot-talk!" laughed the elders, uneasily.

The professors of living and dead languages taught it simple speech.

After a week, it said to them:

"I understand all the words you use. They are very easy. And you cannot quite express what you mean, in any of your tongues. A child of my race——" It stopped, for it had no wish to seem impolite, and then it said, "There is a language that is spoken throughout the universe. If you will allow me——"

And softly and musically it began to utter a babble of meaningless nonsense at which all the professors laughed loudly.

"Parrot-talk!" they jeered. "Pretty Polly! Pretty Polly!"

For they were much annoyed. And they mocked the creature into cowering silence.

The professors of logic came to the same conclusions as the others.

"Your logic is at fault," the creature had told them, despairingly. "I have disproved your conclusions again and again. You will not listen or try to understand."

"Who could understand parrot-talk?"

"I am no parrot, but a man in my own place. Define a man. I walk upright. I think. I collate facts. I imagine. I anticipate. I learn. I speak. What is a man by your definition?"

"Pretty Polly!" said the professors.

They were very angry. One of them hit the creature with his walking-cane. No one likes to be set on a level with a beast. And the beast covered its face with its hands, and was silent.

It was warier when the mathematicians came. It added two and two together for them. They were amazed. It subtracted eight from ten. They wondered at it. It divided twenty by five. They marvelled. It took courage. It said:

"But you have reached a point where your formulae and calculuses fail. There is a simple law—one by which you reached the earth long ago—one by which you can leave it at will——"

The professors were furious.

"Parrot! Parrot!" they shouted.

"No! In my own place——"

The beast fell silent.

Then came the priests, smiling kindly—except to one another. For with each other they argued furiously and loathingly regarding their own views on rule and theory.

"Oh, stop!" said the creature, pleadingly.

It lifted its hands towards them and its golden eyes were full of pity.

"You make everything petty and meaningless," it said. "Let me tell you of the Master-Plan of the Universe. It is so simple and nothing to do with gods or rules, myths or superstition. Nothing to do with fear."

The priests were so outraged that they forgot to hate one another. They screamed wildly with one voice:

"Wicked!"

They fled from the creature, jamming in the cage door in their haste to escape and forget the soul-less, evil thing. And the beast sighed and hid its sorrowful face, and took refuge in increasing silence.

The elders grew to hate it. They disliked the imitating and the parrot-talk, the golden eyes, the sorrow, the pity. They took away its chair, its table, its plate and cup. They ordered it to walk properly—on all fours, like any other beast.

"But in my own place——"

It broke off there. Yet some sort of pride, or stubbornness, or courage, made it refuse to crawl, no matter what they threatened or did.

They sold it to a circus.

A small sum was sent to the farmer who had first found the

thing, and the rest of its price went into the state coffers for making weapons for a pending war.

The man who owned the circus was not especially brutal, as such men go. He was used to training beasts, for he was himself the chief attraction of the show, with his lions and tigers, half-drugged and toothless as they were. He said it was no use being too easy on animals.

"They don't understand over-kindness," said he. "They get to despising you. You have to show who's master."

He showed the creature who was master.

He made it jump through hoops and do simple sums on a blackboard. At first it also tried to speak to the people who came to look at it. It would say, in its soft and bell-clear tones:

"Oh, listen—I can tell you things——"

Everyone was amazed at its cleverness and most entertained by the eager way it spoke. And such parrot-nonsense it talked!

"Hark at it!" they cried. "It wants to tell us things, bless it!"

"About the other side of the moon!"

"The far side of Saturn!"

"Who taught it to say all this stuff?"

"It's saying something about the block in mathematics now!"

"And the language of infinity!"

"Logic!"

"And the Master-Plan!"

They rolled about, helpless with laughter in their ringside seats.

It was even more entertaining to watch the creature doing its sums on the big blackboard, which two attendants would turn so that everyone could admire the cleverness: 2 and 2, and the beautifully-formed 4 that it wrote beneath. 10—8 = 2. 5 into 20—11 from 12.

"How clever it is," said a small girl, admiringly.

Her father smiled.

"It's the trainer who's clever," he said. "The animal knows nothing of what it does. Only what it has been taught. By kindness, of course," he added quickly, as the child looked sad.

"Oh, good," said she, brightening. "I wouldn't like it hurt. It's so sweet."

But even she had to laugh when it came to the hoop-jumping. For the creature hated doing it. And, although the long whip of the trainer never actually touched its grey fur, yet it cowered at the cracking sound. Surprising, if anyone had wondered why. And it ran, upright on its fine furred feet, and graceful in spite of the red and yellow clothes it was wearing, and it jumped through the hoops. And then more hoops were brought. And these were surrounded by inflammable material and set on fire. The audience was enthralled. For the beast was terrified of fire, for some reason. It would shrink back and clutch at its shoulder, its arm, its thigh. It would stare up wildly into the roof of the great circus canopy—as if it could see through it and out to the sky beyond—as though it sought desperately for help that would not come. And it shook and trembled. And the whip cracked. And it cried aloud as it came to each flaming hoop. But it jumped.

And it stopped talking to the people. Sometimes it would almost speak, but then it would give a hunted glance towards the ring-master, and lapse into silence. Yet always it walked and ran and jumped as a man would do these things—upright. Not on all fours, like a proper beast.

And soon a particularly dangerous tightrope dance took the fancy of the people. The beast was sold to a small touring animal-show. It was getting very poor in entertainment value, anyway. It moved sluggishly. Its fur was draggled and dull. It had even stopped screaming at the fiery hoops. And—it was such an eerie, man-like thing to have around. Everyone was glad to see it go.

In the dreary little show where it went, no one even pretended to understand animals. They just showed them in their cages. Their small, fetid cages. To begin with, the keeper would bring the strange creature out to perform for the onlookers. But it was a boring performance. Whip or no whip, hunger or less hunger, the beast could no longer run or jump properly. It shambled round and round, dull-eyed and silent. People merely wondered what sort of animal it was, but not with any great interest. It could hardly even be made to flinch at fire, not even when sparks touched its fur. It was sold to a collector of rare beasts. And he took it to his little menagerie on the edge of his estate near a forest.

He was not really very interested in his creatures. It was a passing hobby for a very rich man. Something to talk about among his friends. Only once he came to inspect his new acquisition. He prodded it with a stick. He thought it rather an ugly, dreary animal.

"I heard that you used to talk, parrot-fashion," said he. "Go on, then, say something."

It only cowered. He prodded it some more.

"I read about you when they had you in the city," said the man, prodding harder. "You used to talk, I know you did. So talk now. You used to say all sorts of clever things. That you were a man in your own place. Go on, tell me you're a man."

"Pretty Polly," mumbled the creature, almost inaudibly.

Nothing would make it speak again.

It was so boring that no one took much notice or care of it. And one night it escaped from its cage.

The last glimpse that anyone saw of it was by a hunter in the deeps of the forest.

It was going slowly looking in terror at rabbits and squirrels. It was weeping aloud and trying desperately to walk on all fours.

THE HAPPY PRINCE

BY OSCAR WILDE

CHOSEN BY
SCOTT O'DELL

IN the world of books one of my first enthusiasms as a young man—along with Lawrence's THE SEA AND SARDINIA, Conrad's NOSTROMO, and THE THREE BLACK PENNIES by Joseph Hergesheimer—was Wilde's THE HOUSE OF POMEGRANATES.

I stumbled upon it by chance on the shelves of a second-hand bookstore. It was a stylish example of the printer's art, this collection of tales for children. Decorative but not decadent, possibly the best illustrations Aubrey Beardsley had done. It caught my eye and I took it home, not at all to read, just to have an attractive book to display on my living room table.

It was not until a year or so later of a wintry night, that pressed for something to read, I was forced to pick up THE HOUSE OF POMEGRANATES. The book entranced me. And of all the tales, especially *The Happy Prince*.

I liked the Prince but even more his dear friend and messenger the Swallow, who wintered in Egypt where a great green snake lived in a palm tree and was fed honey-cakes by twenty priests, and who summered in the north where he fell in love with a river reed:

"'It is a ridiculous attachment,' twittered the other Swallows, 'she has no money, and far too many relations;' and indeed the river was quite full of Reeds."

Many years have passed since *The Happy Prince* was written, dynasties have fallen, fashions have changed. But the tale is still alive, both light-hearted and sad, effortlessly witty and altogether elegant.

SCOTT O'DELL

HIGH above the city, on a tall column, stood the statue of the Happy Prince. He was gilded all over with thin leaves of fine gold, for eyes he had two bright sapphires, and a large red ruby glowed on his sword-hilt.

He was very much admired indeed. "He is as beautiful as a weathercock," remarked one of the Town Councillors who wished to gain a reputation for having artistic tastes; "only not quite so useful," he added, fearing lest people should think him unpractical, which he really was not.

"Why can't you be like the Happy Prince?" asked a sensible mother of her little boy who was crying for the moon. "The Happy Prince never dreams of crying for anything."

"I am glad there is someone in the world who is quite happy," muttered a disappointed man as he gazed at the wonderful statue.

"He looks just like an angel," said the Charity Children as they came out of the cathedral in their bright scarlet cloaks, and their clean white pinafores.

"How do you know?" said the Mathematical Master, "you have never seen one."

"Ah! but we have, in our dreams," answered the children; and the Mathematical Master frowned and looked very severe, for he did not approve of children dreaming.

One night there flew over the city a little Swallow. His friends had gone away to Egypt six weeks before, but he had stayed behind, for he was in love with the most beautiful Reed. He had met her early in the spring as he was flying down the river after a big yellow moth, and had been so attracted by her slender waist that he had stopped to talk to her.

"Shall I love you?" said the Swallow, who liked to come to the point at once, and the Reed made him a low bow. So he flew round and round her, touching the water with his wings, and making silver ripples. This was his courtship, and it lasted all through the summer.

"It is a ridiculous attachment," twittered the other Swallows, "she has no money, and far too many relations;" and indeed the river was quite full of Reeds. Then, when the autumn came, they all flew away.

After they had gone he felt lonely, and began to tire of his lady-love. "She has no conversation," he said, "and I am afraid that she is a coquette, for she is always flirting with the wind." And certainly, whenever the wind blew, the Reed made the most graceful curtsies. "I admit that she is domestic," he continued, "but I love travelling, and my wife, consequently, should love travelling also."

"Will you come away with me?" he said finally to her; but the Reed shook her head, she was so attached to her home.

"You have been trifling with me," he cried. "I am off to the Pyramids. Good-bye!" and he flew away.

All day long he flew, and at night-time he arrived at the city. "Where shall I put up?" he said; "I hope the town has made preparations."

Then he saw the statue on the tall column. "I will put up there," he cried; "it is a fine position with plenty of fresh air." So he alighted just between the feet of the Happy Prince.

"I have a golden bedroom," he said softly to himself as he looked round, and he prepared to go to sleep; but just as he was putting his head under his wing a large drop of water fell on him. "What a curious thing!" he cried, "there is not a single cloud in the sky, the stars are quite clear and bright, and yet it is raining. The climate in the north of Europe is really dreadful. The Reed used to like the rain, but that was merely her selfishness."

Then another drop fell.

"What is the use of a statue if it cannot keep the rain off?" he said; "I must look for a good chimney-pot," and he determined to fly away.

But before he had opened his wings, a third drop fell, and he looked up, and saw—Ah! what did he see?

The eyes of the Happy Prince were filled with tears, and tears were running down his golden cheeks. His face was so beautiful in the moonlight that the little Swallow was filled with pity.

"Who are you?" he said.

"I am the Happy Prince."

"Why are you weeping then?" asked the Swallow; "you have quite drenched me."

"When I was alive and had a human heart," answered the statue, "I did not know what tears were, for I lived in the Palace of Sans Souci, where sorrow is not allowed to enter. In the daytime I played with my companions in the garden, and in the evening I led the dance in the Great Hall. Round the garden ran a very lofty wall, but I never cared to ask what lay beyond it, everything about me was so beautiful. My courtiers called me the Happy Prince, and happy indeed I was, if pleasure be happiness. So I lived, and so I died. And now that I am dead they have set me up here so high that I can see all the ugliness and all the misery of my city, and though my heart is made of lead yet I cannot choose but weep."

"What, is he not solid gold?" said the Swallow to himself. He was too polite to make any personal remarks out loud.

"Far away," continued the statue in a low musical voice, "far away in a little street there is a poor house. One of the windows is open, and through it I can see a woman seated at a table. Her face is thin and worn, and she has coarse red hands, all pricked by the needle, for she is a seamstress. She is embroidering pas- sion-flowers on a satin gown for the loveliest of the Queen's maids-of-honour to wear at the next Court-ball. In a bed in the corner of the room her little boy is lying ill. He has a fever, and is asking for oranges. His mother has nothing to give him but river water, so he is crying. Swallow, Swallow, little Swallow, will you not bring her the ruby out of my sword- hilt? My feet are fastened to this pedestal and I cannot move."

"I am waited for in Egypt," said the Swallow. "My friends are flying up and down the Nile, and talking to the large lotus- flowers. Soon they will be going to sleep in the tomb of the great King. The King is there himself in his painted coffin. He is wrapped in yellow linen, and embalmed with spices. Round his neck is a chain of pale green jade, and his hands are like withered leaves."

"Swallow, Swallow, little Swallow," said the Prince, "will you not stay with me for one night, and be my messenger? The boy is so thirsty, and the mother so sad."

"I don't think I like boys," answered the Swallow. "Last summer, when I was staying on the river, there were two rude boys, the miller's sons, who were always throwing stones at me. They never hit me, of course; we swallows fly far too well for that, and besides, I come of a family famous for its agility; but still, it was a mark of disrespect."

But the Happy Prince looked so sad that the little Swallow was sorry. "It is very cold here," he said; "but I will stay with you for one night, and be your messenger."

"Thank you, little Swallow," said the Prince.

So the Swallow picked out the great ruby from the Prince's sword, and flew away with it in his beak over the roofs of the town.

He passed by the cathedral tower, where the white marble angels were sculptured. He passed by the palace and heard the sound of dancing. A beautiful girl came out on the balcony with her lover. "How wonderful the stars are," he said to her, "and how wonderful is the power of love!" "I hope my dress will be ready in time for the State-ball," she answered; "I have ordered passion-flowers to be embroidered on it; but the seam-stresses are so lazy."

He passed over the river, and saw the lanterns hanging to the masts of the ships. He passed over the Ghetto, and saw the old Jews bargaining with each other, and weighing out money in copper scales. At last he came to the poor house and looked in. The boy was tossing feverishly on his bed, and the mother had fallen asleep, she was so tired. In he hopped, and laid the great ruby on the table beside the woman's thimble. Then he flew round the bed, fanning the boy's forehead with his wings. "How cool I feel," said the boy, "I must be getting better;" and he sank into a delicious slumber.

Then the Swallow flew back to the Happy Prince and told him what he had done. "It is curious," he remarked, "but I feel quite warm now, although it is so cold."

"That is because you have done a good action," said the

Prince. And the little Swallow began to think, and then he fell asleep. Thinking always made him sleepy.

When day broke he flew down to the river and had a bath. "What a remarkable phenomenon," said the Professor of Ornithology as he was passing over the bridge. "A swallow in winter!" And he wrote a long letter about it to the local newspaper. Everyone quoted it, it was full of so many words that they could not understand.

"To-night I go to Egypt," said the Swallow, and he was in high spirits at the prospect. He visited all the public monuments, and sat a long time on top of the church steeple. Wherever he went the Sparrows chirruped, and said to each other, "What a distinguished stranger!" so he enjoyed himself very much.

When the moon rose he flew back to the Happy Prince. "Have you any commissions for Egypt?" he cried. "I am just starting."

"Swallow, Swallow, little Swallow," said the Prince, "will you not stay with me one night longer?"

"I am waited for in Egypt," answered the Swallow. "To-morrow my friends will fly up to the Second Cataract. The river-horse crouches there among the bulrushes, and on a great granite throne sits the God Memnon. All night long he watches the stars, and when the morning star shines he utters one cry of joy, and then he is silent. At noon the yellow lions come down to the water's edge to drink. They have eyes like green beryls, and their roar is louder than the roar of the cataract."

"Swallow, Swallow, little Swallow," said the Prince, "far away across the city I see a young man in a garret. He is leaning over a desk covered with papers, and in a tumbler by his side there is a bunch of withered violets. His hair is brown and crisp, and his lips are red as a pomegranate, and he has large and dreamy eyes. He is trying to finish a play for the Director of the Theatre, but he is too cold to write any more. There is no fire in the grate, and hunger has made him faint."

"I will wait with you one night longer," said the Swallow, who really had a good heart. "Shall I take him another ruby?"

"Alas! I have no ruby now," said the Prince; "my eyes are all that I have left. They are made of rare sapphires, which were brought out of India a thousand years ago. Pluck out one of them and take it to him. He will sell it to the jeweller, and buy food and firewood, and finish his play."

"Dear Prince," said the Swallow, "I cannot do that;" and he began to weep.

"Swallow, Swallow, little Swallow," said the Prince, "do as I command you."

So the Swallow plucked out the Prince's eye, and flew away to the student's garret. It was easy enough to get in, as there was a hole in the roof. Through this he darted, and came into the room. The young man had his head buried in his hands, so he did not hear the flutter of the bird's wings, and when he looked up he found the beautiful sapphire lying on the withered violets.

"I am beginning to be appreciated," he cried; "this is from some great admirer. Now I can finish my play," and he looked quite happy.

The next day the Swallow flew down to the harbour. He sat on the mast of a large vessel and watched the sailors hauling big chests out of the hold with ropes. "Heave a-hoy!" they shouted as each chest came up. "I am going to Egypt!" cried the Swallow, but nobody minded, and when the moon rose he flew back to the Happy Prince.

"I am come to bid you good-bye," he cried.

"Swallow, Swallow, little Swallow," said the Prince, "will you not stay with me one night longer?"

"It is winter," answered the Swallow, "and the chill snow will soon be here. In Egypt the sun is warm on the green palm-trees, and the crocodiles lie in the mud and look lazily about them. My companions are building a nest in the Temple of Baalbec, and the pink and white doves are watching them, and cooing to each other. Dear Prince, I must leave you, but I will never forget you, and next spring I will bring you back two beautiful jewels in place of those you have given away. The ruby shall be redder than a red rose, and the sapphire shall be as blue as the great sea."

"In the square below," said the Happy Prince, "there stands a little match-girl. She has let her matches fall in the gutter, and they are all spoiled. Her father will beat her if she does not bring home some money, and she is crying. She has no shoes or stockings, and her little head is bare. Pluck out my other eye, and give it to her, and her father will not beat her."

"I will stay with you one night longer," said the Swallow, "but I cannot pluck out your eye. You would be quite blind then."

"Swallow, Swallow, little Swallow," said the Prince, "do as I command you."

So he plucked out the Prince's other eye, and darted down with it. He swooped past the match-girl, and slipped the jewel into the palm of her hand. "What a lovely bit of glass," cried the little girl; and she ran home, laughing.

Then the Swallow came back to the Prince. "You are blind now," he said, "so I will stay with you always."

"No, little Swallow," said the poor Prince, "you must go away to Egypt."

"I will stay with you always," said the Swallow, and he slept at the Prince's feet.

All the next day he sat on the Prince's shoulder, and told him stories of what he had seen in strange lands. He told him of the red ibises, who stand in long rows on the banks of the Nile, and catch gold fish in their beaks; of the Sphinx, who is as old as the world itself, and lives in the desert, and knows everything; of the merchants, who walk slowly by the side of their camels, and carry amber beads in their hands; of the King of the Mountains of the Moon, who is as black as ebony, and worships a large crystal; of the great green snake that sleeps in a palm-tree, and has twenty priests to feed it with honey-cakes; and of the pygmies who sail over a big lake on large flat leaves, and are always at war with the butterflies.

"Dear little Swallow," said the Prince, "you tell me of marvellous things, but more marvellous than anything is the suffering of men and of women. There is no Mystery so great as Misery. Fly over my city, little Swallow, and tell me what you see there."

So the Swallow flew over the great city, and saw the rich making merry in their beautiful houses, while the beggars were sitting at the gates. He flew into dark lanes, and saw the white faces of starving children looking out listlessly at the black streets. Under the archway of a bridge two little boys were lying in one another's arms to try to keep themselves warm. "How hungry we are!" they said. "You must not lie here," shouted the Watchman, and they wandered out into the rain.

Then he flew back and told the Prince what he had seen.

"I am covered with fine gold," said the Prince, "you must take it off, leaf by leaf, and give it to my poor; the living always think that gold can make them happy."

Leaf after leaf of the fine gold the Swallow picked off, till the Happy Prince looked quite dull and grey. Leaf after leaf of the fine gold he brought to the poor, and the children's faces grew rosier, and they laughed and played games in the street. "We have bread now!" they cried.

Then the snow came, and after the snow came the frost. The streets looked as if they were made of silver, they were so bright and glistening; long icicles like crystal daggers hung down from the eaves of the houses, everybody went about in furs, and the little boys wore scarlet caps and skated on the ice.

The poor little Swallow grew colder and colder, but he would not leave the Prince, he loved him too well. He picked up crumbs outside the baker's door when the baker was not looking, and tried to keep himself warm by flapping his wings.

But at last he knew that he was going to die. He had just strength to fly up to the Prince's shoulder once more. "Good-bye, dear Prince!" he murmured, "will you let me kiss your hand?"

"I am glad that you are going to Egypt at last, little Swallow," said the Prince, "you have stayed too long here; but you must kiss me on the lips, for I love you."

"It is not to Egypt that I am going," said the Swallow. "I am going to the House of Death. Death is the brother of Sleep, is he not?"

And he kissed the Happy Prince on the lips, and fell down dead at his feet.

At that moment a curious crack sounded inside the statue, as if something had broken. The fact is that the leaden heart had snapped right in two. It certainly was a dreadfully hard frost.

Early the next morning the Mayor was walking in the square below in company with the Town Councillors. As they passed the column he looked up at the statue: "Dear me! how shabby the Happy Prince looks!" he said.

"How shabby indeed!" cried the Town Councillors, who always agreed with the Mayor, and they went up to look at it.

"The ruby has fallen out of his sword, his eyes are gone, and he is golden no longer," said the Mayor; "in fact, he is little better than a beggar!"

"Little better than a beggar," said the Town Councillors.

"And here is actually a dead bird at his feet!" continued the Mayor. "We must really issue a proclamation that birds are not to be allowed to die here." And the Town Clerk made a note of the suggestion.

So they pulled down the statue of the Happy Prince. "As he is no longer beautiful he is no longer useful," said the Art Professor at the University.

Then they melted the statue in a furnace, and the Mayor held a meeting of the Corporation to decide what was to be done with the metal. "We must have another statue, of course," he said, "and it shall be a statue of myself."

"Of myself," said each of the Town Councillors, and they quarrelled. When I last heard of them they were quarrelling still.

"What a strange thing," said the overseer of the workmen at the foundry. "This broken lead heart will not melt in the furnace. We must throw it away." So they threw it on a dust heap where the dead Swallow was also lying.

"Bring me the two most precious things in the city," said God to one of His Angels; and the Angel brought Him the leaden heart and the dead bird.

"You have rightly chosen," said God, "for in my garden of Paradise this little bird shall sing for evermore, and in my city of gold the Happy Prince shall praise me."

LOBO

by Ernest Thompson Seton

chosen by

Joan Phipson

I STARTED to read the stories of Ernest Thompson Seton when I was seven. For three years I snatched feverishly at every one of his books that came my way. I have read them spasmodically ever since. And, going through them again for this collection, I find I read them now at the advanced age of sixty with as much pleasure as when I first began. My critical faculty tells me now —what it was not able to then—that they are perhaps somewhat over-written, that in places they tend to become sentimental. But it tells me, also, that Ernest Thompson Seton must have been one of the first people to write seriously of animals *as animals*. These animals are not sub-people; they do not talk, or have human thoughts. This is mainly due to his own discernment (he confesses in one of his introductions that when he began he used the "archaic" method of animal conversation) and partly due to the stories being basically true. I find his constant theme of the preservation of wild animals and natural things very appropriate to our time and, for those who love animals, com-pulsive reading. I had many favourite stories to choose from, and ended with *Lobo*. It was written in 1894 for *Scribner's Magazine* and was his first story in what he regarded as the new "scientific" method. It seems to me a well-rounded and succinct animal biography. In real life most wild animals come to violent ends, and Lobo was no exception. Ernest Thompson Seton was Canadian, born of English parents, and lived from 1860 to 1946. He was a naturalist and an artist as well as a writer.

JOAN PHIPSON

I

CURRUMPAW is a vast cattle range in northern New Mexico. It is a land of rich pastures and teeming flocks and herds, a land of rolling mesas and precious running waters that at length unite in the Currumpaw River, from which the whole region is named. And the king whose despotic power was felt over its entire extent was an old grey wolf.

Old Lobo, or the king, as the Mexicans called him, was the gigantic leader of a remarkable pack of grey wolves, that had ravaged the Currumpaw Valley for a number of years. All the shepherds and ranchmen knew him well, and, wherever he appeared with his trusty band, terror reigned supreme among the cattle, and wrath and despair among their owners. Old Lobo was a giant among wolves, and was cunning and strong in proportion to his size. His voice at night was well-known and easily distinguished from that of any of his fellows. An ordinary wolf might howl half the night about the herdsman's bivouac without attracting more than a passing notice, but when the deep roar of the old king came booming down the cañon, the watcher bestirred himself and prepared to learn in the morning that fresh and serious inroads had been made among the herds.

Old Lobo's band was but a small one. This I never quite understood, for usually, when a wolf rises to the position and power that he had, he attracts a numerous following. It may be that he had as many as he desired, or perhaps his ferocious temper prevented the increase of his pack. Certain is it that Lobo had only five followers during the latter part of his reign. Each of these, however, was a wolf of renown, most of them were above the ordinary size, one in particular, the second in command, was a veritable giant, but even he was far below the leader in size and prowess. Several of the band, besides the two leaders were especially noted. One of those was a beautiful white wolf, that the Mexicans called Blanca; this was supposed

163

to be a female, possibly Lobo's mate. Another was a yellow wolf of remarkable swiftness, which, according to current stories had, on several occasions, captured an antelope for the pack.

It will be seen, then, that these wolves were thoroughly well-known to the cowboys and shepherds. They were frequently seen and oftener heard, and their lives were intimately associated with those of the cattlemen, who would so gladly have destroyed them. There was not a stockman on the Currumpaw who would not readily have given the value of many steers for the scalp of any one of Lobo's band, but they seemed to possess charmed lives, and defied all manner of devices to kill them. They scorned all hunters, derided all poisons, and continued, for at least five years, to exact their tribute from the Currumpaw ranchers to the extent, many said, of a cow each day. According to this estimate, therefore, the band had killed more than two thousand of the finest stock, for, as was only too well known, they selected the best in every instance.

The old idea that a wolf was constantly in a starving state, and therefore ready to eat anything, was as far as possible from the truth in this case, for these freebooters were always sleek and well-conditioned, and were in fact most fastidious about what they ate. Any animal that had died from natural causes, or that was diseased or tainted, they would not touch, and they even rejected anything that had been killed by the stockmen. Their choice and daily food was the tenderer part of a freshly killed yearling heifer. An old bull or cow they disdained, and though they occasionally took a young calf or colt, it was quite clear that veal or horseflesh was not their favourite diet. It was also known that they were not fond of mutton, although they often amused themselves by killing sheep. One night in November, 1893, Blanca and the yellow wolf killed two hundred and fifty sheep, apparently for the fun of it, and did not eat an ounce of their flesh.

These are examples of many stories which I might repeat, to show the ravages of this destructive band. Many new devices for their extinction were tried each year, but still they lived and throve in spite of all the efforts of their foes. A great price was set on Lobo's head, and in consequence poison in a score of subtle forms was put out for him, but he never failed to detect and avoid it. One thing only he feared—that was firearms, and knowing full well that all men in this region carried them, he was never known to attack or face a human being. Indeed, the set policy of his band was to take refuge in flight whenever, in the daytime, a man was descried, no matter at what distance. Lobo's habit of permitting the pack to eat only that which they themselves had killed, was in numerous cases their salvation, and the keenness of his scent to detect the taint of human hands or the poison itself, completed their immunity.

On one occasion, one of the cowboys heard the too familiar rallying-cry of Old Lobo, and stealthily approaching, he found the Currumpaw pack in a hollow, where they had "rounded up" a small herd of cattle. Lobo sat apart on a knoll, while Blanca, with the rest, was endeavouring to "cut out" a young cow, which they had selected; but the cattle were standing in a compact mass with their heads outward, and presented to the foe a line of horns, unbroken save when some cow, frightened by a fresh onset of the wolves, tried to retreat into the middle of the herd. It was only by taking advantage of these breaks that the wolves had succeeded at all in wounding the selected cow, but she was far from being disabled, and it seemed that Lobo at length lost patience with his followers, for he left his position on the hill, and, uttering a deep roar, dashed toward the herd. The terrified rank broke at his charge, and he sprang in among them. Then the cattle scattered like the pieces of a bursting bomb. Away went the chosen victim, but ere she had gone twenty-five yards Lobo was upon her. Seizing her by the neck he suddenly held back with all his force and so threw her heavily to the ground. The shock must have been tremendous, for the heifer was thrown heels over head. Lobo also turned a somersault, but immediately recovered himself, and his followers falling on the poor cow, killed her in a few seconds. Lobo took no part in the killing—after having thrown the victim, he seemed to say, "Now, why could not some of you have done that at once without wasting so much time?"

The man now rode up shouting, the wolves as usual retired,

and he, having a bottle of strychnine, quickly poisoned the carcass in three places, then went away, knowing they would return to feed, as they had killed the animal themselves. But next morning, on going to look for his expected victims, he found that, although the wolves had eaten the heifer, they had carefully cut out and thrown aside all those parts that had been poisoned.

The dread of this great wolf spread yearly among the ranchmen, and each year a larger price was set on his head, until at last it reached $1,000, an unparalleled wolf-bounty, surely; many a good man has been hunted down for less. Tempted by the promised reward, a Texan ranger named Tannerey came one day galloping up the cañon of the Currumpaw. He had a superb outfit for wolf-hunting—the best of guns and horses, and a pack of enormous wolf-hounds. Far out on the plains of the Pan-handle, he and his dogs had killed many a wolf, and now he never doubted that, within a few days, old Lobo's scalp would dangle at his saddle-bow.

Away they went bravely on their hunt in the grey dawn of a summer morning, and soon the great dogs gave joyous tongue to say that they were already on the track of their quarry. Within two miles, the grizzly band of Currumpaw leaped into view, and the chase grew fast and furious. The part of the wolf-hounds was merely to hold the wolves at bay till the hunter could ride up and shoot them, and this usually was easy on the open plains of Texas; but here a new feature of the country came into play, and showed how well Lobo had chosen his range; for the rocky cañons of the Currumpaw and its tributaries intersect the prairies in every direction. The old wolf at once made for the nearest of these and by crossing it got rid of the horsemen. His band then scattered and thereby scattered the dogs, and when they reunited at a distant point of course all of the dogs did not turn up, and the wolves no longer outnumbered, turned on their pursuers and killed or desperately wounded them all. That night when Tannerey mustered his dogs, only six of them returned, and of these, two were terribly lacerated. This hunter made two other attempts to capture the royal scalp, but neither of them was more successful than the first, and on the last occasion his best horse met its death by a fall; so he gave up the chase in disgust and went back to Texas, leaving Lobo more than ever the despot of the region.

Next year, two other hunters appeared, determined to win the promised bounty. Each believed he could destroy this noted wolf, the first by means of a newly devised poison, which was to be laid out in an entirely new manner; the other, a French Canadian, by poison assisted with certain spells and charms, for he firmly believed that Lobo was a veritable "loup-garou", and could not be killed by ordinary means. But cunningly compounded poisons, charms, and incantations were all of no avail against this grizzly devastator. He made his weekly rounds and daily banquets as aforetime, and before many weeks had passed, Calone and Laloche gave up in despair and went elsewhere to hunt.

In the spring of 1893, after his unsuccessful attempt to capture Lobo, Joe Calone had a humiliating experience, which seems to show that the big wolf simply scorned his enemies, and had absolute confidence in himself. Calone's farm was on a small tributary of the Currumpaw, in a picturesque cañon, and among the rocks of this very cañon, within a thousand yards of the house, old Lobo and his mate selected their den and raised their family that season. There they lived all summer, and killed Joe's cattle, sheep, and dogs, but laughed at all his poisons and traps, and rested securely among the recesses of the cavernous cliffs, while Joe vainly racked his brain for some method of smoking them out, or of reaching them with dynamite. But they escaped entirely unscathed, and continued their ravages as before. "There's where he lived all last summer," said Joe, pointing to the face of the cliff, "and I couldn't do a thing with him. I was like a fool to him."

II

This history, gathered so far from the cowboys, I found hard to believe until in the fall of 1893, I made the acquaintance of the wily marauder, and at length came to know him more thoroughly than anyone else. Some years before, in the Bingo days, I had been a wolf-hunter, but my occupations since then had been of another sort, chaining me to stool and desk. I was much in need of a change, and when a friend, who was also a ranch-owner on the Currumpaw, asked me to come to New Mexico and try if I could do anything with this predatory pack, I accepted the invitation and, eager to make the acquaintance of its king, was as soon as possible among the mesas of that region. I spent some time riding about to learn the country, and at intervals, my guide would point to the skeleton of a cow to which the hide still adhered, and remark, "That's some of his work."

It became quite clear to me that, in this rough country, it was useless to think of pursuing Lobo with hounds and horses, so that poison or traps were the only available expedients. At present we had no traps large enough, so I set to work with poison.

I need not enter into the details of a hundred devices that I employed to circumvent this "loup-garou"; there was no combination of strychnine, arsenic, cyanide, or prussic acid, that I did not essay; there was no manner of flesh that I did not try as bait; but morning after morning, as I rode forth to learn the result, I found that all my efforts had been useless. The old king was too cunning for me. A single instance will show his wonderful sagacity. Acting on the hint of an old trapper, I melted some cheese together with the kidney fat of a freshly killed heifer, stewing it in a china dish, and cutting it with a bone knife to avoid the taint of metal. When the mixture was cool, I cut it into lumps, and making a hole in one side of each lump, I inserted a large dose of strychnine and cyanide, contained in a capsule that was impermeable by any odour; finally I sealed the holes up with pieces of the cheese itself. During the whole process, I wore a pair of gloves steeped in the hot blood of the heifer, and even avoided breathing on the baits. When all was ready, I put them in a raw-hide bag rubbed all over with blood, and rode forth dragging the liver and kidneys of the beef at the end of a rope. With this I made a ten-mile circuit, dropping a bait at each quarter of a mile, and taking the utmost care, always, not to touch any with my hands.

Lobo, generally, came into this part of the range in the early part of each week, and passed the latter part, it was supposed, around the base of Sierra Grande. This was Monday, and that same evening, as we were about to retire, I heard the deep bass howl of his majesty. On hearing it one of the boys briefly remarked, "There he is, we'll see."

The next morning I went forth, eager to know the result. I soon came on the fresh trail of the robbers, with Lobo in the lead—his track was always easily distinguished. An ordinary wolf's forefoot is $4\frac{1}{2}$ inches long, that of a large wolf $4\frac{3}{4}$ inches, but Lobo's, as measured a number of times, was $5\frac{1}{2}$ inches from claw to heel; I afterward found that his other proportions were commensurate, for he stood three feet high at the shoulder, and weighed 150 pounds. His trail, therefore, though obscured by those of his followers, was never difficult to trace. The pack had soon found the track of my drag, and as usual followed it. I could see that Lobo had come to the first bait, sniffed about it, and finally had picked it up.

Then I could not conceal my delight. "I've got him at last," I exclaimed; "I shall find him stark within a mile," and I galloped on with eager eyes fixed on the great broad track in the dust. It led me to the second bait and that also was gone. How I exulted—I surely have him now and perhaps several of his band. But there was the broad paw-mark still on the drag; and though I stood in the stirrup and scanned the plain I saw nothing that looked like a dead wolf. Again I followed—to find now that the third bait was gone—and the king-wolf's track led on to the fourth, there to learn that he had not really taken a bait at all, but had merely carried them in his mouth. Then having piled the three on the fourth, he scattered filth over them to express his utter contempt for my devices. After this he left my drag and went about his business with the pack he guarded so effectively.

This is only one of many similar experiences which convinced me that poison would never avail to destroy this robber, and though I continued to use it while awaiting the arrival of the traps, it was only because it was meanwhile a sure means of killing many prairie wolves and other destructive vermin.

About this time there came under my observation an incident that will illustrate Lobo's diabolic cunning. These wolves had at least one pursuit which was merely an amusement, it was stampeding and killing sheep, though they rarely ate them. The sheep are usually kept in flocks of from one thousand to three thousand under one or more shepherds. At night they are gathered in the most sheltered place available, and a herdsman sleeps on each side of the flock to give additional protection. Sheep are such senseless creatures that they are liable to be stampeded by the veriest trifle, but they have deeply ingrained in their nature one, perhaps only one, strong weakness, namely, to follow their leader. And this the shepherds turn to good account by putting half a dozen goats in the flock of sheep. The latter recognize the superior intelligence of their bearded cousins, and when a night alarm occurs they crowd around them, and usually are thus saved from a stampede and are easily protected. But it was not always so. One night late in last November, two Perico shepherds were aroused by an onset of wolves. Their flocks huddled around the goats, which being neither fools nor cowards, stood their ground and were bravely defiant; but alas for them, no common wolf was heading this attack. Old Lobo, the were-wolf, knew as well as the shepherds that the goats were the moral force of the flock, so hastily running over the backs of the densely packed sheep, he fell on these leaders, slew them all in a few minutes, and soon had the luckless sheep stampeding in a thousand different directions. For weeks afterward I was almost daily accosted by some anxious shepherd, who asked, "Have you seen any stray OTO sheep lately?" and usually I was obliged to say I had; one day it was, "Yes, I came on some five or six carcasses by Diamond Springs;" or another, it was to the effect that I had seen a small "bunch" running on the Malpai Mesa; or again, "No, but Juan Meira saw about twenty, freshly killed, on the Cedra Monte two days ago."

At length the wolf traps arrived, and with two men I worked a whole week to get them properly set out. We spared no labour or pains, I adopted every device I could think of that might help to ensure success. The second day after the traps arrived, I rode around to inspect, and soon came upon Lobo's trail running from trap to trap. In the dust I could read the whole story of his doings that night. He had trotted along in the darkness, and although the traps were so carefully concealed, he had instantly detected the first one. Stopping the onward march of the pack, he had cautiously scratched around it until he had disclosed the trap, the chain, and the log, then left them wholly exposed to view with the trap still unsprung, and passing on he treated over a dozen traps in the same fashion. Very soon I noticed that he stopped and turned aside as soon as he detected suspicious signs on the trail and a new plan to outwit him at once suggested itself. I set the traps in the form of an H; that is, with a row of traps on each side of the trail, and one on the trail for the cross-bar of the H. Before long, I had an opportunity to count another failure. Lobo came trotting along the trail, and was fairly between the parallel lines before he detected the single trap in the trail, but he stopped in time, and why or how he knew enough I cannot tell, but the Angel of the wild things must have been with him, but without turning an inch to the right or left, he slowly and cautiously backed on his own tracks, putting each paw exactly in its old track until he was off the dangerous ground. Then returning at one side he scratched clods and stones with his hind feet till he had sprung every trap. This he did on many other occasions, and although I varied my methods and redoubled my precautions, he was never deceived, his sagacity seemed never at fault, and he might have been pursuing his career of rapine to-day, but for an unfortunate alliance that proved his ruin and added his name to the long list of heroes who, unassailable when alone, have fallen through the in-discretion of a trusted ally.

III

Once or twice, I had found indications that everything was not quite right in the Currumpaw pack. There were signs of irregularity, I thought; for instance there was clearly the trail of a smaller wolf running ahead of the leader, at times, and this I could not understand until a cowboy made a remark which explained the matter.

"I saw them today," he said, "and the wild one that breaks away is Blanca." Then the truth dawned upon me, and I added, "Now, I know that Blanca is a she-wolf, because were a he-wolf to act thus, Lobo would kill him at once."

This suggested a new plan. I killed a heifer, and set one or two rather obvious traps about the carcass. Then cutting off the head, which is considered useless offal, and quite beneath the notice of a wolf, I set it a little apart and around it placed six powerful steel traps properly deodorized and concealed with the utmost care. During my operations I kept my hands, boots, and implements smeared with fresh blood, and afterwards sprinkled the ground with the same, as though it had flowed from the head; and when the traps were buried in the dust I brushed the place over with the skin of a coyote, and with a foot of the same animal made a number of tracks over the traps. The head was so placed that there was a narrow passage between it and some tussocks, and in this passage I buried two of my best traps, fastening them to the head itself.

Wolves have a habit of approaching every carcass they get wind of, in order to examine it, even when they have no intention of eating of it, and I hoped that this habit would bring the Currumpaw pack within reach of my latest stratagem. I did not doubt that Lobo would detect my handiwork about the meat, and prevent the pack approaching it, but I did build some hopes on the head, for it looked as though it had been thrown aside as useless.

Next morning, I sallied forth to inspect the traps, and there, oh, joy! were the tracks of the pack, and the place where the beef-head and its traps had been was empty. A hasty study of the trail showed that Lobo had kept the pack from approaching the meat, but one, a small wolf, had evidently gone on to examine the head as it lay apart and had walked right into one of the traps.

We set out on the trail, and within a mile discovered that the hapless wolf was Blanca. Away she went, however at a gallop and although encumbered by the beef-head, which weighed over fifty pounds, she speedily distanced my companion who was on foot. But we overtook her when she reached the rocks, for the horns of the cow's head became caught and held her fast. She was the handsomest wolf I had ever seen. Her coat was in perfect condition and nearly white.

She turned to fight, and raising her voice in the rallying cry of her race, sent a long howl rolling over the cañon. From far away upon the mesa came a deep response, the cry of Old Lobo. That was her last call, for now we had closed in on her, and all her energy and breath were devoted to combat.

Then followed the inevitable tragedy, the idea of which I shrank from afterward more than at the time. We each threw a lasso over the neck of the doomed wolf, and strained our horses in opposite directions until the blood burst from her mouth, her eyes glazed, her limbs stiffened and then fell limp. Homeward then we rode, carrying the dead wolf, and exulting over this, the first death-blow we had been able to inflict on the Currumpaw pack.

At intervals during the tragedy, and afterward as we rode homeward, we heard the roar of Lobo as he wandered about on the distant mesas, where he seemed to be searching for Blanca. He had never really deserted her, but knowing that he could not save her, his deep-rooted dread of firearms had been too much for him when he saw us approaching. All that day we heard him wailing as he roamed in his quest, and I remarked at length to one of the boys, "Now, indeed, I truly know that Blanca was his mate."

As evening fell he seemed to be coming toward the home cañon, for his voice sounded continually nearer. There was an unmistakable note of sorrow in it now. It was no longer the loud, defiant howl, but a long, plaintive wail; "Blanca! Blanca!" he seemed to call. And as night came down, I noticed that he was not far from the place where we had overtaken her. At length he seemed to find the trail, and when he came to the spot where we had killed her, his heart-broken wailing was piteous to hear. It was sadder than I could possibly have believed. Even the stolid cowboys noticed it, and said they had "never heard a wolf carry on like that before". He seemed to know exactly what had taken place, for her blood had stained the place of her death.

Then he took up the trail of the horses and followed it to the ranch-house. Whether in hopes of finding her there, or in quest of revenge, I know not, but the latter was what he found, for he surprised our unfortunate watchdog outside and tore him to little bits within fifty yards of the door. He evidently came alone this time, for I found one trail next morning, and he had galloped about in a reckless manner that was very unusual with him. I had half expected this, and had set a number of additional traps about the pasture. Afterwards I found that he had indeed fallen into one of these, but such was his strength, he had torn himself loose and cast it aside.

I believed that he would continue in the neighbourhood until he found her body at least, so I concentrated all my energies on this one enterprise of catching him before he left the region, and while yet in this reckless mood. Then I realized what a mistake I had made in killing Blanca, for by using her as a decoy I might have secured him the next night.

I gathered in all the traps I could command, one hundred and thirty strong steel wolf-traps, and set them in fours in every trail that led into the cañon; each trap was separately fastened to a log, and each log was separately buried. In burying them, I carefully removed the sod and every particle of earth that was lifted we put in blankets, so that after the sod was replaced and all was finished the eye could detect no trace of human handi-work. When the traps were concealed I trailed the body of poor Blanca over each place, and made of it a drag that circled all about the ranch, and finally I took off one of her paws and made with it a line of tracks over each trap. Every precaution and device known to me I used, and retired at a late hour to await the result.

Once during the night I thought I heard Old Lobo, but was not sure of it. Next day I rode around, but darkness came on before I completed the circuit of the north cañon, and I had nothing to report. At supper one of the cowboys said, "There was a great row among the cattle in the north cañon this morning, maybe there is something in the traps there." It was afternoon of the next day before I got to the place referred to, and as I drew near a great grizzly form arose from the ground, vainly endeavouring to escape, and there revealed before me stood Lobo, King of the Currumpaw, firmly held in the traps. Poor old hero, he had never ceased to search for his darling, and when he found the trail her body had made he followed it recklessly, and so fell into the snare prepared for him. There he lay in the iron grasp of all four traps, perfectly helpless, and all around him were numerous tracks showing how the cattle had gathered about him to insult the fallen despot, without daring to approach within his reach. For two days and two nights he had lain there, and now was worn out with struggling. Yet, when I went near him, he rose up with bristling mane and raised his voice, and for the last time made the cañon reverberate with his deep bass roar, a call for help, the muster call of his band. But there was none to answer him, and, left alone in his extremity, he whirled about with all his strength and made a desperate effort to get at me. All in vain, each trap was a dead drag of over three hundred pounds, and in their relentless fourfold grasp, with great steel jaws on every foot, and the heavy logs and chains all entangled together, he was absolutely powerless. How his huge ivory tusks did grind on those cruel chains, and when I ventured to touch him with my rifle-barrel he left grooves on it which are there to this day. His eyes glared green with hate and fury, and his jaws snapped with a hollow "chop", as he vainly endeavoured to reach me and my trembling horse. But he was worn out with hunger and struggling and loss of blood, and he soon sank exhausted to the ground.

Something like compunction came over me, as I prepared to deal out to him that which so many had suffered at his hands.

"Grand old outlaw, hero of a thousand lawless raids, in a few minutes you will be but a great load of carrion. It cannot be otherwise." Then I swung my lasso and sent it whistling over his head. But not so fast; he was yet far from being subdued, and, before the supple coils had fallen on his neck he seized the noose and, with one fierce chop, cut through its hard thick strands, and dropped it in two pieces at his feet.

Of course I had my rifle as a last resource, but I did not wish to spoil his royal hide, so I galloped back to the camp and returned with a cowboy and a fresh lasso. We threw to our victim a stick of wood which he seized in his teeth, and before he could relinquish it our lassoes whistled through the air and tightened on his neck.

Yet before the light had died from his fierce eyes, I cried, "Stay, we will not kill him; let us take him alive to the camp." He was so completely powerless now that it was easy to put a stout stick through his mouth, behind his tusks, and then lash his jaws with a heavy cord which was also fastened to the stick. The stick kept the cord in, and the cord kept the stick in so he was harmless. As soon as he felt his jaws were tied he made no further resistance, and uttered no sound, but looked calmly at us and seemed to say, "Well, you have got me at last, do as you please with me." And from that time he took no more notice of us.

We tied his feet securely, but he never groaned, nor growled, nor turned his head. Then with our united strength we were just able to put him on my horse. His breath came evenly as though sleeping, and his eyes were bright and clear again, but did not rest on us. Afar on the great rolling mesas they were fixed, his passing kingdom, where his famous band was now scattered. And he gazed till the pony descended the pathway into the cañon, and the rocks cut off the view.

By travelling slowly we reached the ranch in safety, and after securing him with a collar and a strong chain, we staked him out in the pasture and removed the cords. Then for the first time I could examine him closely, and proved how unreliable is vulgar report when a living hero or tyrant is concerned. He had *not* a collar of gold about his neck, nor was there on his shoulders an inverted cross to denote that he had leagued himself with Satan. But I did find on one haunch a great broad scar, that tradition says was the fang-mark of Juno, the leader of Tannerey's wolf-hounds—a mark which she gave him the moment before he stretched her lifeless on the sand of the cañon.

I set meat and water beside him, but he paid no heed. He lay calmly on his breast, and gazed with those steadfast yellow eyes away past me down through the gateway on the cañon, over the open plains—his plains—nor moved a muscle when I touched him. When the sun went down he was still gazing fixedly across the prairie. I expected he would call up his band when night came, and prepared for them, but he had called once in his extremity, and none had come; he would never call again.

A lion shorn of his strength, an eagle robbed of his freedom, or a dove bereft of his mate, all die, it is said, of a broken heart; and who will aver that this grim bandit could bear the three-fold brunt, heart-whole? This only I know, that when the morning dawned, he was lying there still in his position of calm repose, his body unwounded, but his spirit was gone—the old King-wolf was dead.

I took the chain from his neck, a cowboy helped me to carry him to the shed where lay the remains of Blanca, and as we laid him beside her, the cattle-man exclaimed; "There, you *would* come to her, now you are together again."

The Water Woman and Her Lover
by Ralph Prince
chosen by Andrew Salkey

I SUPPOSE the best reason I'm able to give for having chosen *The Water Woman and Her Lover* is that I've always liked the kind of story it is: a nice, exciting, strange, sort of believable *legend*. And it's the legend part of it that grabs me every time. In fact, *everybody's* legends, myths, folk tales and stories of similar appeal mean a great deal to me. Guyana is particularly rich in legends. Perhaps it is the best endowed in that way of all the countries in the English-speaking Caribbean. Guyana draws on many different national and racial sources for its distinctive Guyanese folk literature: Carib, Arawak, African, Indian, Chinese, Portuguese, Dutch and British. *The Water Woman and Her Lover* is a beautiful, haunting legend often told by the people of Essequibo, out of the store of their oral tradition, and here re-told in writing by Ralph Prince, the Antiguan short story writer.

ANDREW SALKEY

IT'S an old Essequibo tale they used to tell in whispers. But even as they whispered the tale they were afraid the wind might blow their whisperings into the river where the water woman lived. They were afraid the water woman might hear their whisperings and return to haunt them as she had haunted her lover.

It's a strange story. Here it is from the beginning:

There was an old koker near Parika, through which water passed to and from the Essequibo river, for drainage of the lands in the area. On moonlight nights a naked woman was often seen sitting near the koker, with her back to the road and her face to the river.

She was a fair-skinned woman, and she had long, black, shiny hair rolling over her shoulders and down her back. Below her waist she was like a fish. When the moon was bright, especially at full-moon time, you could see her sitting on the koker, combing her long, black, shiny hair. You could see very dimly just a part of her face—a side view. But if you stepped nearer to get a closer look she would disappear. Without even turning her head to see who was coming, she would plunge into the river with a splash and vanish. They called her Water Mama.

People used to come from Salem, Tuschen, Naamryck and other parts of the east bank of the Essequibo river to see this mysterious creature. They would wait in the bush near the koker from early morning, and watch to see her rise from the river. But no matter how closely they watched, they would never see her when she came from the water. For a long time they would wait, and watch the koker bathed in moonlight. Then suddenly, as if she had sprung from nowhere, the water woman would appear sitting near the koker, completely naked, facing the river, and combing her long, black hair.

There was a strong belief among the villagers in the area that riches would come to anyone who found Water Mama's comb, or a lock of her hair. So they used to stay awake all night at the koker, and then early in the morning, even before the sun rose, they would search around where she had sat combing her hair. But they never found anything. Only the water that had drained off her body remained behind—and also a strong fishy smell.

The old people said that after looking at Water Mama or searching near the koker for her hair and her comb, you were always left feeling haunted and afraid. They told stories of people found sleeping, as if in a trance, while walking away from the koker. They warned that if a man watched her too long, and searched for her hair and her comb too often, he would dream about her. And if the man loved her and she loved him, she would haunt him in his dreams. And that would be the end of him, they said, because she was a creature of the devil. These warnings did not frighten the younger and more adventurous men from the villages around. They kept coming from near and far to gaze at Water Mama. After watching her and searching for her hair and her comb, they always had that haunted, fearful feeling. And many mornings, even as they walked away from the koker, they slept, as in a trance. But still they returned night after night to stare in wonder at that strange, mysterious woman.

At last something happened—something the old people had always said would happen—a man fell in love with the water woman. Some say he was from Salem. Some say he came from Naamryck. Others say he hailed from Parika, not far from the koker. Where he came from is not definitely known; but it is certain that he was a young man, tall and dark and big, with broad shoulders. His name was John, and they called him Big John because of his size.

When Big John had first heard of Water Mama he laughed and said she was a jumbie. But as time went by he heard so many strange things about her that he became curious. And so one moonlight night he went to the koker to look at the water woman.

He had waited for nearly an hour, and watched the moonlight shining on the koker and the river. His old doubts had returned and he was about to leave when he saw something strange, something that "mek he head rise", as the old folks say when telling the story. He saw a naked woman, sitting near the koker. A moment before, he had seen no one there. Then suddenly he saw this strange woman sitting in the moonlight and combing her long, black hair. It shone brightly in the moonlight.

Big John made a few steps towards her to see her more clearly. Then suddenly she was gone. Without even turning her head around to look at him, she plunged into the river with a big splash and vanished. Where he had seen her sitting, there was a pool of water. And then arose a strong, fishy smell. A feeling of dread overcame him.

He then set out to get away from there. He tried to run but could only walk. And even as he began walking, his steps were slow and his eyes were heavy with sleep. And that is the way he went home, walking and staggering, barely able to open his eyes now and then to see where he was going, walking and sleeping, as in a trance.

The next morning when Big John awoke and remembered what he had seen and experienced the night before, he became afraid. He vowed never to go back to the koker to look at the water woman. But that night the moon rose, flooding the land in silver, glistening in the trees, sparkling on the river. He became enchanted. His thoughts turned to the riverside and the strange woman combing her long, black hair.

And so later that night he stood near the koker waiting and watching for the strange woman to appear. Just like the night before, she appeared suddenly near the koker, combing her hair in the moonlight. Big John stepped towards her but she plunged into the river and disappeared. And once again he had that feeling of dread, followed by drowsiness as he walked home.

This went on for several nights, with Big John becoming more and more fascinated as he watched the water woman combing her hair in the moonlight. After the third night he no longer felt afraid, and he walked in the pool of water she left behind. Sometimes he waited until morning and searched around for locks of her hair and her comb, but he never found them.

After a few months of this waiting and watching, Big John felt sad and lost. He had fallen in love with the strange woman.

183

But he could not get near to her. And so he stopped going to the riverside to watch her.

When the moon had gone and the dark nights came back he began to drop her from his mind. But in another month the moon returned, flooding the land in silver, gleaming in the trees, sparkling on the river, and he remembered the water woman, and he longed to see her combing her hair again.

And on that very night the moon returned, he had a strange dream. He saw the water woman sitting near the koker, combing her long, black hair shining in the moonlight. She sat with her back to the river and her face full towards him. As she combed her hair she smiled with him, enchanting him with her beauty. He stepped forward to get a closer look, but she did not move. And so at last he saw her clearly, her bright eyes, her lovely face, her teeth sparkling as she smiled, and her body below her waist tapered off like a fish. She was the most beautiful creature he had ever seen.

He stretched out his hands to touch her, and she gave him her comb and said, "Take this to remember me by."

Then she jumped into the river and disappeared.

When he awoke the next morning he remembered the dream. He felt happy as he told his friends what he had seen in the dream. But they were afraid for him, and they warned him:

"Is haunt she hauntin' you."

"She goin' mek you dream an' dream till you don' know wha' to do wid youself."

"When she ready she goin' do wha' she like wid you."

"Big John you better watch youself wid de water woman."

"De water woman goin' haunt you to de en'."

These warnings made Big John laugh, and he told them:

"She can' do me anyt'ing in a dream."

But they warned him again:

"You forget 'bout de water woman, but she don' forget 'bout you."

"Is you start it when you watch she so much at de koker."

"Now you 'rouse she an' she want you. Da is de story now, she want you."

Big John laughed off these warnings and told them that noth-

THE WATER WOMAN AND HER LOVER

ing was going to happen to him as nothing could come from a dream.

But later that day he saw something strange. It made him shiver with dread. On the floor near his bed was a comb. He could not believe his eyes. It looked very much like the comb the water woman had given to him in the dream. He wondered how a comb he had seen in a dream could get into his room.

When he told his friends about finding the comb they said: "Is bes' for you to go 'way from here."

"Is you start it when you watch she so much at de koker."

That night he had another dream. In this dream he saw the water woman sitting in the moonlight. He stepped even closer to her than before, and she smiled with him.

For the first time since he had seen her, she was not combing her hair, and she had no comb in her hand. She pulled out a few strands of her hair and gave them to him and said, "Keep these to remember me by." And he took them in his hands and smiled with her. In another instant she was gone with a splash into the river.

The next morning Big John awoke with a smile as he remembered the dream. But as he sat up in the bed he found himself with a few strands of hair in his hands. His eyes opened wide in surprise. It was only then that he realized that he was getting caught in something strange.

And so the dreams went on, night after night. They became like magnets drawing Big John to bed early every night, and holding him fast in sleep till morning. They no longer made him feel afraid on awakening.

In one dream the water woman gave him a conch shell. On awakening the next morning he found sand on his bed and grains of sand in both hands. One night he dreamt that he and the water woman played along the river bank, splashing each other with water. The next morning he found his bed wet, and water splashed all over the room.

Big John told his friends about these dreams, and they warned him that the water woman had him under a spell. They were right, he kept on dreaming about her night after night.

Then came his last dream. The water woman stood by the

riverside holding a large bundle to her bosom. She smiled and said: "You have my comb and strands of my hair. I have given you other little gifts to remember me by. Tonight I shall give you money to make you rich. If you keep it a secret you will stay on earth and enjoy it. If you do not keep it a secret, you must come with me and be my lover for ever."

She hurled the bundle to him, and then jumped into the river and was gone.

When Big John awoke the next morning he found the floor of the room covered with tens of thousands of five-dollar bills, piled up high in heaps. It took him a long time to gather them and count them. It was a vast fortune.

Big John was too excited to keep the news about the dream and the fortune it had brought all to himself. He went around the village and told some of his closest friends about it. When they went with him to his house and saw those great piles of money, their eyes bulged and their mouths opened wide in amazement.

Then they made a wild scramble for it. They fought among themselves all that afternoon for the money. Some of them got away with little fortunes. Some ran away with their pockets bulging with notes. Others were left with notes that got torn up in the scrambling and fighting. Big John himself was beaten by the others and got nothing. They ran away and left him.

What happened to Big John after that no one knows. Some say he dreamt again of the water woman that night and she took him away in the dream. Some say he went to the koker several nights to look for her but never found her, and so he drowned himself in the river. Others say that the water woman sent her water people for him, and that they took him to live with her in her home at the bottom of the river.

But if you go down to the koker near Parika on any night of the full moon, you will see the water woman sitting with her back to the road and her face to the river, combing her long, black, shiny hair in the moonlight. You will also see a tall, big man with broad shoulders standing close beside her.

The Loaded Dog

by Henry Lawson

chosen by Ivan Southall

HENRY LAWSON was a tragic figure in the story of Australian writing. His was a sad, hard life in a hard land. I am not certain that he should be called *great*, though there are people who have not the slightest doubt about it. Sometimes I wonder whether those who profoundly admire his "deceptively easy style" raise him to heights that would make him giddy if he were still around.

Henry Lawson wrote uniquely Australian stories, hard and sad they were—those words again—but sometimes so sentimental that modern readers can become a little embarrassed. Yet Henry Lawson wrote of reality, of the colonial privation and poverty he knew at first hand around the turn of the century. Australia was not then "the lucky country".

I was a year old when Lawson died—in 1922—and 13 years later I proudly owned a two-volume collection of his works bought for five shillings saved a penny at a time from selling newspapers on street corners. (A Special Privilege Offer it was! We had them in those days, too!) I didn't "go much" for Lawson's sad stories—any more than I do now—but his funny ones were different altogether. *The Loaded Dog* I read again and again and remembered it also from Primary School, from kids reading it in classroom exercises, kids of forty years ago rocking with laughter.

The Loaded Dog is a simple story and might strike you as cruel (if you're in a gentle mood), but if it doesn't make you laugh out loud there might not be much in the world that ever will.

IVAN SOUTHALL

DAVE REGAN, Jim Bently, and Andy Page were sinking a shaft at Stony Creek in search of a rich gold quartz reef which was supposed to exist in the vicinity. There is always a rich reef supposed to exist in the vicinity; the only questions are whether it is ten feet or hundreds beneath the surface, and in which direction. They had struck some pretty solid rock, also water which kept them baling. They used the old-fashioned blasting-powder and time-fuse. They'd make a sausage or cartridge of blasting-powder in a skin of strong calico or canvas, get the drill-hole as dry as possible, drop in the cartridge with some dry dust, and wad and ram with stiff clay and broken brick. Then they'd light the fuse and get out of the hole and wait. The result was usually an ugly pot-hole in the bottom of the shaft and half a barrow-load of broken rock.

There was plenty of fish in the creek, fresh-water bream, cod, cat-fish, and tailers. The party were fond of fish, and Andy and Dave of fishing. Andy would fish for three hours at a stretch if encouraged by a "nibble" or a "bite" now and then —say once in twenty minutes. The butcher was always willing to give meat in exchange for fish when they caught more than they could eat; but now it was winter, and these fish wouldn't bite. However, the creek was low, just a chain of muddy waterholes, from the hole with a few bucketfuls in it to the sizable pool with an average depth of six or seven feet, and they could get fish by bailing out the smaller holes or muddying up the water in the larger ones till the fish rose to the surface. There was the cat-fish, with spikes growing out of the sides of its head, and if you got pricked you'd know it, as Dave said. Andy took off his boots, tucked up his trousers, and went into a hole one day to stir up the mud with his feet, and he knew it. Dave scooped one out with his hand and got pricked, and he knew it too; his arm swelled, and the pain throbbed up into his shoulder, and down into his stomach, too, he said, like a toothache he had once, and kept him awake for two nights— only the toothache pain had a "burred edge," Dave said.

Dave got an idea.

"Why not blow the fish up in the big waterhole with a cartridge?" he said. "I'll try it."

He thought the thing out and Andy Page worked it out. Andy usually put Dave's theories into practice if they were practicable, or bore the blame for the failure and the chaffing of his mates if they weren't.

He made a cartridge about three times the size of those they used in the rock. Jim Bently said it was big enough to blow the bottom out of the river. The idea was to sink the cartridge in the water with the open end of the fuse attached to a float on the surface, ready for lighting. Andy dipped the cartridge in melted bees'-wax to make it watertight. "We'll have to leave it some time before we light it," said Dave, "to give the fish time to get over their scare when we put it in, and come nosing round again; so we'll want it well watertight."

Round the cartridge Andy, at Dave's suggestion, bound a strip of sail canvas. Dave's schemes were elaborate, and he often worked his inventions out to nothing. The cartridge was rigid and solid enough now, but Andy and Dave wanted to be sure. Andy sewed on another layer of canvas, and stood it carefully against a tent-peg, where he'd know where to find it, and wound the fuse loosely round it. Then he went to the camp-fire to try some potatoes which were boiling in their jackets in a billy, and to see about frying some chops for dinner. Dave and Jim were at work in the claim that morning.

They had a big black young retriever dog—or rather an overgrown pup, a big, foolish, four-footed mate, who was always slobbering round them and lashing their legs with his heavy tail that swung round like a stock-whip. Most of his head was usually a red, idiotic slobbering grin of appreciation of his own silliness. He seemed to take life, the world, his two-legged mates, and his own instinct as a huge joke. He'd retrieve anything; he carted back most of the camp rubbish that Andy threw away. They had a cat that died in hot weather, and Andy threw it a good distance away in the scrub; and early one morning the dog found the cat, after it had been dead a week or so, and carried it back to camp, and laid it just inside the tent-flaps, where it could best make its presence known when the mates should rise and begin to sniff suspiciously in the sickly smothering atmosphere of the summer sunrise. He used to retrieve them when they went in swimming; he'd jump in after them, and take their hands in his mouth, and try to swim out with them, and scratch their naked bodies with his paws. They loved him for his good-heartedness and his foolishness, but when they wished to enjoy a swim they had to tie him up in camp.

He watched Andy with great interest all the morning making the cartridge, and hindered him considerably, trying to help; but about noon he went off to the claim to see how Dave and Jim were getting on, and to come home to dinner with them. Andy saw them coming, and put a panful of mutton-chops on the fire. Andy was cook to-day; Dave and Jim stood with their backs to the fire, as bushmen do in all weathers, waiting till dinner should be ready. The retriever went nosing round after something he seemed to have missed.

Andy's brain still worked on the cartridge; his eye was caught by the glare of an empty kerosene-tin lying in the bushes, and it struck him that it wouldn't be a bad idea to sink the cartridge packed with clay, sand, or stones in the tin, to increase the force of the explosion. He may have been all out, from a scientific point of view, but the notion looked all right to him. Jim Bently, by the way, wasn't interested in their "damned silliness." Andy noticed an empty treacle-tin—the sort with the little tin neck or spout soldered on to the top for the convenience of pouring out the treacle—and it struck him that this would have made the best kind of cartridge-case: he would only have had to pour in the powder, stick the fuse in through the neck, and cork and seal it with bees'-wax. He was turning to suggest this to Dave, when Dave glanced over his shoulder to see how the chops were doing—and bolted. He explained afterwards that he thought he heard the pan spluttering extra, and looked to see if the chops were burning. Jim Bently looked behind and bolted after Dave. Andy stood stock-still, staring after them.

"Run, Andy! Run!" they shouted back at him. "Run! Look

behind you, you fool!" Andy turned slowly and looked, and there close behind him, was the retriever with the cartridge in his mouth—wedged into his broadest and silliest grin. And that wasn't all. The dog had come round the fire to Andy, and the loose end of the fuse had trailed and waggled over the burning sticks into the blaze; Andy had slit and nicked the firing end of the fuse well, and now it was hissing and spitting properly.

Andy's legs started with a jolt; his legs started before his brain did, and he made after Dave and Jim. And the dog followed Andy.

Dave and Jim were good runners—Jim the best—for a short distance; Andy was slow and heavy, but he had the strength and the wind and could last. The dog capered round him, delighted as a dog could be to find his mates, as he thought, on for a frolic. Dave and Jim kept shouting back, "Don't foller us! Don't foller us, you stupid fool!" But Andy kept on, no matter how they dodged. They could never explain, any more than the dog, why they followed each other, but so they ran, Dave keeping in Jim's track in all its turnings, Andy after Dave, and the dog circling round Andy—the live fuse swishing in all directions and hissing and spluttering and stinking. Jim yelling to Dave not to follow him, Dave shouting to Andy to go in another direction—to "spread out", and Andy roaring at the dog to go home. Then Andy's brain began to work, stimulated by the crisis: he tried to get a running kick at the dog, but the dog dodged; he snatched up sticks and stones and threw them at the dog and ran on again. The retriever saw that he'd made a mistake about Andy, and left him and bounded after Dave. Dave, who had the presence of mind to think that the fuse's time wasn't up yet, made a dive and a grab for the dog, caught him by the tail, and as he swung round snatched the cartridge out of his mouth and flung it as far as he could; the dog immediately bounded after it and retrieved it. Dave roared and cursed at the dog, who, seeing that Dave was offended, left him and went after Jim, who was well ahead. Jim swung to a sapling and went up it like a native bear; it was a young sapling, and Jim couldn't safely get more than ten or twelve feet from the ground. The dog laid the cartridge, as carefully as if it were a kitten, at the foot of the sapling, and capered and leaped and whooped joyously round under Jim. The big pup reckoned that this was part of the lark—he was all right now—it was Jim who was out for a spree. The fuse sounded as if it were going a mile a minute. Jim tried to climb higher and the sapling bent and cracked. Jim fell on his feet and ran. The dog swooped on the cartridge and followed. It all took but a very few moments. Jim ran to a digger's hole, about ten feet deep, and dropped down into it—landing on soft mud—and was safe. The dog grinned sardonically down on him, over the edge, for a moment, as if he thought it would be a good lark to drop the cartridge down on Jim.

"Go away, Tommy," said Jim feebly, "go away."

The dog bounded off after Dave, who was the only one in sight now; Andy had dropped behind a log, where he lay flat on his face, having suddenly remembered a picture of the Russo-Turkish war with a circle of Turks lying flat on their faces (as if they were ashamed) round a newly-arrived shell.

There was a small hotel or shanty on the creek, on the main road, not far from the claim. Dave was desperate, the time flew much faster in his stimulated imagination than it did in reality, so he made for the shanty. There were several casual bushmen on the veranda and in the bar; Dave rushed into the bar, banging the door to behind him. "My dog!" he gasped, in reply to the astonished stare of the publican, "the blanky retriever—he's got a live cartridge in his mouth——"

The retriever, finding the front door shut against him, had bounded round and in by the back way, and now stood smiling in the doorway leading from the passage, the cartridge still in his mouth and the fuse spluttering. They burst out of that bar. Tommy bounded first after one and then after another, for, being a young dog, he tried to make friends with everybody.

The bushmen ran round corners, and some shut themselves in the stable. There was a new weather-board and corrugated-iron kitchen and wash-house on piles in the backyard, with some women washing clothes inside. Dave and the publican bundled in there and shut the door—the publican cursing Dave and calling him a crimson fool, in hurried tones, and wanting to know what the hell he came here for.

The retriever went in under the kitchen, amongst the piles, but, luckily for those inside, there was a vicious yellow mongrel cattle-dog sulking and nursing his nastiness under there—a sneaking, fighting, thieving canine, whom neighbours had tried for years to shoot or poison. Tommy saw his danger—he'd had experience from this dog—and started out and across the yard, still sticking to the cartridge. Half-way across the yard the yellow dog caught him and nipped him. Tommy dropped the cartridge, gave one terrified yell, and took to the bush. The yellow dog followed him to the fence and then ran back to see what he had dropped. Nearly a dozen other dogs came from round all the corners and under the buildings—spidery, thievish, bold-blooded kangaroo dogs, mongrel sheep- and cattle-dogs, vicious black and yellow dogs—that slip after you in the dark, nip your heels, and vanish without explaining—and yapping, yelping small fry. They kept at a respectable distance round the nasty yellow dog, for it was dangerous to go near him when he thought he had found something which might be good for a dog or cat. He sniffed at the cartridge twice, and was just taking a third cautious sniff when——

It was very good blasting-powder—a new brand that Dave had recently got up from Sydney; and the cartridge had been excellently well made. Andy was very patient and painstaking in all he did, and nearly as handy as the average sailor with needles, twine, canvas and rope.

Bushmen say that that kitchen jumped off its piles and on again. When the smoke and dust cleared away, the remains of the nasty yellow dog were lying against the paling fence of the yard looking as if he had been kicked into a fire by a horse and afterwards rolled in the dust under a barrow, and finally thrown against the fence from a distance. Several saddle-horses, which had been "hanging-up" round the veranda, were galloping wildly down the road in clouds of dust, with broken bridle-reins flying; and from a circle round the outskirts, from every point of the compass in the scrub, came the yelping of dogs. Two of them went home, to the place where they were born, thirty miles away, and reached it the same night and stayed there; it was not till towards evening that the rest came back cautiously to make inquiries. One was trying to walk on two legs, and most of 'em looked more or less singed; and a little, singed, stumpy-tailed dog, who had been in the habit of hopping the back half of him along on one leg, had reason to be glad that he'd saved up the other leg all those years, for he needed it now. There was one old one-eyed cattle-dog round that shanty for years afterwards, who couldn't stand the smell of a gun being cleaned. He it was who had taken an interest, only second to that of the yellow dog, in the cartridge. Bushmen said that it was amusing to slip up on his blind side and stick a dirty ramrod under his nose: he wouldn't wait to bring his solitary eye to bear—he'd take to the bush and stay out all night.

For half an hour or so after the explosion there were several bushmen round behind the stable who crouched, doubled up, against the wall, or rolled gently on the dust, trying to laugh without shrieking. There were two white women in hysterics at the house, and a half-caste rushing aimlessly round with a dipper of cold water. The publican was holding his wife tight and begging her between her squawks, to "hold up for my sake, Mary, or I'll lam the life out of ye."

Dave decided to apologize later on, "when things had settled a bit," and went back to camp. And the dog that had done it all, Tommy, the great, idiotic mongrel retriever, came slobbering round Dave and lashing his legs with his tail, and trotted home after him, smiling his broadest, longest, and reddest smile of amiability, and apparently satisfied for one afternoon with the fun he'd had.

Andy chained the dog up securely, and cooked some more chops, while Dave went to help Jim out of the hole.

And most of this is why, for years afterwards, lanky, easy-going bushmen, riding lazily past Dave's camp, would cry, in a lazy drawl and with just a hint of the nasal twang:

" 'Ello, Da-a-ve! How's the fishin' getting on, Da-a-ve?"

A PIECE
OF PIE

BY DAMON RUNYON
chosen by
JOHN ROWE TOWNSEND

Damon Runyon did not care for the title of author. He was a newspaper-man and proud of it. According to a memoir by Don Iddon, he was "perhaps the greatest reporter America ever produced. He could write every kind of story—baseball games, boxing matches . . . colour columns and straight news, editorials and front page leads—anything and everything that goes into a newspaper."

Runyon was a remarkable short story writer, too. His work is very American, and not to everybody's taste; but I like it enormously, and this is my choice. His stories are, I think, a reporter's stories. They are busy and full of action. Their range of bizarre and shady characters, and the extraordinary style and language that came to be called Runyonese, arise from the way of life of a man whose beat was Broadway and who talked endlessly to all kinds of people.

A Piece of Pie is a true short story: a single episode described from start to finish; rounded, satisfying, complete. There is nothing subtle or sensitive about it, and it is humorous rather than witty, but these are not defects in a story about something so unsubtle as an eating match. It has the pungent individual flavour of Runyon, and it deals richly with a subject dear to his heart; for—to quote Don Iddon again—"he was a great eater and would talk about food for hours."

JOHN ROWE TOWNSEND

ON Boylston Street, in the City of Boston, Mass., there is a joint where you can get as nice a broiled lobster as anybody ever slaps a lip over, and who is in there one evening partaking of this tidbit but a character by the name of Horse Thief and me.

This Horse Thief is called Horsey for short, and he is not called by this name because he ever steals a horse but because it is the consensus of public opinion from coast to coast that he may steal one if the opportunity presents.

Personally, I consider Horsey a very fine character, because any time he is holding anything he is willing to share his good fortune with one and all, and at this time in Boston he is holding plenty. It is the time we make the race meeting at Suffolk Down, and Horsey gets to going very good, indeed, and in fact he is now a character of means, and is my host against the broiled lobster.

Well, at a table next to us are four or five characters who all seem to be well-dressed, and stout-set, and red-faced, and prosperous-looking, and who all speak with the true Boston accent, which consists of many ah's and very few r's. Characters such as these are familiar to anybody who is ever in Boston very much, and they are bound to be politicians, retired cops, or contractors, because Boston is really quite infested with characters of this nature.

I am paying no attention to them, because they are drinking local ale, and talking loud, and long ago I learn that when a Boston character is engaged in aleing himself up, it is a good idea to let him alone, because the best you can get out of him is maybe a boff on the beezer. But Horsey is in there on the old Ear-ie, and very much interested in their conversation, and finally I listen myself just to hear what is attracting his attention, when one of the characters speaks as follows:

"Well," he says, "I am willing to bet ten thousand dollars that he can outeat anybody in the United States any time."

Now at this, Horsey gets right up and steps over to the table and bows and smiles in a friendly way on one and all, and says:

"Gentlemen," he says, "pardon the intrusion, and excuse me for billing in, but," he says, "do I understand you are speaking of a great eater who resides in your fair city?"

Well, these Boston characters all gaze at Horsey in such a hostile manner that I am expecting any one of them to get up and request him to let them miss him, but he keeps on bowing and smiling, and they can see that he is a gentleman, and finally one of them says:

"Yes," he says, "we are speaking of a character by the name of Joel Duffle. He is without doubt the greatest eater alive. He just wins a unique wager. He bets a character from Bangor, Me., that he can eat a whole window display of oysters in this very restaurant, and he not only eats all the oysters but he then wishes to wager that he can also eat the shells, but," he says, "it seems that the character from Bangor, Me., unfortunately taps out on the first proposition and has nothing with which to bet on the second."

"Very interesting," Horsey says. "Very interesting, if true, but," he says, "unless my ears deceive me, I hear one of you state that he is willing to wager ten thousand dollars on this eater of yours against anybody in the United States."

"Your ears are perfect," another of the Boston characters says. "I state it, although," he says, "I admit it is a sort of figure of speech. But I state it all right," he says, "and never let it be said that a Conway ever pigs it on a betting proposition."

"Well," Horsey says, "I do not have a tenner on me at the moment, but," he says, "I have here a thousand dollars to put up as a forfeit that I can produce a character who will outeat your party for ten thousand, and as much more as you care to put up."

And with this, Horsey outs with a bundle of coarse notes and tosses it on the table, and right away one of the Boston characters, whose name turns out to be Carroll, slaps his hand on the money and says:

"Bet."

Well, now this is prompt action to be sure, and if there is one thing I admire more than anything else, it is action, and I can see that these are characters of true sporting instincts and I commence wondering where I can raise a few dibs to take a piece of Horsey's proposition, because of course I know that he has nobody in mind to do the eating for his side but Nicely-Nicely Jones.

And knowing Nicely-Nicely Jones, I am prepared to wager all the money I can possibly raise that he can outeat anything that walks on two legs. In fact, I will take a chance on Nicely-Nicely against anything on four legs, except maybe an elephant, and at that he may give the elephant a photo finish.

I do not say that Nicely-Nicely is the greatest eater in all history, but what I do say is he belongs up there as a contender. In fact, Professor D, who is a professor in a college out West before he turns to playing the horses for a livelihood, and who makes a study of history in his time, says he will not be surprised but what Nicely-Nicely figures one-two.

Professor D says we must always remember that Nicely-Nicely eats under the handicaps of modern civilization, which require that an eater use a knife and fork, or anyway a knife, while in the old days eating with the hands was a popular custom and much faster. Professor D says he has no doubt that under the old rules Nicely-Nicely will hang up a record that will endure through the ages, but of course maybe Professor D overlays Nicely-Nicely somewhat.

Well, now that the match is agreed upon, naturally Horsey and the Boston characters begin discussing where it is to take place, and one of the Boston characters suggests a neutral ground, such as New London, Conn., or Providence, R.I., but Horsey holds out for New York, and it seems that Boston characters are always ready to visit New York, so he does not meet with any great opposition on this point.

They all agree on a date four weeks later so as to give the principals plenty of time to get ready, although Horsey and I know that this is really unnecessary as far as Nicely-Nicely is concerned, because one thing about him is he is always in condition to eat.

This Nicely-Nicely Jones is a character who is maybe five feet eight inches tall, and about five feet nine inches wide, and when he is in good shape he will weigh upward of two hundred and eighty-three pounds. He is a horse player by trade, and eating is really just a hobby, but he is undoubtedly a wonderful eater even when he is not hungry.

Well, as soon as Horsey and I return to New York, we hasten to Mindy's restaurant on Broadway and relate the bet Horsey makes in Boston, and right away so many citizens, including Mindy himself, wish to take a piece of the proposition that it is oversubscribed by a large sum in no time.

Then Mindy remarks that he does not see Nicely-Nicely Jones for a month of Sundays, and then everybody present remembers that they do not see Nicely-Nicely around lately, either, and this leads to a discussion of where Nicely-Nicely can be, although up to this moment if nobody sees Nicely-Nicely but once in the next ten years it will be considered sufficient.

Well, Willie the Worrier, who is a bookmaker by trade, is among those present, and he remembers the last time he looks for Nicely-Nicely hoping to collect a marker of some years' standing, Nicely-Nicely is living at the Rest Hotel on West Forty-ninth Street, and nothing will do Horsey but I must go with him over to the Rest to make inquiry for Nicely-Nicely, and there we learn that he leaves a forwarding address away up on Morningside Heights in care of somebody by the name of Slocum.

So Horsey calls a short, and away we go to this address, which turns out to be a five-story walk-up apartment, and a card downstairs shows that Slocum lives on the top floor. It takes Horsey and me ten minutes to walk up the five flights as we are by no means accustomed to exercise of this nature, and when we finally reach a door marked Slocum, we are plumb tuckered out, and have to sit down on the top step and rest a while.

Then I ring the bell at this door marked Slocum, and who appears but a tall young Judy with black hair who is without doubt beautiful, but who is so skinny we have to look twice to see her, and when I ask her if she can give me any information about a party named Nicely-Nicely Jones, she says to me like this:

"I guess you mean Quentin," she says. "Yes," she says, "Quentin is here. Come in, gentlemen."

So we step into an apartment, and as we do so a thin, sickly looking character gets up out of a chair by the window, and in a weak voice says good evening. It is a good evening, at that, so Horsey and I say good evening right back at him, very polite, and then we stand there waiting for Nicely-Nicely to appear, when the beautiful skinny young Judy says:

"Well," she says, "this is Mr. Quentin Jones."

Then Horsey and I take another swivel at the thin character, and we can see that it is nobody but Nicely-Nicely, at that, but the way he changes since we last observe him is practically shocking to us both, because he is undoubtedly all shrunk up. In fact, he looks as if he is about half what he is in his prime, and his face is pale and thin, and his eyes are away back in his head, and while we both shake hands with him it is some time before either of us is able to speak. Then Horsey finally says:

"Nicely," he says, "can we have a few words with you in private on a very important proposition?"

Well, at this, and before Nicely-Nicely can answer aye, yes or no, the beautiful skinny young Judy goes out of the room and slams a door behind her, and Nicely-Nicely says:

"My fiancée, Miss Hilda Slocum," he says. "She is a wonderful character. We are to be married as soon as I lose twenty pounds more. It will take a couple of weeks longer," he says.

"My goodness gracious, Nicely," Horsey says. "What do you mean lose twenty pounds more? You are practically emaciated now. Are you just out of a sick bed, or what?"

"Why," Nicely-Nicely says, "certainly I am not out of a sick bed. I am never healthier in my life. I am on a diet. I lose eighty-three pounds in two months, and am now down to two hundred. I feel great," he says. "It is all because of my fiancée, Miss Hilda Slocum. She rescues me from gluttony and obesity, or anyway," Nicely-Nicely says, "this is what Miss Hilda Slocum calls it. My, I feel good. I love Miss Hilda Slocum very much," Nicely-Nicely says. "It is a case of love at first sight on both sides the day we meet in the subway. I am wedged in one of the turnstile gates, and she kindly pushes on me from behind until I wiggle through. I can see she has a kind heart, so I date her up for a movie that night and propose to her while the newsreel is on. But," Nicely-Nicely says, "Hilda tells me at once that she will never marry a fat slob. She says I must put myself in her hands and she will reduce me by scientific methods and then she will become my ever-loving wife, but not before.

"So," Nicely-Nicely says, "I come to live here with Miss Hilda Slocum and her mother, so she can supervise my diet. Her mother is thinner than Hilda. And I surely feel great," Nicely-Nicely says. "Look," he says.

And with this, he pulls out the waistband of his pants, and shows enough spare space to hide War Admiral in, but the effort seems to be a strain on him, and he has to sit down in his chair again.

"My goodness gracious," Horsey says. "What do you eat, Nicely?"

"Well," Nicely-Nicely says, "I eat anything that does not contain starch, but," he says, "of course everything worth eating contains starch, so I really do not eat much of anything whatever. My fiancée, Miss Hilda Slocum, arranges my diet. She is an expert dietician and runs a widely known department in a diet magazine by the name of *Let's Keep House*."

Then Horsey tells Nicely-Nicely of how he is matched to eat against this Joel Duffle, of Boston, for a nice side bet, and how he has a forfeit of a thousand dollars already posted for appearance, and how many of Nicely-Nicely's admirers along Broadway are looking to win themselves out of all their troubles by betting on him, and at first Nicely-Nicely listens with great interest, and his eyes are shining like six bits, but then he becomes very sad, and says:

"It is no use, gentlemen," he says. "My fiancée, Miss Hilda Slocum, will never hear of me going off my diet even for a little while. Only yesterday I try to talk her into letting me have a little pumpernickel instead of toasted whole wheat bread, and she says if I even think of such a thing again, she will break our engagement. Horsey," he says, "do you ever eat toasted whole wheat bread for a month hand running? Toasted?" he says.

"No," Horsey says. "What I eat is nice, white French bread, and corn muffins, and hot biscuits with gravy on them."

"Stop," Nicely-Nicely says. "You are eating yourself into an early grave, and, furthermore," he says, "you are breaking my heart. But," he says, "the more I think of my following depending on me in this emergency, the sadder it makes me feel to think I am unable to oblige them. However," he says, "let us call Miss Hilda Slocum in on an outside chance and see what her reactions to your proposition are."

So we call Miss Hilda Slocum in, and Horsey explains our predicament in putting so much faith in Nicely-Nicely only to find him dieting, and Miss Hilda Slocum's reactions are to order Horsey and me out of the joint with instructions never to darken her door again, and when we are a block away we can still hear her voice speaking very firmly to Nicely-Nicely.

Well, personally, I figure this ends the matter, for I can see that Miss Hilda Slocum is a most determined character, indeed, and the chances are it does end it, at that, if Horsey does not happen to get a wonderful break.

He is at Belmont Park one afternoon, and he has a real good thing in a jump race, and when a brisk young character in a hard straw hat and eyeglasses comes along and asks him what he likes, Horsey mentions this good thing, figuring he will move himself in for a few dibs if the good thing connects.

Well, it connects all right, and the brisk young character is very grateful to Horsey for his information, and is giving him plenty of much-obliges, and nothing else, and Horsey is about to mention that they do not accept much-obliges at his hotel, when the brisk young character mentions that he is nobody but Mr. McBurgle and that he is the editor of the *Let's Keep House* magazine, and for Horsey to drop in and see him any time he is around his way.

Naturally, Horsey remembers what Nicely-Nicely says about Miss Hilda Slocum working for this *Let's Keep House* magazine, and he relates the story of the eating contest to Mr. McBurgle and asks him if he will kindly use his influence with Miss Hilda Slocum to get her to release Nicely-Nicely from his diet long enough for the contest. Then Horsey gives Mr. McBurgle a tip on another winner, and Mr. McBurgle must use plenty of influence on Miss Hilda Slocum at once, as the next day she calls Horsey up at his hotel before he is out of bed, and speaks to him as follows:

"Of course," Miss Hilda Slocum says, "I will never change my attitude about Quentin, but," she says, "I can appreciate that he feels very bad about you gentlemen relying on him and having to disappoint you. He feels that he lets you down, which is by no means true, but it weighs upon his mind. It is interfering with his diet.

"Now," Miss Hilda Slocum says, "I do not approve of your contest, because," she says, "it is placing a premium on gluttony, but I have a friend by the name of Miss Violette Shumberger who may answer your purpose. She is my dearest friend from childhood, but it is only because I love her dearly that this friendship endures. She is extremely fond of eating," Miss Hilda Slocum says. "In spite of my pleadings, and my warnings, and my own example, she persists in food. It is disgusting to me but I finally learn that it is no use arguing with her.

"She remains my dearest friend," Miss Hilda Slocum says, "though she continues her practice of eating, and I am informed that she is phenomenal in this respect. In fact," she says, "Nicely-Nicely tells me to say to you that if Miss Violette Shumberger can perform the eating exploits I relate to him from hearsay she is a lily. Good-bye," Miss Hilda Slocum says. "You cannot have Nicely-Nicely."

Well, nobody cares much about this idea of a stand-in for Nicely-Nicely in such a situation, and especially a Judy that no one ever hears of before, and many citizens are in favor of pulling out of the contest altogether. But Horsey has his thousand-dollar forfeit to think of, and as no one can suggest anyone else, he finally arranges a personal meet with the Judy suggested by Miss Hilda Slocum.

He comes into Mindy's one evening with a female character who is so fat it is necessary to push three tables together to give her room for her lap, and it seems that this character is Miss Violette Shumberger. She weighs maybe two hundred and fifty pounds, but she is by no means an old Judy, and by no means bad-looking. She has a face the size of a town clock and enough chins for a fire escape, but she has a nice smile and pretty teeth, and a laugh that is so hearty it knocks the whipped cream off an order of strawberry shortcake on a table fifty feet away and arouses the indignation of a customer by the name of Goldstein who is about to consume same.

Well, Horsey's idea in bringing her into Mindy's is to get some kind of line on her eating form, and she is clocked by many experts when she starts putting on the hot meat, and it is agreed by one and all that she is by no means a selling-plater. In fact, by the time she gets through, even Mindy admits she has plenty of class, and the upshot of it all is Miss Violette Shumberger is chosen to eat against Joel Duffle.

Maybe you hear something of this great eating contest that comes off in New York one night in the early summer of 1937. Of course eating contests are by no means anything new, and in fact they are quite an old-fashioned pastime in some sections of this country, such as the South and East, but this is the first big public contest of the kind in years, and it creates no little comment along Broadway.

In fact, there is some mention of it in the blats, and it is not a frivolous proposition in any respect, and more dough is wagered on it than any other eating contest in history, with Joel Duffle a 6 to 5 favorite over Miss Violette Shumberger all the way through.

This Joel Duffle comes to New York several days before the contest with the character by the name of Conway, and requests a meet with Miss Violette Shumberger to agree on the final details and who shows up with Miss Violette Shumberger as her coach and adviser but Nicely-Nicely Jones. He is even thinner and more peaked-looking than when Horsey and I see him last, but he says he feels great, and that he is within six pounds of his marriage to Miss Hilda Slocum.

Well, it seems that his presence is really due to Miss Hilda Slocum herself, because she says that after getting her dearest friend Miss Violette Shumberger into this jackpot, it is only fair to do all she can to help her win it, and the only way she can think of is to let Nicely-Nicely give Violette the benefit of his experience and advice.

But afterward we learn that what really happens is that this editor, Mr. McBurgle, gets greatly interested in the contest, and when he discovers that in spite of his influence, Miss Hilda Slocum declines to permit Nicely-Nicely to personally compete, but puts in a pinch eater, he is quite indignant and insists on her letting Nicely-Nicely school Violette.

Furthermore we afterward learn that when Nicely-Nicely returns to the apartment on Morningside Heights after giving Violette a lesson, Miss Hilda Slocum always smells his breath to see if he indulges in any food during his absence.

Well, this Joel Duffle is a tall character with stooped shoulders, and a sad expression, and he does not look as if he can eat his way out of a tea shoppe, but as soon as he commences to discuss the details of the contest, anybody can see that he knows what time it is in situations such as this. In fact, Nicely-Nicely says he can tell at once from the way Joel Duffle talks that he is a dangerous opponent, and he says while Miss Violette Shumberger impresses him as an improving eater, he is only sorry she does not have more seasoning.

This Joel Duffle suggests that the contest consist of twelve courses of strictly American food, each side to be allowed to pick six dishes, doing the picking in rotation, and specifying the weight and quantity of the course selected to any amount the contestant making the pick desires, and each course is to be divided for eating exactly in half, and after Miss Violette Shumberger and Nicely-Nicely whisper together a while, they say the terms are quite satisfactory.

Then Horsey tosses a coin for the first pick, and Joel Duffle says heads, and it is heads, and he chooses, as the first course, two quarts of ripe olives, twelve bunches of celery, and four pounds of shelled nuts, all this to be split fifty-fifty between them. Miss Violette Shumberger names twelve dozen cherry-stone clams as the second course, and Joel Duffle says two gallons of Philadelphia pepper-pot soup as the third.

Well, Miss Violette Shumberger and Nicely-Nicely whisper together again, and Violette puts in two five-pound striped bass, the heads and tails not to count in the eating, and Joel Duffle names a twenty-two pound roast turkey. Each vegetable is rated as one course, and Miss Violette Shumberger asks for twelve pounds of mashed potatoes with brown gravy. Joel Duffle says two dozen ears of corn on the cob, and Violette replies with two quarts of lima beans. Joel Duffle calls for twelve bunches of asparagus cooked in butter, and Violette mentions ten pounds of stewed new peas.

This gets them down to the salad, and it is Joel Duffle's play, so he says six pounds of mixed green salad with vinegar and oil dressing, and now Miss Violette Shumberger has the final selection, which is the dessert. She says it is a pumpkin pie, two feet across, and not less than three inches deep.

It is agreed that they must eat with knife, fork or spoon, but speed is not to count, and there is to be no time limit, except they cannot pause more than two consecutive minutes at any stage, except in case of hiccoughs. They can drink anything, and as much as they please, but liquids are not to count in the scoring. The decision is to be strictly on the amount of food consumed, and the judges are to take account of anything left on the plates after a course, but not of loose chewings on bosom or vest up to an ounce. The losing side is to pay for the food, and in case of a tie they are to eat it off immediately on ham and eggs only.

Well, the scene of this contest is the second-floor dining-room of Mindy's restaurant, which is closed to the general public for the occasion, and only parties immediately concerned in the contest are admitted. The contestants are seated on either side of a big table in the center of the room, and each contestant has three waiters.

No talking and no rooting from the spectators is permitted, but of course in any eating contest the principals may speak to each other if they wish, though smart eaters never wish to do this, as talking only wastes energy, and about all they ever say to each other is please pass the mustard.

About fifty characters from Boston are present to witness the contest, and the same number of citizens of New York are admitted, and among them is this editor, Mr. McBurgle, and he is around asking Horsey if he thinks Miss Violette Shumberger is as good a thing as the jumper at the race track.

Nicely-Nicely arrives on the scene quite early, and his appearance is really most distressing to his old friends and admirers, as by this time he is shy so much weight that he is a pitiful scene, to be sure, but he tells Horsey and me that he thinks Miss Violette Shumberger has a good chance.

"Of course," he says, "she is green. She does not know how to pace herself in competition. But," he says, "she has a wonderful style. I love to watch her eat. She likes the same things I do in the days when I am eating. She is a wonderful character, too. Do you ever notice her smile?" Nicely-Nicely says.

"But," he says, "she is the dearest friend of my fiancée, Miss Hilda Slocum, so let us not speak of this. I try to get Hilda to come to see the contest, but she says it is repulsive. Well, anyway," Nicely-Nicely says, "I manage to borrow a few dibs, and am wagering on Miss Violette Shumberger. By the way," he says, "if you happen to think of it, notice her smile."

Well, Nicely-Nicely takes a chair about ten feet behind Miss Violette Shumberger, which is as close as the judges will allow him, and he is warned by them that no coaching from the corners will be permitted, but of course Nicely-Nicely knows this rule as well as they do, and furthermore by this time his exertions seem to have left him without any more energy.

There are three judges, and they are all from neutral territory. One of these judges is a party from Baltimore, Md., by the name of Packard, who runs a restaurant, and another is a party from Providence, R.I., by the name of Croppers, who is a sausage manufacturer. The third judge is an old Judy by the name of Mrs. Rhubarb, who comes from Philadelphia, and once keeps an actors' boarding-house, and is considered an excellent judge of eaters.

Well, Mindy is the official starter, and at 8.30 p.m. sharp, when there is still much betting among the spectators, he outs with his watch, and says like this:

"Are you ready, Boston? Are you ready, New York?"

Miss Violette Shumberger and Joel Duffle both nod their heads, and Mindy says commence, and the contest is on, with

Joel Duffle getting the jump at once on the celery and olives and nuts.

It is apparent that this Joel Duffle is one of these rough-and-tumble eaters that you can hear quite a distance off, especially on clams and soups. He is also an eyebrow eater, an eater whose eyebrows go up as high as the part in his hair as he eats, and this type of eater is undoubtedly very efficient.

In fact, the way Joel Duffle goes through the groceries down to the turkey causes the Broadway spectators some uneasiness, and they are whispering to each other that they only wish the old Nicely-Nicely is in there. But personally, I like the way Miss Violette Shumberger eats without undue excitement, and with great zest. She cannot keep close to Joel Duffle in the matter of speed in the early stages of the contest, as she seems to enjoy chewing her food, but I observe that as it goes along she pulls up on him, and I figure this is not because she is stepping up her pace, but because he is slowing down.

When the turkey finally comes on, and is split in two halves right down the middle, Miss Violette Shumberger looks greatly disappointed, and she speaks for the first time as follows:

"Why," she says, "where is the stuffing?"

Well, it seems that nobody mentions any stuffing for the turkey to the chef, so he does not make any stuffing, and Miss Violette Shumberger's disappointment is so plain to be seen that the confidence of the Boston characters is somewhat shaken. They can see that a Judy who can pack away as much fodder as Miss Violette Shumberger has to date, and then beef for stuffing, is really quite an eater.

In fact, Joel Duffle looks quite startled when he observes Miss Violette Shumberger's disappointment, and he gazes at her with great respect as she disposes of her share of the turkey, and the mashed potatoes, and one thing and another in such a manner that she moves up on the pumpkin pie on dead even terms with him. In fact, there is little to choose between them at this point, although the judge from Baltimore is calling the attention of the other judges to a turkey leg that he claims Miss Violette Shumberger does not clean as neatly as Joel Duffle does his, but the other judges dismiss this as a technicality.

Then the waiters bring on the pumpkin pie, and it is without doubt quite a large pie, and in fact it is about the size of a man-hole cover, and I can see Joel Duffle is observing this pie with a strange expression on his face, although to tell the truth I do not care for the expression on Miss Violette Shumberger's face either.

Well, the pie is cut in two dead center, and one half is placed before Miss Violette Shumberger and the other half before Joel Duffle, and he does not take more than two bites before I see him loosen his waistband and take a big swig of water, and thinks I to myself, he is now down to a slow walk, and the pie will decide the whole heat, and I am only wishing I am able to wager a little more dough on Miss Violette Shumberger. But about this moment, and before she as much as touches her pie, all of a sudden Violette turns her head and motions to Nicely-Nicely to approach her, and as he approaches, she whispers in his ear.

Now at this, the Boston character by the name of Conway jumps up and claims a foul and several other Boston characters join him in this claim, and so does Joel Duffle, although after-ward even the Boston characters admit that Joel Duffle is no gentleman to make such a claim against a lady.

Well, there is some confusion over this, and the judges hold a conference, and they rule that there is certainly no foul in the actual eating that they can see, because Miss Violette Shum-berger does not touch her pie so far.

But they say that whether it is a foul otherwise all depends on whether Miss Violette Shumberger is requesting advice on the contest from Nicely-Nicely and the judge from Providence, R.I., wishes to know if Nicely-Nicely will kindly relate what passes between him and Violette so they may make a decision.

"Why," Nicely-Nicely says, "all she asks me is can I get her another piece of pie when she finishes the one in front of her."

Now at this, Joel Duffle throws down his knife, and pushes back his plate with all but two bites of his pie left on it, and says to the Boston characters like this:

"Gentlemen," he says, "I am licked. I cannot eat another mouthful. You must admit I put up a game battle, but," he says, "it is useless for me to go on against this Judy who is asking for more pie before she even starts on what is before her. I am almost dying as it is, and I do not wish to destroy myself in a hopeless effort. Gentlemen," he says, "she is not human."

Well, of course this amounts to throwing in the old napkin and Nicely-Nicely stands up on his chair, and says:

"Three cheers for Miss Violette Shumberger!"

Then Nicely-Nicely gives the first cheer in person, but the effort overtaxes his strength, and he falls off the chair in a faint just as Joel Duffle collapses under the table, and the doctors at the Clinic Hospital are greatly baffled to receive, from the same address at the same time, one patient who is suffering from undernourishment, and another patient who is unconscious from over-eating.

Well, in the meantime, after the excitement subsides, and wagers are settled, we take Miss Violette Shumberger to the main floor in Mindy's for a midnight snack, and when she speaks of her wonderful triumph, she is disposed to give much credit to Nicely-Nicely Jones.

"You see," Violette says, "what I really whisper to him is that I am a goner. I whisper to him that I cannot possibly take one bite of the pie if my life depends on it, and if he has any bets down to try and hedge them off as quickly as possible.

"I fear," she says, "that Nicely-Nicely will be greatly disappointed in my showing, but I have a confession to make to him when he gets out of the hospital. I forget about the contest," Violette says, "and eat my regular dinner of pig's knuckles and sauerkraut an hour before the contest starts and," she says, "I have no doubt this tends to affect my form somewhat. So," she says, "I owe everything to Nicely-Nicely's quick thinking."

It is several weeks after the great eating contest that I run into Miss Hilda Slocum on Broadway and it seems to me that she looks much better nourished than the last time I see her, and when I mention this she says:

"Yes," she says, "I cease dieting. I learn my lesson," she says. "I learn that male characters do not appreciate anybody who tries to ward off surplus tissue. What male characters wish is substance. Why," she says, "only a week ago my editor, Mr.

McBurgle, tells me he will love to take me dancing if only I get something on me for him to take hold of. I am very fond of dancing," she says.

"But," I say, "what of Nicely-Nicely Jones? I do not see him around lately."

"Why," Miss Hilda Slocum says, "do you not hear what this cad does? Why, as soon as he is strong enough to leave the hospital, he elopes with my dearest friend, Miss Violette Shumberger, leaving me a note saying something about two souls with but a single thought. They are down in Florida running a barbecue stand, and," she says, "the chances are, eating like seven mules."

"Miss Slocum," I says, "can I interest you in a portion of Mindy's chicken fricassee?"

"With dumplings?" Miss Hilda Slocum says. "Yes," she says, "you can. Afterward I have a date to go dancing with Mr. McBurgle. I am crazy about dancing," she says.

The Story of
Jorkel Hayforks

by George Mackay Brown

chosen by
Jill Paton Walsh

I LIKE the work of George Mackay Brown so much, because it makes a gift of Orkney to me, so that those remote and fascinating northern islands, which I have never visited, shine in my mind with the radiance that usually belongs only to places one has known, and loved as a child. It is very hard to choose just one of his stories to show what I mean, for almost his best quality is the way the place makes all times one for him, and you have to read quite a way into a story before you can be sure if it is happening now, or in the middle ages, or among the Vikings. But I have decided on this one because I particularly admire it for an author's reason. I have often thought that the kind of literature people read would affect their view of themselves; the style of the writer would influence the "life style" of the readers. Don't you think, for example, that more people fell unhappily in love, in the Romantic era? Or look at the fun Jane Austen got out of the view of life that reading Gothic novels had given her heroine, in NORTHANGER ABBEY! The modern psychological novel encourages us all to live indoors a good deal, lovingly tending to selfscape; but the Vikings, those harsh bold men, wrote a literature of sagas, in which neither inner selves, nor landscape, nor feelings play much part, but only words and deeds. It seems to me that only by using their own stark way of story telling could one get a Viking story to feel right—to be in the right key—, and I have a spoiled and unfinished novel of my own to convince me that the cold simple style of the sagas, like a Viking grey steel sword, is a fiendishly difficult weapon for modern hands. But here is George Mackay Brown, triumphantly, unselfconsciously, bringing to his Viking tales a Viking tone of voice. There must be something special in his northern Orkney skies; and somehow, someday, I must get there to see for myself.

JILL PATON WALSH

THE week before midsummer Jorkel and six others took ship at Bergen in Norway and sailed west two days with a good wind behind them. They made land at Whalsay in Shetland and were well entertained at a farm there by a man called Veig. After they had had supper one of Jorkel's men played the harp and recited some verses. The name of this poet was Finn.

As soon as Finn had sat down, Brenda, the daughter of Veig the Shetlander, came to her father and said, "Offer Finn a horse and a piece of land, so that he will be pleased to stay here."

Veig made the offer to Finn, but Finn said, "We are sailing to Orkney on a certain urgent matter in the morning. I can't stay."

Veig repeated Finn's remark to Brenda.

At midnight when the men were drinking round the fire, Brenda rose out of bed and said to her father Veig, "I can't get to sleep. Offer Finn a gold arm-band and a silver ring to stay here in Shetland."

Veig called Finn aside and made this offer. Finn said, "I am a poor man and a happy man, and gold and women would distract me from the making of verses. Besides, we have an appointment to keep in Orkney on midsummer day."

Veig told Brenda what Finn had said.

At dawn, though the ale keg was empty, the men were still sitting at the fire. Some of them were lying under the benches drunk, but Finn was discussing metres with the Shetlanders. "I would argue better," said Finn, "if I was not so dry."

Soon after that Brenda came in and offered Finn a cup of ale.

With the froth still wet on his beard, Finn turned to Brenda and said, "Did you brew this ale, woman?" Brenda said that she alone had made it. Then Finn said, "On account of this ale I will stay for a while with you here in Shetland."

Then the sun got up and the Norwegians stirred themselves

and went on board their ship. But Finn was nowhere to be found, and the door of Brenda's room was barred. Jorkel was very angry about that.

They say that Finn made no more poems after that day. Brenda bore him twelve children. He died there in Shetland before there was a grey hair in his beard. He was drunk most days till his death, and he would drink from no cup but Brenda's. He was totally dependent on her always. It was thought rather a pity that such a promising poet should make such an ordinary end.

"She bewitched him, that bitch," said Jorkel.

In the afternoon of the same day, Jorkel's ship reached Fair Isle. They saw some sheep on a hillside there. Flan, who was a blacksmith back in Norway, said they were fine sheep. "And my wife," said he, "will be looking for a present from the west. I will bring her a fleece from Fair Isle."

Before they could stop Flan he leapt overboard and swam ashore. The sheep were grazing at the edge of a high cliff. Flan climbed up this face, disturbing the sea birds that were there, and laid hands on the first sheep he saw. He was raising his axe to despatch the ewe when another sheep ran terrified between his legs and toppled him over the edge of the crag, so that the sea birds were wildly agitated for the second time that day.

"Flan's descent is much quicker than his going up," said Jorkel. "What does a blacksmith know about shepherding?"

They anchored that night under the cliffs of Fair Isle.

They left Fair Isle at dawn and had a rough crossing to the Orkneys. There was a strong wind from the east and the sea fell into the ship in cold grey lumps, so that they were kept busy with the bailing pans.

Then Mund who had a farm east in Sweden laid down his bailing pan.

He said, "I have made deep furrows in the land with my plough but I did not believe there could be furrows in the world like this."

The men went on bailing.

218

Later Mund said, "When Grettir lay dying in his bed at Gothenburg last summer his face was like milk. Is my face that colour?"

Jorkel said his face was more of a green colour, and urged the men to bail all the harder, since now Mund was taking no part in the game.

At noon Mund said, "I was always a gay man at midsummer, but I do not expect to be dancing round at Johnsmas fire this year."

The men went on bailing, until presently the wind shifted into the north and moderated, so that they were able to cook a meal of stewed rabbit and to open a keg of ale.

But when they brought the meat and ale to Mund, they found him lying very still and cold against a thwart.

"Mund will not be needing dinner any more," said Jorkel.

They reached Papa Westray soon after that. There were some decent farms in the island, and an ale-house near the shore, and a small monastery with a dozen bald-headed brothers beside a loch.

The people of the island gave them a hospitable welcome, and sold them fish and mutton, and showed them where the best wells were.

The twelve brothers trooped into the church for vespers.

After the necessary business of victualling had been transacted, the Norwegians went into the ale-house to drink.

They played draughts and sang choruses so long as there was ale in the barrel. Then, when the keeper of the ale-house was opening a new barrel, Jorkel noticed that Thord was missing.

"He will have gone after the women of Papa Westray," said Sweyn. Thord was known to be a great lecher back home in Norway.

The church bell rang for compline.

There was some fighting in the ale-house when they were midway through the second barrel, but by that time they were too drunk to hurt each other much. When things had quietened down, Jorkel remarked that Thord was still absent.

"No doubt he is stealing eggs and cheese, so that we can

vary our diet on the ship," said Valt. Thord was a famous thief on the hills of southern Norway, when it was night and everyone was sitting round the fires inside and there was no moon.

They went on drinking till the lights of yesterday and to-morrow met in a brief twilight and their senses were reeling with ale and fatigue.

"This is a strange voyage," said Jorkel. "It seems we are to lose a man at every station of the way."

They heard the bell of the church ringing. Jorkel went to the door of the ale-house. Thirteen hooded figures passed under the arch to sing matins.

Jorkel returned to the ale-barrel and said, "It seems that Thord has repented of his drinking and whoring and thieving. Yesterday there were twelve holy men in Papa Westray. This morning I counted thirteen."

He lay down beside his companions, and they slept late into the morning.

Now there were only three men on the ship, Jorkel and Sweyn and Valt.

"We will not stop until we reach Hoy," said Jorkel. "Every time we stop there is one kind of trouble or another."

They were among the northern Orkneys now, sailing through a wide firth with islands all around.

It turned out that none of the three knew where exactly Hoy was.

Sweyn said, "There is a man in that low island over there. He has a mask on and he is taking honey from his hives. I will go ashore and ask him where Hoy is."

"Be careful," said Jorkel. "We will have difficulty in getting to Hoy if there are only two of us left to work the ship."

Sweyn waded ashore and said to the bee-keeper, "Be good enough to tell us how we can recognize the island of Hoy."

The man took off his mask and replied courteously that they would have to sail west between the islands until they reached the open ocean, and then keeping the coast of Hrossey on the port side and sailing south they would see in the distance two blue hills rising out of the sea. These blue hills were Hoy.

Sweyn thanked him and asked if he was getting plenty of honey.

The man replied that it was a bad year for honey. The bees had been as dull as the weather.

"Still," the bee-keeper said, "the next comb I take from the hive will be a gift for you."

Sweyn was deeply touched by the courtesy and kindness of the bee-keeper.

It happened that as the man was bending over the hive, a bee came on the wind and settled on his neck and stung him.

The bee-keeper gave a cry of annoyance and shook off the bee.

Sweyn was angry at the way the insects repaid with in-gratitude the gentleness of the Orkney bee-keeper. He suddenly brought his axe down on the hive and clove it in two.

Jorkel and Valt were watching from the ship, and they saw Sweyn run screaming round the island with a cloud of bees after him. It was as if he was being pelted with hot sharp sonorous hail stones.

Sweyn ran down into the ebb and covered himself with seaweed.

When Jorkel and Valt reached him, he told them where Hoy was. Then his face turned blind and blue and swollen and he died.

Jorkel and Valt got horses at a farm called the Bu in Hoy and rode between the two hills till they came to a place called Rackwick. There was a farm there and five men were working in the hayfield. It was a warm bright day, and the faces of the labourers shone with sweat.

Jorkel asked them if a man called Arkol lived nearby.

"Arkol is the grieve at this farm," said one of the labourers, "but he often sleeps late."

"We work in the daytime," said another, "but Arkol does most of his labouring at night."

"Arkol is a great man for the women," said a third, and winked.

Jorkel said he thought that would be the man they were looking for.

Presently the labourers stopped to rest and they invited Jorkel and Valt to share their bread and ale. They sat under a wall where there was shadow and Valt told all that had happened to them from the time they left Bergen. But Jorkel sat quietly and seemed preoccupied. They noticed too that he did not eat or drink much.

"Who is the owner of this farm?" said Valt when he had finished his story of the voyage.

The labourers said the farmer in Rackwick was a man called John. They spoke highly of him. He was a good master to them.

Just then a man with a dark beard crossed the field. He ordered the labourers to resume their work, and then looked suspiciously at Jorkel and Valt. They were rather scruffy and dirty after their voyage.

Jorkel asked him if his name was Arkol Dagson.

The man yawned once or twice and said that it was.

"In that case," said Jorkel, "I must tell you that my sister Ingirid in Bergen bore you a son at the beginning of June."

Arkol made no answer but yawned again. Then he laughed.

"And I want to know," said Jorkel, "if you will pay for the fostering of the child."

Arkol said he would not discuss so intimate a matter with two tramps. So far he had not been in the habit of paying for the fostering of any child that he had fathered, and he doubted whether it was wise to begin now, especially as Norway was so far away. Furthermore, he could hardly be expected to believe the unsupported testimony of two tramps, one of whom claimed to be Ingirid's brother. Ingirid had been a most lovely and gently-reared girl, and Arkol did not think the scare-crow standing before him could really be the brother of such a delightful bedmate. Besides, he had been busy all night in another sweet bed, and now he was very tired, and he begged the two gentlemen of the roads to excuse him.

Jorkel said, "Will you pay now for the fostering of your son?"

Arkol turned away and yawned.

Jorkel drove his dagger into Arkol's throat, so that he fell dead at once on the field.

The labourers jumped down from the haystack and ran at Jorkel and Valt with their forks.

"I wish the others were here now," said Jorkel as he turned to face them. "Now I would be glad to have Finn and Flan and Mund and Thord and Sweyn at my side."

Valt was quickly pronged to death there, and though Jorkel defended himself well and was still on his feet when John of Rackwick appeared on the scene, he was so severely lacerated that he lay between life and death in the farm for more than a week.

The three farm girls looked after him well till he recovered. They hovered around him day and night with oil and sweet water and beeswax.

On the day they took the last bandages from Jorkel's arm, John of Rackwick came to him and said mildly, "Arkol, my grieve, was in many ways an evil lecherous man, and for that he must answer to a higher lord than the Earl of Orkney or the King of Norway. But also he was a loyal servant of mine, and because of that you must pay me as compensation your ship that is anchored off Selwick. You are welcome to stay here in Hoy, Jorkel, for as long as you like. There is a small vacant croft on the side of the hill that will support a cow and an ox and a few sheep. It will be a tame life for a young man, but now you are disabled because of the hay forks, and if you till your field carefully nothing could be more pleasing to God."

Jorkel accepted that offer. He lived there at Upland for the rest of his life. In Orkney he was nicknamed "Hayforks". He put by a little money each harvest so that one day he would be able to return to Norway, but the years passed and he could never get a passage.

The summer before his death Jorkel went to Papa Westray in a fishing boat. At the church there he inquired for Thord, and presently Thord came out to meet him. They were two old men now, bald and toothless. They embraced each other under the arch. They were like two boys laughing at each other over an immense distance, thin affectionate lost voices.

Jorkel took a purse from his belt and counted five pieces of silver into Thord's hand. "I have been saving this money for forty years," he said, "so that some day I could go home to Norway. But it is too late. Who would know me in Bergen now? I should prepare, instead, for the last, longest journey. Will you arrange for masses to be said in your church for Finn and Flan and Mund and Sweyn and Valt?"

Thord said that masses would certainly be offered for those dead men and for Jorkel himself too. Then he embraced Jorkel and blessed him. Jorkel turned round. He was at peace. The long silver scars of the hayforks troubled his body no longer.

Half-way to the boat he turned back. He gave Thord another silver coin. "Say a mass for Arkol Dagson also," he said.

They smiled at each other, crinkling their old eyes.

The
Invisible Boy

by Ray Bradbury

chosen by Patricia Wrightson

GOOD fantasy is a prismatic thing, changing its lights and colours while you look at it. Even less than other fiction does it look the same to any two people. So when one finds Ray Bradbury's work on the shelf labelled SCIENCE FICTION there is no need to be surprised. Yet I always am.

To me it seems that Bradbury's work is not at all concerned with the speculations of science fiction. It is only incidentally fantasy at all. True, it does tingle with electric strangeness and glow mysteriously with the light of other worlds; but Bradbury's fantasy works in reverse. It leads always into the heart of the most homely reality. A time machine takes you back to ancient dawn—to prove the infinite value of a butterfly. The world disintegrates in the testing of the final Device—and you watch a woman's hand wither while her embroidery burns, the world's funeral fire reflected in her needle. From space, sunfire, witchery, the hulk of a dinosaur, the electric hum of a powerhouse, Bradbury distills the essence of small humanity. He does it with a profound understanding and love of small humanity that makes the word "compassion" seem pretentious.

The result, of course, is poetry. And true to Bradbury, the poetry is often concentrated in a dewdrop or conveyed in the idiom of simple people. It is not the breadth and richness of his devices that makes Ray Bradbury my favourite writer of short stories. It is the breadth and richness of his humanity.

To show it I have chosen one of the stories that does not employ any large or rich device: the small story of a lonely old woman and a boy. This story has no electric tingle, no rainbow-lights of fantasy, no immensity of space. Whatever richness it displays is Bradbury's own.

PATRICIA WRIGHTSON

S HE took the great iron spoon and the mummified frog and gave it a bash and made dust of it, and talked to the dust while she ground it in her stony fists quickly. Her beady gray bird-eyes flickered at the cabin. Each time she looked, a head in the small thin window ducked as if she'd fired off a shotgun.

"Charlie!" cried Old Lady. "You come outa there! I'm fixing a lizard magic to unlock that rusty door! You come out now and I won't make the earth shake or the trees go up in fire or the sun set at high noon!"

The only sound was the warm mountain light on the high turpentine trees, a tufted squirrel chittering around and around on a green-furred log, the ants moving in a fine brown line at Old Lady's bare, blue-veined feet.

"You been starving in there two days, darn you!" she panted, chiming the spoon against a flat rock, causing the plump gray miracle bag to swing at her waist. Sweating sour, she rose and marched at the cabin, bearing the pulverized flesh. "Come out, now!" She flicked a pinch of powder inside the lock. "All right, I'll come get you!" she wheezed.

She spun the knob with one walnut-colored hand, first one way, then the other. "O Lord," she intoned, "fling this door wide!"

When nothing flung, she added yet another philtre and held her breath. Her long blue untidy skirt rustled as she peered into her bag of darkness to see if she had any scaly monsters there, any charm finer than the frog she'd killed months ago for such a crisis as this.

She heard Charlie breathing against the door. His folks had pranced off into some Ozark town early this week, leaving him, and he'd run almost six miles to Old Lady for company—she was by way of being an aunt or cousin or some such, and he didn't mind her fashions.

But then, two days ago, Old Lady, having gotten used to the

boy around, decided to keep him for convenient company. She pricked her thin shoulder bone, drew out three blood pearls, spat wet over her right elbow, tromped on a crunch-cricket, and at the same instant clawed her left hand at Charlie, crying, "My son you are, you are my son, for all eternity!"

Charlie, bounding like a startled hare, had crashed off into the bush, heading for home.

But Old Lady, skittering quick as a gingham lizard, cornered him in a dead end, and Charlie holed up in this old hermit's cabin and wouldn't come out, no matter how she whammed door, window, or knothole with amber-colored fist or trounced her ritual fires, explaining to him that he was certainly her son *now*, all right.

"Charlie, you *there?*" she asked, cutting holes in the door planks with her bright little slippery eyes.

"I'm all of me here," he replied finally, very tired.

Maybe he would fall out on the ground any moment. She wrestled the knob hopefully. Perhaps a pinch too much frog powder had grated the lock wrong. She always overdid or under-did her miracles, she mused angrily, never doing them just *exact*, Devil take it!

"Charlie, I only wants someone to night-prattle to, someone to warm hands with at the fire. Someone to fetch kindling for me mornings, and fight off the spunks that come creeping of early fogs! I ain't got no fetching on you for myself, son, just for your company." She smacked her lips. "Tell you what, Charles, you come out and I *teach* you things!"

"What things?" he suspicioned.

"Teach you how to buy cheap, sell high. Catch a snow weasel, cut off its head, carry it warm in your hind pocket. There!"

"Aw," said Charlie.

She made haste. "Teach you to make yourself shotproof. So if anyone bangs at you with a gun, nothing happens."

When Charlie stayed silent, she gave him the secret in a high fluttering whisper. "Dig and stitch mouse-ear roots on Friday during full moon, and wear 'em around your neck in a white silk."

"You're crazy," Charlie said.

"Teach you how to stop blood or make animals stand frozen or make blind horses see, all them things I'll teach you! Teach you to cure a swelled-up cow and unbewitch a goat. Show you how to make yourself invisible!"

"Oh," said Charlie.

Old Lady's heart beat like a Salvation tambourine.

The knob turned from the other side.

"You," said Charlie, "are funning me."

"No, I'm not," exclaimed Old Lady. "Oh, Charlie, why, I'll make you like a window, see right through you. Why, child, you'll be surprised!"

"Real invisible?"

"Real invisible!"

"You won't fetch on to me if I walk out?"

"Won't touch a bristle of you, son."

"Well," he drawled reluctantly, "all right."

The door opened. Charlie stood in his bare feet, head down, chin against chest. "Make me invisible," he said.

"First we got to catch us a bat," said Old Lady. "Start lookin'!"

She gave him some jerky beef for his hunger and watched him climb a tree. He went high up and high up and it was nice seeing him there and it was nice having him here and all about after so many years alone with nothing to say good morning to but bird-droppings and silvery snail tracks.

Pretty soon a bat with a broken wing fluttered down out of the tree. Old Lady snatched it up, beating warm and shrieking between its porcelain white teeth, and Charlie dropped down after it, hand upon clenched hand, yelling.

That night, with the moon nibbling at the spiced pine cones, Old Lady extracted a long silver needle from under her wide blue dress. Gumming her excitement and secret anticipation, she sighted up the dead bat and held the cold needle steady-steady.

She had long ago realized that her miracles, despite all perspirations and salts and sulphurs, failed. But she had always dreamt that one day the miracles might start functioning, might spring up in crimson flowers and silver stars to prove that God had forgiven her for her pink body and her pink thoughts and her warm body and her warm thoughts as a young miss. But so far God had made no sign and said no word, but nobody knew this except Old Lady.

"Ready?" she asked Charlie, who crouched cross-kneed, wrapping his pretty legs in long goose-pimpled arms, his mouth open, making teeth. "Ready," he whispered, shivering.

"There!" She plunged the needle deep in the bat's right eye. "So!"

"Oh!" screamed Charlie, wadding up his face.

"Now I wrap it in gingham, and here, put it in your pocket, keep it there, bat and all. Go on!"

He pocketed the charm.

"Charlie!" she shrieked fearfully. "Charlie, where *are* you? I can't *see* you, child!"

"Here!" He jumped so the light ran in red streaks up his body. "I'm here, Old Lady!" He stared wildly at his arms, legs, chest, and toes. "I'm here!"

Her eyes looked as if they were watching a thousand fireflies crisscrossing each other in the wild night air.

"Charlie, oh, you went *fast!* Quick as a hummingbird! Oh, Charlie, come *back* to me!"

"But I'm *here!*" he wailed.

"Where?"

"By the fire, the fire! And—and I can see myself. I'm not invisible at all!"

Old Lady rocked on her lean flanks. "Course *you* can see *you!* Every invisible person knows himself. Otherwise, how could you eat, walk, or get around places? Charlie, touch me. Touch me so I *know* you."

Uneasily he put out a hand.

She pretended to jerk, startled, at his touch. "*Ah!*"

"You mean to say you can't *find* me?" he asked. "Truly?"

"Not the least half rump of you!"

She found a tree to stare at, and stared at it with shining eyes, careful not to glance at him. "Why, I sure *did* a trick *that* time!" She sighed with wonder. "Whooeee. Quickest invisible I *ever* made! Charlie. Charlie, how you *feel?*"

230

"Like creek water—all stirred."

"You'll settle."

Then after a pause she added, "Well, what you going to do now, Charlie, since you're invisible?"

All sorts of things shot through his brain, she could tell. Adventures stood up and danced like hell-fire in his eyes, and his mouth, just hanging, told what it meant to be a boy who imagined himself like the mountain winds. In a cold dream he said, "I'll run across wheat fields, climb snow mountains, steal white chickens off'n farms. I'll kick pink pigs when they ain't looking. I'll pinch pretty girls' legs when they sleep, snap their garters in schoolrooms." Charlie looked at Old Lady, and from the shiny tips of her eyes she saw something wicked shape his face. "And other things I'll do, I'll do, I will," he said.

"Don't try nothing on me," warned Old Lady. "I'm brittle as spring ice and I don't take handling." Then: "What about your folks?"

"My folks?"

"You can't fetch yourself home looking like that. Scare the inside ribbons out of them. Your mother'd faint straight back like timber falling. Think they want you about the house to stumble over and your ma have to call you every three minutes, even though you're in the room next her elbow?"

Charlie had not considered it. He sort of simmered down and whispered out a little "Gosh" and felt of his long bones carefully.

"You'll be mighty lonesome. People looking through you like a water glass, people knocking you aside because they didn't reckon you to be underfoot. And women, Charlie, *women*——"

He swallowed. "What about women?"

"No woman will be giving you a second stare. And no woman wants to be kissed by a boy's mouth they can't even *find!*"

Charlie dug his bare toe in the soil contemplatively. He pouted. "Well, I'll stay invisible, anyway, for a spell. I'll have me some fun. I'll just be pretty careful, is all. I'll stay out from in front of wagons and horses and Pa. Pa shoots at the nariest sound." Charlie blinked. "Why, with me invisible, someday Pa might just up and fill me with buckshot, thinkin' I was a hill squirrel in the doorway. Oh . . ."

231

Old Lady nodded at a tree. "That's likely."

"Well," he decided slowly, "I'll stay invisible for to-night, and to-morrow you can fix me back all whole again, Old Lady."

"Now if that ain't just like a critter, always wanting to be what he can't be," remarked Old Lady to a beetle on a log.

"What you mean?" said Charlie.

"Why," she explained, "it was real hard work, fixing you up. It'll take a little *time* for it to wear off. Like a coat of paint wears off, boy."

"You!" he cried. "You did this to me! Now you make me back, you make me seeable!"

"Hush," she said. "It'll wear off, a hand or a foot at a time."

"How'll it look, me around the hills with just one hand showing!"

"Like a five-winged bird hopping on the stones and bramble."

"Or a foot showing!"

"Like a small pink rabbit jumping thicket."

"Or my head floating!"

"Like a hairy balloon at the carnival!"

"How long before I'm *whole?*" he asked.

She deliberated that it might pretty well be an entire year.

He groaned. He began to sob and bite his lips and make fists. "You magicked me, you did this, you did this thing to me. Now I won't be able to run home!"

She winked. "But you *can* stay here, child, stay on with me real comfort-like, and I'll keep you fat and saucy."

He flung it out: "You did this on purpose! You mean old hag, you want to keep me here!"

He ran off through the shrubs on the instant.

"Charlie, come back!"

No answer but the pattern of his feet on the soft dark turf, and his wet choking cry which passed swiftly off and away.

She waited and then kindled herself a fire. "He'll be back," she whispered. And thinking inward on herself, she said, "And now I'll have me my company through spring and into late summer. Then, when I'm tired of him and want a silence, I'll send him home."

Charlie returned noiselessly with the first gray of dawn, gliding over the rimed turf to where Old Lady sprawled like a bleached stick before the scattered ashes.

He sat on some creek pebbles and stared at her.

She didn't dare look at him or beyond. He had made no sound, so how could she know he was anywhere about? She couldn't.

He sat there, tear marks on his cheeks.

Pretending to be just waking—but she had found no sleep from one end of the night to the other—Old Lady stood up, grunting and yawning, and turned in a circle to the dawn.

"Charlie?"

Her eyes passed from pines to soil, to sky, to the far hills. She called out his name, over and over again, and she felt like staring plumb straight at him, but she stopped herself. "Charlie? Oh, Charles!" she called, and heard the echoes say the very same.

He sat, beginning to grin a bit, suddenly, knowing he was close to her, yet she must feel alone. Perhaps he felt the growing of a secret power, perhaps he felt secure from the world, certainly he was *pleased* with his invisibility.

She said aloud, "Now where *can* that boy be? If he only made a noise so I could tell just where he is, maybe I'd fry him a breakfast."

She prepared the morning victuals, irritated at his continuous quiet. She sizzled bacon on a hickory stick. "The smell of it will draw his nose," she muttered.

While her back was turned he swiped all the frying bacon and devoured it tastily.

She whirled, crying out, "Lord!"

She eyed the clearing suspiciously. "Charlie, that *you?*"

Charlie wiped his mouth clean on his wrists.

She trotted about the clearing, making like she was trying to locate him. Finally, with a clever thought, acting blind, she headed straight for him, groping. "Charlie, where *are* you?"

A lightning streak, he evaded her, bobbing, ducking.

It took all her will power not to give chase; but you can't chase invisible boys, so she sat down, scowling, sputtering, and tried to

233

fry more bacon. But every fresh strip she cut he would steal bubbling off the fire and run away far. Finally, cheeks burning, she cried, "I know where you are! Right *there!* I hear you run!" She pointed to one side of him, not too accurate. He ran again. "Now you're there!" she shouted. "There, and there!" pointing to all the places he was in the next five minutes. "I hear you press a grass blade, knock a flower, snap a twig. I got fine shell ears, delicate as roses. They can hear the stars moving!"

Silently he galloped off among the pines, his voice trailing back, "Can't hear me when I'm set on a rock. I'll just *set!*"

All day he sat on an observatory rock in the clear wind, motionless and sucking his tongue.

Old Lady gathered wood in the deep forest, feeling his eyes weaseling on her spine. She wanted to babble: "Oh, I see you, I see you! I was only fooling about invisible boys! You're right there!" But she swallowed her gall and gummed it tight.

The following morning he did the spiteful things. He began leaping from behind trees. He made toad-faces, frog-faces, spider-faces at her, clenching down his lips with his fingers, popping his raw eyes, pushing up his nostrils so you could peer in and see his brain thinking.

Once she dropped her kindling. She pretended it was a blue jay startled her.

He made a motion as if to strangle her.

She trembled a little.

He made another move as if to bang her shins and spit on her cheek.

These motions she bore without a lid-flicker or a mouth-twitch.

He stuck out his tongue, making strange bad noises. He wiggled his loose ears so she wanted to laugh, and finally she did laugh and explained it away quickly by saying, "Sat on a salamander! Whew, how it poked!"

By high noon the whole madness boiled to a terrible peak.

For it was at that exact hour that Charlie came racing down the valley stark boy-naked!

Old Lady nearly fell flat with shock!

"Charlie!" she almost cried.

Charlie raced naked up one side of a hill and naked down the other—naked as day, naked as the moon, raw as the sun and a newborn chick, his feet shimmering and rushing like the wings of a low-skimming hummingbird.

Old Lady's tongue locked in her mouth. What could she say? Charlie, go dress? For *shame? Stop* that? *Could* she? Oh, Charlie, Charlie, God! Could she say that now? *Well?*

Upon the big rock, she witnessed him dancing up and down, naked as the day of his birth, stomping bare feet, smacking his hands on his knees and sucking in and out his white stomach like blowing and deflating a circus balloon.

She shut her eyes tight and prayed.

After three hours of this she pleaded, "Charlie, Charlie, come here! I got something to *tell* you!"

Like a fallen leaf he came, dressed again, praise the Lord.

"Charlie," she said, looking at the pine trees, "I see your right toe. *There* it is."

"You do?" he said.

"Yes," she said very sadly. "There it is like a horny toad on the grass. And there, up there's your left ear hanging on the air like a pink butterfly."

Charlie danced. "I'm forming in, I'm forming in!"

Old Lady nodded. "Here comes your ankle!"

"Gimme *both* my feet!" ordered Charlie.

"You got 'em."

"How about my hands?"

"I see one crawling on your knee like a daddy longlegs."

"How about the other one?"

"It's crawling too."

"I got a body?"

"Shaping up fine."

"I'll need my head to go home, Old Lady."

To go home, she thought wearily. "No!" she said, stubborn and angry. "No, you ain't got no head. No head at all," she cried. She'd leave that to the very last. "No head, no head," she insisted.

"No head?" he wailed.

"Yes, oh my God, yes, yes, you got your blamed head!" she

snapped, giving up. "Now, fetch me back my bat with the needle in his eye!"

He flung it at her. "Haaaa-yoooo!" His yelling went all up the valley, and long after he had run toward home she heard his echoes, racing.

Then she plucked up her kindling with a great dry weariness and started back toward her shack, sighing, talking. And Charlie followed her all the way, *really* invisible now, so she couldn't see him, just hear him, like a pine cone dropping or a deep underground stream trickling, or a squirrel clambering a bough; and over the fire at twilight she and Charlie sat, him so invisible, and her feeding him bacon he wouldn't take, so she ate it herself, and then she fixed some magic and fell asleep with Charlie, made out of sticks and rags and pebbles, but still warm and her very own son, slumbering and nice in her shaking mother arms . . . and they talked about golden things in drowsy voices until dawn made the fire slowly, slowly wither out. . . .

The Choosers

JOAN AIKEN, daughter of the American poet Conrad Aiken, was born in Rye, Sussex. She was educated at home until the age of 12, then went to Wychwood School, Oxford (where, foraging in the very good library, she first came across Laurence Housman's stories). Her first job was in the BBC but "I soon became bored as all I had to do was rule lines on the back of index cards." She moved to the United Nations London Information Service; later married and had two children. She returned to work as features editor on *Argosy* magazine, and to a spell as an advertising copywriter at J. Walter Thompson. She is now a full-time writer, having had over 25 books published. She alternates between adult thrillers and children's books: her children's books include ALL YOU'VE EVER WANTED, THE WOLVES OF WILLOUGHBY CHASE (which won the 1969 *Guardian* Award), NIGHT BIRDS ON NANTUCKET and A HARP OF FISHBONES; and her most recent adult thriller is DIED ON A RAINY SUNDAY. She has also written two children's plays.

HONOR ARUNDEL was born in North Wales, the fifth in a family of six; she was educated at a boarding school in Kent and at Somerville College, Oxford. From there she went to London where she worked as a typist, a journalist on the *Daily Worker* and an engineer in an aircraft repair shop. In 1953 she moved to Edinburgh, after a spell as a film critic. She married the actor Alex McCrindle. Her two youngest daughters are at Edinburgh University and live at the top of one of the highest houses in Edinburgh, familiar to readers of THE HIGH HOUSE. Honor Arundel's books all have a Scottish setting and the Scottish Arts Council granted her one of their first-ever Awards to a children's writer for her book A FAMILY FAILING. Her other titles include THE LONGEST WEEKEND, EMMA'S ISLAND, EMMA IN LOVE, THE TERRIBLE TEMPTATION and THE BLANKET WORD. Her books are translated into a number of languages and many of them have been Junior Literary Guild choices in America. Honor Arundel died in June, 1973, just as this anthology was going to press.

JOHN CHRISTOPHER was born in 1922, halfway between the two villages of Knowsley and (in those days) Huyton. He was unwillingly removed to Hampshire at the age of ten and subsequently educated at Peter Symond's School, Winchester. Following the publication of his novel, THE DEATH OF GRASS, in 1957 he became a full-time writer. For the last six years he has concentrated chiefly on writing children's books, which are generally classed as science-fiction but seem to get more of their inspiration from the past than from the future. He is married with a son and four daughters, and lives in Guernsey. His children's books include THE WHITE MOUNTAINS, THE CITY OF GOLD AND LEAD, and THE POOL OF FIRE (the *Tripods* trilogy); THE GUARDIANS (*Guardian Award*, 1970); THE PRINCE IN WAITING, BEYOND THE BURNING LANDS, and THE SWORD OF THE SPIRITS (the *Prince* trilogy). He is a winner of the American Christopher Award for his children's books.

WILLIAM (BILL) CLEAVER, a native of Seattle, Washington, is the son of an attorney and received his education in private schools in British Columbia. In his young life he was devoted to swimming, tennis, chess and philately and showed vigorous ability as a fiction writer but this potential remained dormant until his marriage shortly after the close of World War II. VERA CLEAVER was born in Virgil, South Dakota and, influenced by her maternal grandfather who was a newspaper publisher, began writing fiction at the age of six. She was educated at various schools in South Dakota, Nebraska, Wyoming and Florida and in 1945 married Bill Cleaver. The Cleavers have lived in Japan and France, Washington state, North Carolina and California and now make their home in Florida. Together they have written a number of short stories for magazines and ten books. WHERE THE LILIES BLOOM was a nominee for a National Book Award in 1970 and GROVER was a nominee for a National Book Award in 1971. Their other titles include THE MOCK REVOLT, I WOULD RATHER BE A TURNIP, ELLEN GRAE and LADY ELLEN GRAE.

ELIZABETH COATSWORTH is one of America's most well-loved and distinguished writers for young people. She is the author of over 60 books, one of which, THE CAT WHO WENT TO HEAVEN, won the Newbery Medal in 1931. With her husband, the great naturalist and writer Henry Beston, she travelled widely in Europe, Central America, North Africa, and the Orient, and the old farm house in Maine where she has continued to live since her husband's death is crammed with fascinating treasures found on her travels. Elizabeth Coatsworth was born in Buffalo, New York, but has lived most of her life in Maine and her deep love for the Maine countryside and people is evident in much of her writing. She is also a considerable poet—poetry being her favourite form of writing. Her many books include HERE I STAY, AWAY GOES SALLY, THE PRINCESS AND THE LION, FIVE BUSHEL FARM, and THE FAIR AMERICAN.

HELEN CRESSWELL was born and bred in a Nottingham suburb, and later went to Kings College, London, where she gained a BA Honours degree in English. Since she had to do something to earn money until she could keep herself by writing alone, she did a variety of things, from pretending to train as a fashion buyer to coaching backward readers in Primary Schools. She is now married to Brian Rowe and they have two daughters. They live at Eakring, a small north Nottinghamshire village, in a Georgian farmhouse on a hill. Helen Cresswell has written over forty books for children. Three of these, THE PIEMAKERS, THE NIGHT-WATCHMEN and UP THE PIER have been commended for the Library Association Carnegie Medal. Six of her books have been adapted for television and read on JACKANORY, and she has recently written five television plays for children centred around a girl called LIZZIE DRIPPING. These are being filmed on location in Eakring and are also to be published in book form. She has just completed her first adult television play. When she is not writing she tends to be thinking, reading or roaming the countryside, and sometimes all three at once. She enjoys gardening, collecting antiques, listening to music and sitting in country graveyards.

PETER DICKINSON was never interested in authors when he was young. For instance he read every Henty book he could lay hands on, and still Henty was only five letters on the back of each book. If you'd said to him "Peter, I want you to meet Mr. Henty," he'd have been irritated at the intrusion—this strange man coming between the reader and the story on the feeble pretext of having written the stuff down. He still thinks this was a very correct attitude. He himself was born in Zambia in 1927, was educated in an old-fashioned way (that means badly), and was on the staff of *Punch* for 17 years. He has written five rather complicated thrillers, two of which won prizes for being the best crime novels of the year. His first three children's books (THE WEATHERMONGER, HEARTSEASE and THE DEVIL'S CHILDREN) are usually classed as Science Fiction but really only just count. As soon as people try to class him he writes something which doesn't fit the class. He married an Admiral's daughter and has two tall daughters and two rough sons. His most recent novels are THE GIFT and THE DANCING BEAR.

JANE GARDAM was born in 1928 at Coatham on the North-East coast of Yorkshire, and until she was 18 only left it for visits to her grandparents' farm in West Cumberland. Then in heavy tweeds and a green felt hat with a feather bought for her by her Auntie Mabel she appeared at London University (Bedford College) to read English Literature. After her degree she stayed for three more years doing post-graduate research, and then worked as a journalist on several magazines, including a spell with *Time and Tide* working for C. V. Wedgwood, who was then the Literary Editor. Jane Gardam is married to a Q.C., has three children, and lives in Wimbledon, London. She travels when she can with her husband, who works as far away as Borneo, but still feels most at home in the north of England, where she rents a small stone farmhouse on the Westmorland fells. She walks a great deal and at speed in Yorkshire and the Lake District. Her three published books to date are A FEW FAIR DAYS, A LONG WAY FROM VERONA (Runner-up, Guardian Award 1972; Spring Book Festival Honor Book, U.S.A.) and THE SUMMER AFTER THE FUNERAL.

MOLLIE HUNTER (Maureen Mollie Hunter McIlwraith) was born in 1922 in the Scottish village of Longniddry, East Lothian, one of five children of an Irish father and Scottish mother. She spent her childhood and early adulthood in the Lowlands, but has lived for the past twenty years in the Highlands with her husband and two sons. Her main interests are folk-lore on which she bases such fantasy stories as THE HAUNTED MOUNTAIN (Scottish Arts Council Award 1973), and Scottish history, from which she draws material for such novels as THE LOTHIAN RUN and THE THIRTEENTH MEMBER. Mollie Hunter was a poet, freelance journalist and playwright before turning to novels, and sees her writing career as having been influenced by her parents, both of whom had "the gift of the gab". She considers the small glen where she now lives to be the most beautiful spot on earth, and loves to walk for hours with her two enormous dogs. Her most recently published book, A SOUND OF CHARIOTS, has been acclaimed on both sides of the Atlantic.

JOAN LINGARD began to write as a child and always wrote about places she had never been to which seemed so much more exciting than "dull old Belfast where I lived from two to eighteen and where nothing ever happened." The Belfast background, however, provided Joan Lingard with the material for a number of adult novels and after reading the sixth of these, THE LORD ON OUR SIDE, Honor Arundel suggested to Joan Lingard that she should write about Ulster for young readers. From this suggestion grew three books: THE TWELFTH DAY OF JULY, ACROSS THE BARRICADES and INTO EXILE; books in which Joan Lingard explored the Ulster situation with the understanding born of experience—things did indeed happen in Belfast and they were things she wanted young readers to know about. Joan Lingard was born in Edinburgh, and returned there to train as a teacher. She now lives with her three daughters in Cheshire. She is a successful television script writer, and has contributed regularly to a number of long-running Scottish television productions. Her special pleasure is to be by the sea, but she also enjoys walking in cities and travelling.

ANDRE NORTON was born in Cleveland, Ohio, and before she became a full-time writer she worked for many years as a children's librarian in the Cleveland Public Library. She is the author of many novels, and is widely regarded as one of the leading science fiction writers of today. Her science fiction titles include MOON OF THREE RINGS, ICE CROWN and EXILES OF THE STARS. She has also written a number of fantasy stories for younger children, including OCTAGON MAGIC and FUR MAGIC; and has published a memoir of childhood in rural Ohio, BERTIE AND MAY, which she wrote with her mother, Bertha Stemm Norton. Andre Norton is interested in folklore, history and social history, and collects science fiction, diaries, and Victorian novels. She now lives in Florida.

SCOTT O'DELL writes: "Los Angeles was a frontier town when I was born there. It had more horses than automobiles, more jack rabbits than people. My father was a railroad man so we moved a lot, but never far. Wherever we went, it was into frontier country. There was San Pedro, which is part of Los Angeles. And Rattlesnake Island, where we lived in a house on stilts where the waves came up and washed under us every day. That is why, I suppose, the feel of the frontier and the sound of the sea are in my books." After graduation from college (Stanford and the University of Wisconsin) Scott O'Dell worked as a movie cameraman, had a spell in the Air Force during World War II, and several years as a book editor on a Los Angeles newspaper. He has devoted the past twenty years to writing and has been awarded the coveted Hans Christian Andersen Award for his children's books. He now lives with his wife in California, spends a great deal of his time sailing, enjoys fishing, gardening, and anything to do with the sea. His books include ISLAND OF THE BLUE DOLPHINS (Newbery Medal, 1960), THE KING'S FIFTH, THE BLACK PEARL and SING DOWN THE MOON, the latter having grown from a summer spent with the Navaho Indians.

JOAN PHIPSON was born of English parents in Australia in 1912. She was taken to England to be christened and was there when World War I broke out, subsequently living in India for 18 months while her father was at the

Front in France. She was educated in Australia at Frensham, but her education was interrupted by return visits to England. After leaving school Joan Phipson did a secretarial course in England, and then returned to Australia to work as a school librarian, and a copy and script writer for radio. In World War II she was a telegraphist in the WAAF. At the end of the war she married and "retired to breed sheep, cattle and two children". She also began to write children's books, and the many she has had published include THE BOUNDARY RIDERS, THE FAMILY CONSPIRACY, IT HAPPENED ONE SUMMER, BIRKIN, BASS AND BILLY MARTIN and POLLY'S TIGER. Except for occasional visits abroad, she has remained living in the country at Mandurama, N.S.W. Joan Phipson has several times been a winner of the Australian Children's Book of the Year Award.

ANDREW SALKEY was born of Jamaican parents in Colon, Panama, in 1928. He has lived in England since 1952, at present in London with his wife and two sons. He is a novelist, poet, travel writer, children's author, anthologist, and radio journalist. ANANCY'S SCORE, a collection of Jamaican folk tales, is his only book of short stories; his long poem JAMAICA, was awarded the Thomas Helmore Poetry Prize in 1955. His children's books include HURRICANE, (Deutscher Kinderbuchpreis, 1967), DROUGHT, JONAH SIMPSON and EARTHQUAKE. Andrew Salkey has edited many anthologies of Caribbean writing, including WEST INDIAN STORIES, STORIES FROM THE CARIBBEAN, WRITING IN CUBA SINCE THE REVOLUTION, and BREAK-LIGHT, a poetry anthology. He was awarded a Guggenheim Fellowship for creative writing in 1960. His interests include the cinema, collecting Caribbean paintings and African wood-carvings, and reading books about Cuba, Chile, China and Tanzania, countries in whose contemporary development he is very interested.

IVAN SOUTHALL was born near Melbourne in 1921. He left school at fourteen hoping to be a journalist, an ambition not realized. First he was a process engraver in a newspaper office, then a pilot in the Royal Australian Air Force (winning the D.F.C. in 1944) and from 1947 has lived in the Australian "bush". Many of his books have been for children. He has won the Australian Children's Book of the Year Award three times, for ASH ROAD, TO THE WILD SKY, and BREAD AND HONEY. JOSH won the Carnegie Medal in 1971. Between 1967 and 1969, in a voluntary capacity, Mr. Southall helped establish the Knoxbrooke Training Centre for the Intellectually Handicapped at Fern Tree Gully in Victoria and is still involved in its management. Mr. Southall and his English-born wife, Joy, have four children and two grandchildren.

JOHN ROWE TOWNSEND was born in Leeds and educated at Leeds Grammar School and Cambridge University, where he edited the undergraduate newspaper. In 1949 he joined what was then the *Manchester Guardian*, and from 1955 to 1969 was editor of its weekly international edition. He resigned this post to have more time for writing and lecturing, but retained a connection with the *Guardian* as children's books editor. His novels for children and young people include GUMBLE'S YARD, HELL'S EDGE and THE INTRUDER, which was serialised on ITV in 1972. Both HELL'S EDGE and THE INTRUDER were runners-up for the Carnegie Medal, and THE INTRUDER won a Silver Pen from the English Centre of International P.E.N. and two American awards. Mr. Townsend has also edited an anthology of modern poetry, written two books about children's literature—WRITTEN FOR CHILDREN and A SENSE OF STORY—and taught courses in children's literature in American universities. He has three children of his own and lives in Cheshire.

JILL PATON WALSH was born and brought up in North Finchley, London, and was educated at St. Michael's Convent. From there she went to St. Anne's College, Oxford, and read English, choosing a mediaeval and philological course. Still at Oxford she took a Diploma of Education, and then taught English for three years, during which time she married. She left teaching when her son was born, and soon after began to write. Jill Paton Walsh now has three children and lives in a Victorian house in Richmond. She is interested in cooking, carpentry, sewing and photography. Her books include THE DOLPHIN CROSSING, FIREWEED, FAREWELL GREAT KING, GOLDENGROVE and THE DAWNSTONE.

PATRICIA WRIGHTSON was born at Lismore in New South Wales, daughter of a country solicitor and third in a family of six. She attended several State schools, including the State Correspondence School for isolated children; spent a period as a boarder in a private school but "couldn't stand the homesickness." Her teachers all suspected she was a potential writer, but she claims that her own courage to attempt writing diminished as her appreciation of literature grew. After having two children of her own, Patricia Wrightson began her writing career, realising that "their lives would be rather arid if I really had nothing worth saying to children". For twenty years Patricia Wrightson worked as a hospital administrator; she is now the Editor of the N.S.W. Department of Education's *School Magazine*, which has a monthly circulation of half a million. She lives in Sydney. Her many published books include DOWN TO EARTH, THE CROOKED SNAKE, THE ROCKS OF HONEY and "I OWN THE RACECOURSE!" (A RACECOURSE FOR ANDY).

The Chosen Authors

RAY BRADBURY, the distinguished American writer of science fiction, was born in 1920. He now lives in Los Angeles.

GEORGE MacKAY BROWN was born in 1921 in Stromness, Orkney, the setting of his stories and poems. He read English at Edinburgh University, now lives and works in Orkney.

WALTER DE LA MARE was born in Kent in 1873 and died in 1956. He was made a Companion of Honour in 1948 for his services to literature, and was awarded the Order of Merit in 1953.

NICHOLAS STUART GRAY was born in Scotland in 1921. He is an actor and playwright, and was a founder of the London Children's Theatre.

DOROTHY K. HAYNES was born in Lanark in 1918 and is a frequent contributor to literary periodicals and journals throughout Britain.

LAURENCE HOUSMAN, the English novelist, dramatist, and illustrator, was born in 1865 and died in 1959.

SARAH ORNE JEWETT was born in New England in 1849 and died in 1909. Most of her writing is set in her native Maine and vividly describes New England life.

MacKINLAY KANTOR, the American writer, was born in 1904. His novel, *Andersonville*, was awarded a Pulitzer Prize.

HENRY LAWSON, one of the most famous of all Australian writers, was born in 1867 and died in Sydney in 1922. He lived for a while in New Zealand and also in England.

LIAM O'FLAHERTY was born in Ireland in 1897. Although he is widely travelled, most of his novels are concerned with Irish life and politics.

ARTHUR PORGES is an American writer of science fiction and short stories. *The Ruum* was first published in 1953.

RALPH PRINCE comes from Antigua, one of the Leeward Islands in the Caribbean archipelago. He now lives in Guyana.

DAMON RUNYON, who lived from 1884 until 1946, was an American writer noted for his stories about colourful Broadway characters, the most famous of which was *Guys and Dolls*.

ERNEST THOMPSON SETON, the naturalist, writer, and illustrator, was born in England in 1860 but later lived in Canada. He died in 1946.

FRANK STOCKTON, novelist and classic short story writer, was born in America in 1834 and died in 1902.

THEODORE STURGEON was born in 1918 in New York City. He has an international reputation for his science fiction novels and collections. He is also an accomplished guitarist.

OSCAR WILDE, the controversial poet, dramatist, and novelist, was born in Ireland in 1854. He lived mainly in London, but died in Paris, bitter and financially ruined, in 1900.